THE NEW NEIGHBOUR

MIRANDA RIJKS

INKUBATOR
BOOKS

Published by Inkubator Books
www.inkubatorbooks.com

Copyright © 2021 by Miranda Rijks

ISBN (Paperback): 978-1-915275-02-8
ISBN (eBook): 978-1-915275-03-5

Miranda Rijks has asserted her right to be identified as the
author of this work.

THE NEW NEIGHBOUR is a work of fiction. People, places,
events, and situations are the product of the author's
imagination. Any resemblance to actual persons, living or
dead is entirely coincidental.

PROLOGUE

It gets dark so late during this time of year, and I need to make sure that everyone is fast asleep, so it's one o'clock in the morning when I step out, ready to do my Good Samaritan deed. If truth be told, I'm a bit nervous, but needs must. It's not like I'm hurting anyone. I've put the tools in a dark grey holdall, which is slung over my shoulder, and a torch is strapped around my forehead. I take a deep breath and creep outside. It's pitch black, and my heart is thumping, but then I think about the consequences of my actions and how happy she'll be. I grin when I think about the smile it'll put on her face. Yes, it's definitely worth it.

I sneak out through the back of our garden, opening the gate to the public footpath that runs behind our house. The gate creaks, and I hold my breath, annoyed that I've forgotten to oil it. Nothing stirs, but then an owl hoots, and I nearly jump out of my skin. I let out a snort, idiot that I am. I creep along the footpath and then haul myself up onto the top of the fence. The tools in my backpack jangle, but no one is going to hear. And then I jump. It's a long way down and tough on the knees, even for someone as fit as me. I stay crouched down for a moment just to be sure, but there's silence, so I creep along the perimeter of the garden, keeping my head down low so that the light illuminates my feet. When I'm in the right place, I open the backpack and take out the saw. At least I think I'm in the right place.

I do a few cuts and realise this is going to be a lot tougher than I imagined.

Then I hear something. My heart is hammering and my breathing heavy. I switch the light off on my head torch.

What the hell?

A light comes on in one of the rooms upstairs, and the curtains are drawn back.

No! This isn't meant to be happening.

'Oi, you! What are you doing?'

I dump the saw and run. The very worst thing that could happen would be if I get caught, but even that's not the end of the world. But I'm young and fit, and actually, it's quite funny, so I laugh as I sprint across the lawn and down the side of the house. As I race into the driveway at the front of the house, I glance backwards over my shoulder. I can't see anyone following me, but I'm not going to stop now. I carry on running, my trainers giving me a good grip, down their short drive and then onto the lane.

Bang!

It feels like I've been punched in the gut. Pain radiates through my chest, and I gasp for breath. What happened? I'm on the tarmac, little bits of gravel stuck in the palms of my hands and on my left cheek.

It hurts like hell. For a moment, I think I'm dead, but then I open my eyes, and the moon is still hanging in the sky. I glance up and see the outline of a big car.

I've been hit by a car in the middle of the night on a private road. Thrown up into the air and tossed around like a rag doll. I've been hit by a car that hasn't got its lights on. Who the hell is driving a car here at this time of night?

There's silence. I manage to crawl to the side of the road, away from those big wheels, and although my leg and chest are screaming with pain, I stagger to my feet. I'm okay, though. It was the shock of it that knocked me for six.

'Are you all right?' The voice is familiar.

'Yeah. Yeah, I'm fine,' I say as I stand upright. I fix my eyes on the moon to stop the trees and the stars from spinning around me. And then the car drives away, slowly, along the road towards our house. But it's one in the morning, and what is it doing?

I touch my head, and my hand comes away sticky. I'm bleeding.

'Help!' I shout, but my voice doesn't carry through the dark night. I think I must be more hurt than I assumed. I sink back down onto the road. It's summer, so it's not cold, but the grit and gravel bite the palms of my hands. I need to give myself five minutes or so, and then I'll make my way back home and clean myself up.

But then I hear footsteps. Thank goodness, they're coming back. I'm going to get help. The moon throws a milky light, and the moving shadow gets nearer and nearer. Then a bright light is shone into my eyes, just briefly, but enough to totally blind me.

'Help!' I say. 'I'm more injured than I first thought.'

Then a searing pain.

And blackness.

1

My little salon is at the front of the house with a window that looks onto our drive and the private road beyond. It has its own door, which means my clients don't need to walk through the house. The setup really couldn't be more perfect, yet running a little nail and beauty salon wasn't even on my radar when we bought this house six years ago. It was the location that sold it to us. Mike wanted to be within a twenty-minute commute of his architect's practice in Horsham, and I wanted space, countryside, and a good primary school for the kids. A community would have been nice, but unfortunately, we didn't get that. The neighbours keep to themselves around here.

Nevertheless, whenever I drive up the lane, a narrow country road with overgrown bramble hedges and clusters of oak and beech trees, their boughs hanging low and scattering acorns and leaves on the verges, I feel a deep sense of gratitude. I wanted the countryside idyll, and I've got it. I can't decide which season I like the best—early summer when the sides of the roads are filled with heavily scented wild garlic and the woods are a carpet of mauve from the mass of bluebells, or the autumn when shiny chestnut conkers roll along the lane and acorns crunch underfoot. But this year has been different, and I've barely noticed the passing of the seasons, yet the damp cold is already with us, and the weather forecasters are threatening an unseasonably harsh winter.

'How are you keeping, dear?' Mrs Ponder asks me, jolting me back into the present.

I'm on automatic, filing down her nails. 'We're fine, thank you. Harper started nursery school in September.'

'They grow up so quickly, do the little ones.' She frowns and stares out the window. 'There's a removal lorry,' she says.

I pause, the nail file held aloft, and follow her gaze. It's the size of a Luton van with the name *Carefree Removals* emblazoned with big red letters on the side, not one of those large 7.5 tonne HGV types that we had when we moved into this house. The van pulls into the house opposite ours, the house that has stood empty for the past five months.

'Well, it'll be nice for you to have new neighbours,' Mrs Ponder says, wriggling her fingers and bringing my attention back to her nails. 'Let's hope it's a happier home for the newcomers.'

'Indeed.'

'What's the house like? Is it the same as yours?'

'I've never been inside, but I think it's a similar layout to this one.'

'You're very lucky, living in such a big house.'

I nod. I know I'm lucky. Lucky beyond my wildest dreams.

Mrs Ponder has deep ridges across her nails, and I work rapidly to smooth them out. Sometimes I wonder what I'm doing painting people's nails, shaping brows, and removing unwanted hair, all the while listening to the minutiae of my clients' lives, hoping that they will leave my home feeling a little better about themselves than they did when they arrived. I don't need to be doing this. In fact, Mike tried to dissuade me, but now that Harry and Harper are both at school, I want to be doing something useful. I hate having to ask Mike for money to spend on myself.

I was an architect too. In fact, I was Mike's boss for a while, and back then, I envisaged that I would be designing buildings for the rest of my life. But I had a difficult pregnancy with Harry and was in and out of hospital, and it became obvious very early on that I couldn't be a mother and a high-flying architect. Life isn't fair. And so I quit, and I suppose it was just as well that I did because I couldn't have coped with my precious, complicated boy as well as being on building sites at the crack of dawn. We're lucky because Mike earns well, and during the three years we were together before Harry was born, combined with the sale of my one-bedroom apartment, I squirrelled away a nice little nest egg, which made a good contribution to the purchase of our home. Mike moved to a different firm about five years ago and is now an architect working for a commercial practice where they design shopping centres and municipal buildings, hospitals and hotels. He loves his job, which is just as well because he spends so much time doing it. As the firm grew and they employed more staff, I had hoped that his workload might ease a little. It seems to have had the opposite result, and these past few months have been particularly all-consuming. Mike works crazy hours. He's home late, and he often goes into the office at the weekends. He's turning into an absent parent despite the fact that we all sleep under the same roof.

'Perhaps they'll have children,' Mrs Ponder says. It takes me a moment to realise she's talking about the new neighbours. 'Young ones, like yours. Has there been any more about the awful incident? Such a tragedy.'

'No. No one has been charged, and the inquest is done and dusted.'

'It's got to have been one of those gypsies from the camp up the hill,' Mrs Ponder says. 'They drive like idiot lunatics.'

I don't reply. I know that's what many of the locals think because it's easier to blame a tragedy on people who aren't like us, isn't it? But I don't agree with that viewpoint. Just because they live in mobile homes or caravans and move from one area to the next doesn't mean that they have any less of a moral compass. Clearly, the police agree with me because they haven't arrested anyone.

'Well, let's hope for happier times,' Mrs Ponder says. 'I think you've done well staying in this house. As lovely as it is, I'm not sure that I would have stayed put.'

I try to stop myself from raising my eyebrows. Bad things occur wherever one might live, and although I try not to think about it when I drive past the spot where it happened, it never crossed my mind that we should move away. This is our dream house. It's got four bedrooms and three bath-rooms, with a large open plan kitchen, which if it isn't viewed too closely could easily be featured in an interior design magazine. The garden is surrounded on two sides by mature trees, mainly beeches and silver birch, although we have one statement oak tree that must be at least a couple of hundred years old. I have a particular affinity with that tree, and although I'm no tree hugger, I wish I could talk to it and learn its life story. Mike planted lots of croci underneath it, and in the spring, we have a carpet of yellows and mauves. At the back of the house is a wide patio with steps that lead down to the lawn, which slopes down towards a large field, which this year was planted with rape seed. I love the golden glow that shimmers through the trees. It's tranquil here too, the sounds of the chirping birds and the tapping woodpecker and the wind rustling through the trees broken only by the planes leaving or arriving into Gatwick airport or the distant thrum of traffic from the A24 when the wind is blowing in an easterly direction. We've spent a lot of money on doing up the house and garden, building a new oak-framed conservatory onto the living room, pruning the trees and filling up the borders with English country garden perennials such as delphinium and peonies that get nibbled by the tiptoeing hungry deer. Neither Mike nor I imagined we would take to gardening, but when you have as magical a spot as we do, it screams out for care and attention. Surprisingly, we both enjoy our time in the garden. Inside the house, I've made new curtains for all of the bedrooms. Mike used to spend his spare time in his garden shed, doing woodwork or potting out plants, but I can count on one hand the number of hours he's spent in the garden this year. Yes, it's really our countryside idyll and forever home. Mike said we might even build a swimming pool next year if he gets his expected bonus, but frankly, I'd rather have him around more so he can actually enjoy what we've already got. I know how lucky we are to be living such a comfortable existence.

I finish painting Mrs Ponder's nails in the sugary pink-orange colour that she always chooses, and pop her fingers inside the LED nail lamp. As I'm tidying up, I glance outside. From the front of our house, I have a view to the front of the Walkers' home, Number Two The Close. I've never under-stood why the houses weren't given names more suited to the locality. Bluebell Cottage or Robin's Nest, perhaps. I looked into it shortly after we moved in, but the bureaucracy involved in changing a house name is ridiculous. There's a woman standing next to the removal's van with her back to me, and I wonder if we'll become friends. Our houses are too far apart to make out her age, but that doesn't matter. I have an eclectic array of friends of all ages.

After Mrs Ponder leaves, I hurry into the kitchen. It's a country-style kitchen with hand-painted cupboards in pale grey and white Silestone countertops. Originally tasteful and expensive looking, installed and meticulously maintained by the previous owners of the house who bought the property from new, it's now looking a bit worse for wear, scratched and marked, predominantly by Harry, although Lupin, our black Labrador, has made his own contribution.

Three of the five houses on The Close (including ours) were built ten years ago when the Abbott seniors got planning permission for the small development. The Abbotts are third-generation farmers. Their son, Jack Abbott, and his wife, Josie, along with their three young children, live in the old farmhouse now, our neighbours to the left. I never met Mrs Abbott senior, who passed away some years ago, and I gather that Mr Abbott is in a care home. Their home is a typical build for this part of Sussex, with tile hung exterior walls and low ceilings with beams. They have a number of barns and outbuildings that are part of the farm and accessed from the main road, while their house shares the private road of The Close. The other original house on The Close is more modest and owned by the Quinns who, according to Josie, have lived there for over forty years. She let slip once that her parents-in-law made the Quinns an offer far above market value to buy their house off them so they could build another two or three new properties on the site. Apparently, the Quinns refused. Now in their early seventies, they said it was their forever home, and they intended to see out their years there.

Yesterday evening, I made a Victoria sponge, intending to give it to the kids for tea today, but they'll have to make do with some shop-bought biscuits as their teatime treat. I take the cake out of the larder and sprinkle some icing sugar over the top of it, carefully placing it onto some aluminium foil before easing it into a pale grey cake tin. Striding into the living room, I rummage in the drawer of an antique dresser, given to us by Mike's mother, and find a handful of unused cards. There's an inoffensive one with painted flowers on the front and no wording inside. I scrawl a *Welcome to The Close* message and sign it with all four of our names.

I put my coat on, and Lupin looks up at me expectantly. 'Sorry, you're staying here.' I bend down to stroke the dog, then pick up the cake tin and card and walk out the back door. In the past, if I were nipping out for ten minutes, I might have left the door unlocked. I don't anymore.

As I'm walking from our driveway to the private lane that links the five houses, the new neighbour's removal van is leaving. That was quick. Perhaps there's another bigger lorry on its way.

Even though the house at number two has only been empty for five months, it already has a neglected feel, with the previously tidy front garden covered with fallen leaves and the wheelie bin lying on its side. Or perhaps I'm projecting in the knowledge of what happened. Our house and number two are similar in design, with red bricks and anthracite grey metal window frames. I take a deep breath and stride up to the black front door, pressing the electronic doorbell.

I barely have time to step away when the door swings open.

'Hello!' the woman says. At a guess, she's early forties, and although her shoulder-length mid-brown hair looks as if she's just walked out of a hair salon, there's something tired about her thin face. It's lined, and when she smiles at me, I notice that her teeth are crooked and slightly yellow, perhaps the teeth of a heavy smoker.

'I just wanted to come and say welcome to The Close. I'm Isobel Floyd, and I live in the house opposite with my husband, Mike, and kids, Harper and Harry. This is for you.' I hold out the tin with the cake in it. She draws her chin backwards, and her eyes widen.

'Wow, I didn't think people actually did that anymore!' She levers off the lid and peers inside the tin. 'You baked a cake just for me? That's so kind. You must come in.'

She stands back and beckons me through into the hallway. She's wearing a tightly fitted dress in a leopard print with high-heel boots, most definitely not the sort of clothes most people wear when moving into a new home.

'Come through and excuse the mess.' She leads the way into the kitchen. Even though the house is a similar shape to ours, there's nothing else that's the same. The whitewashed walls are bare with picture hooks and faded squares suggesting where paintings once hung. The kitchen is totally different, smaller with a bank of white cupboards and vinyl-covered countertops.

'This house must look very different to how you last saw it,' she says. 'It's always strange seeing properties when they're empty.'

I smile tightly because I never stepped inside this house before.

'My name's Linette Smith. As you probably know, I'm renting this house, although I'd love to live permanently somewhere like this. It's a dream. The removal guys have just left, and the only thing I've unpacked is the box with the kettle and some mugs. Will you join me for a cuppa and a piece of your delicious-looking cake?'

'Thank you,' I say as I glance around. There's very little furniture here, and what there is looks shabby. The table has a brown Formica top and metal legs like a camping table, and the chairs are white plastic.

'Take a pew,' she says. 'And sorry about the state of my stuff. I've just split up from my husband, and he got to keep all of our things.' She turns away from me, and I think that she's wiping her eyes. This must be very hard for her. She puts the kettle on and turns around to face me again. 'I wanted to rent somewhere furnished, but I fell in love with this house and garden. It has a lovely feel about it.'

I smile.

'How do you take your tea?'

'Just milk, please,' I say.

'It's UHT. All I've got,' she says with an apologetic grimace.

'That's fine.' I smile at her.

Linette carries two chipped navy mugs to the table and sits down opposite me. The table wobbles violently.

'I'm so excited about living here and can't wait to get to know you all. Tell me about your kids.'

'Harry is six, and Harper is four. They both go to the local village school, although Harper only started this term. How about you? Do you have any children?' I glance around but can't see any toys or family photos. I hope I haven't put my foot in it.

She shakes her head and pulls a sad face. 'Didn't happen for us, and now it's likely too late. Such is life. What's it like living here?'

'Perfect. Really, it's a dream come true for Mike and me. Where have you moved from?'

'Crawley direction. I need to know the gossip.' She leans forwards and rubs the palms of her hands together. 'What are the other neighbours like? Do you all get on?'

I can feel the edge of my lips quiver slightly as I force them into a smile. It's obvious that she doesn't know what happened here, that she has no idea of the tragedy that befell the previous residents of this house. But I'm not going to be the person to tell her. I don't want to ruin the first day in her new home.

'Spill the beans.' She laughs. 'I want to know what they're like.'

'Josie and Jack Abbott live in the farmhouse as you drive

into The Close. They've got three young children, and Jack farms all the land around here. Next door to you are Mr and Mrs Quinn. They're an older couple and keep themselves to themselves. I believe they've lived here for over forty years. And on the other side of you at the end of The Close is Thomas Adler. He lives alone and predominantly works from home.'

'A single man!' Linette winks at me.

'Mmm,' I say noncommittally.

'And do you all socialise?'

'Not really. People keep to themselves around here, probably because we're not in the village itself. I get to meet local people because I have a little beauty business, doing nails and brows and stuff, and of course, school has been helpful for making friends.'

'The school gates aren't an option for me, so I'm going to have to come up with another way of meeting people.' She gazes at the ceiling for a moment. 'I know. I'll have a drinks party and invite all the neighbours.'

'That's very kind,' I murmur, thinking, *Good luck with that.*

2

When you live in a lovely house in a tranquil setting, you can be lulled into a false sense of security, that nothing bad can happen to you. So when nineteen-year-old Wilson Walker was killed in a hit-and-run accident at the junction of our private road and the lane, it rocked everyone's worlds. Of course, it was beyond horrific for the Walkers, but I think we were all very deeply affected. I certainly was, still am, if truth be told. It makes you look at life differently, and I hug my children tighter, keep a closer eye on them and never let them out of sight, especially when there are cars around.

The Walkers moved into their house about four years ago. Mona Walker reminded me of a dormouse, the type of woman who walked around with slightly rounded shoulders, her eyes on the ground, as if she wanted to shrink in on herself. Her husband, Keith Walker, couldn't have been more different. He was a hulk, brutish in appearance, with bulging biceps, a thick, dark beard and a confrontational way of talking to people, standing with his hands on his hips and his jaw jutting forwards. Not that I ever heard him raise his voice.

He kept to himself like everyone around here, muttering a terse hello should it be unavoidable. I invited Mona over a couple of times shortly after they moved in, but she said she was working or was too busy. I soon got the hint. I liked their two sons, though. Wilson was at college somewhere locally, and he used to do odd jobs and gardening for neighbours. His younger brother, Ollie, was thirteen or fourteen. A polite boy who always smiled at us, Ollie had offered to babysit Harry and Harper, but we never took him up on that.

The Walker family moved away about a month after Wilson died. They didn't tell anyone they were going. A removal lorry arrived, and off they went. I don't blame them. It must have been horrific driving past the spot where their son was mown down. And here we are, six months on, and the driver of the car who killed him still hasn't been found. On the grapevine, I've heard that the inquest is closed and that's that.

I'm relieved that Linette doesn't know what happened, but I suppose she'll find out soon enough. All the same, it's not going to be me who tells her.

As I'm walking back from Linette's house, holding my empty cake tin, I see Josie lifting shopping bags out of a new car. She's wearing her old Barbour, skinny jeans and wellington boots. It's her uniform, and I remember the first time I saw her in a dress, it was a shock. She's got a great figure and scrubs up well, but she normally doesn't bother with anything as prosaic as makeup. Her mid-brown hair is scraped back into a ponytail, and there's a ruddiness to her cheeks from so much time spent outdoors. This morning, she was driving her Audi, but now she's in an aged Fiesta. I wonder if her car is in the garage. I wave, and she nods. That's all I get these days.

Josie and I used to be reasonably close. We were both pregnant at the same time, me with Harper and her with her youngest, Molly. In theory, we had lots in common. We both had a difficult start in life. She was adopted aged two and spent years tracking down her birth father, only to discover he had died a decade earlier. I was adopted by my third foster family, and I have no desire to seek out my birth parents. Mum is the mother I have known for the best part of my life, and every day I thank my lucky stars that she came into my life. It's thanks to her and a particularly enlightened teacher at my secondary school, who noticed early on that I was good at art and maths and spent most of my time doodling draw-ings in my exercise books, that I found my vocation so early on and made it to university. Architecture is often seen as the domain of the middle classes. I've broken that trend.

Josie and I never had an easy friendship such as I have with most of my girlfriends and, particularly, the people I used to work with, but we helped each other out from time to time, and I felt that she was there for me should I need it and vice versa. That's changed. Looking back, it's been a gradual shift since well before Wilson's death, but recently, it's like Josie positively dislikes me. She doesn't look me in the eye and never seeks me out for a chat. I wonder if I've done some-thing to offend her, and I've been meaning to have a heart-to-heart with her, but the time hasn't been right until now. Feeling brave after my positive chat with Linette, I hurry towards her driveway.

'Would you like me to pick up your kids from school this afternoon?' I shout across the lane.

'No, thanks,' she says, slamming the boot shut and turning her back to me, walking away towards the house.

Those two words knock the stuffing out of me. I know it's stupid to feel wounded by her, but we're both making the same journey, morning and afternoon, and our children are even in the same classes, so it's ridiculous that she's not letting me help out. I see her every day, often several times a day, and this froideur can't carry on. I`m determined to find out what the problem is.

LATER IN THE AFTERNOON, I'm standing at the school gates, chatting to the mother of Harper's best friend, when I spot Josie.

'Can you excuse me a moment?' I say and wend my way through the throng of parents.

I tap Josie on the arm, and she jumps. She tries to disguise her scowl when she realises it's me.

'Can I have a quick word?' I ask quietly.

She shrugs.

'Is everything all right? It's just you seem to be avoiding me at the moment, and I was wondering if I've done anything to upset you.'

She sighs. 'It's not about you, Isobel. Everything's fine.'

'Come on, Josie. It's obvious that everything isn't all right. I just wanted to be able to help you out from time to time.'

'You can't. Look, I appreciate the offer, but I don't need anything from you.'

'Maybe not, but I'm your neighbour and friend, so if I can help, I'd like to.'

She sighs heavily. 'Things are tough at the moment, but it'll pass.' She wraps her arms around her torso and glances at her black wellington boots. I get the sense she feels she's already told me too much. I flounder to find something else to say.

'Is your car in the garage?'

'What? No. For God's sake! I just wish everyone would mind their own business. If you must know, it's my new car. I've downsized.'

'Oh.' That explains things. I know life has been tough for farmers the past few years, and I guess the Abbotts have financial difficulties. It explains why Josie hasn't come to the school mums' nights out during the past six months.

'Have you met our new neighbour?' I ask, eager to keep the conversation going.

'Yes, she seems nice enough.'

And then the children start pouring out of school, and I reckon Josie is as relieved as me that our awkward chat is over.

BACK AT HOME, I bundle the kids inside and step on an envelope that has been pushed through the letterbox. It's a note from Linette asking me over for a coffee next Tuesday, including her mobile number for an RSVP. That's kind of her. It should really be me inviting her over to my house. I check my diary, and I've only got a couple of clients from midday onwards, so ten a.m. is fine. I text her to say thank you.

By the time Mike gets home, Harper is already in bed in her pale pink palace, surrounded by her vast collection of cuddly toys, and Harry is creating havoc in his bedroom. He's the type of child who is either manic or subdued. There seems to be little in the middle ground, and it makes it exhausting for everyone, particularly me. Mike's footsteps are slow and heavy as he climbs the stairs.

'Daddy!' Harry screeches as he careens out of his room, slamming himself into Mike's legs.

'Hello, monster!' Mike says. But there's a lethargy to his voice. When he comes into Harper's room, he gives me a cursory kiss on my cheek and sits down heavily on Harper's bed.

'A tough day?' I ask.

'Yes.'

As he's saying goodnight to the children, I look at him. I mean really look, not the sort of quick glance we tend to give our spouses, the sort of glance that our brains fill in due to familiarity. I try to see Mike with fresh eyes. He's a good-looking man, tall and slender, with dark honey-coloured curly hair and sparkling green eyes, but his face has a greyish tinge, and the rings under his eyes have a purple hue. His shoulders slouch, and I notice that he has ink on his hands. Mike has always been fastidious about his hands, with long fingers and neatly cut nails. They're the tools of his trade despite the current reality that CAD designs have overtaken any need to draw buildings in pen and ink. But Mike still likes to sketch old-style even if most of his work is done on the computer. He looks really tired, and I wonder with a jolt whether he's ill.

If I'm being honest with myself, things haven't been great between us this past year. He has been working increasingly long hours, and when he's home, he's often snappy and complains how exhausted he is. I've suggested that I could close up my little salon and go back to work, something that in many ways, I'd love to do, but he's insistent that we don't need an additional income and that I'm the vital cog that keeps our family functioning. When I asked whether he could work shorter hours, he said he enjoys the job, that things will get better next year when they recruit yet more staff. From time to time, I feel a great surge of resentment that he is still able to do the job that I loved, but then I look at the children and I know that I've made the right decision. Life is hard enough for Harry without having two absent parents.

As every year passes, Mike discusses his work with me less and less. To begin with, I thought it was because he was worried that I might feel left out and that perhaps he was rubbing salt into the wound. Now I wonder whether he's simply lost respect for me, that my opinions are irrelevant because I've been out of the industry for too long. Or perhaps I'm just reading too much into it. I suppose it's normal for dialogue and romance to slowly evaporate in a marriage, especially when neither of us makes a concerted effort to prioritise our relationship. For Mike, work comes first. For me, it's the children.

I'M NOT A NATURAL COOK, and actually, I'm not that interested in food. It's a necessity, and I sometimes envy those people who relish and appreciate food in the same way that I appreciate drawing and design. I have perfected a staple of meals, and I rotate them. I once asked Mike if he minded, and he said that he's just grateful he has a meal on the table at the end of a long day. His mum was a nurse, and she worked throughout his childhood, so he was brought up on ready-made meals. Tonight, I've made salmon en croute with baby potatoes and peas, and I'm pouring him a glass of chilled Pinot Grigio. Occasionally, I take stock and snigger. I wonder what my drug-addicted birth mother would think about her oh-so-very-posh middle-class daughter.

'Linette has invited me over,' I say. 'The new neighbour.' I wait for a response but don't get one.

'Are you listening?'

'What, sorry. I was miles away.'

'You're always miles away.' I'm unable to control the snappiness in my voice. I can't help myself from asking the same question again. 'Is work too much?'

'No, of course not. I enjoy it.' He carries on eating, and the sound of him chewing his puff pastry grates on my nerves.

'You look really tired, Mike.'

'Probably because I am.' He takes a large swig of wine. During the past year, we always have a bottle open, and whilst I rarely drink, he has at least two glasses a night and often a couple of beers too.

'Are you feeling okay?'

'Yup.'

'Aren't you sleeping well?'

'We've been here before. There's a lot on, Isobel. Just let it go.'

'Perhaps you could ask Pete for another assistant?'

'That's sure as hell not going to happen. We've got some big projects on at the moment, but things should calm down after Christmas.'

'You need a holiday.'

He grunts. 'Fat chance.'

'I mean a few days away, just you and me. Mum can look after the kids. We could go somewhere in Devon, by the sea.'

'I can't take any holiday, Isobel. There's too much going on at work.'

'Come on, Mike. You look exhausted, ill even. How about a long weekend? You could manage that, surely?'

He clenches his jaw and takes another large sip of wine.

'Otherwise, you need to go to the doctor. Have a check-up, make sure that you're not low on vitamins and minerals. Or you might have a thyroid issue. You remember how your dad was knackered all the time?'

'I know you mean well, but let it go!' He makes an exaggerated sigh. 'I'm not going to the bloody doctor. There's nothing wrong with me other than I've got too much work on. It would be a problem if I didn't enjoy it, but I do.'

I can feel tears welling up. It's pathetic. All I want is for Mike to be relaxed and as happy as he always used to be. I'm not hungry and shove the food to the side of my plate, placing my cutlery neatly in the middle of it.

'Look, I'm sorry,' Mike says, reaching across the table and placing his hand over mine. 'I know I've been distant, and I know you've had the full burden of caring for the kids. I'll go away for a long weekend if you insist.'

'I'm not insisting,' I say, pulling my hand away. 'I think you need it. We both do.'

'Fair enough. Book something, but double-check with Janine first. She's in control of my diary.'

I nod. Janine is the firm's office manager and secretary to the partners. She's a kindly middle-aged woman who seems to be the glue that sticks the firm together.

When we've finished eating, for the first time in ages, Mike offers to help with clearing up. I tell him to go and put his feet up and then feel that familiar surge of resentment. I'm not a fifties housewife. I tell myself that this stage won't last forever, that we'll get our marriage back on track, and I will return to work at some point. It's becoming a familiar mantra.

Later that evening, I do an online search for a country house hotel overlooking the sea in Devon. I find a delightful-looking spa hotel with views over the English Channel, and unsurprisingly for early November, there is plenty of availability. Hopefully, this will be just what we need.

3

I'm a few minutes late for coffee at Linette's house. It was a particularly difficult morning with Harry. He refuses to eat any food that is the colour brown. Normally, I manage that by feeding him with cornflakes and a boiled egg for breakfast. I've found some corn-based bread that is a vile shade of yellow, and he'll happily drink freshly squeezed orange juice. I know some mothers look at me with rolling eyes, as if I'm pandering to my spoiled son's obsequious behaviour, but instinctively, I've known Harry was a bit different—or special, as I like to say—since he was a baby.

This morning, he announced he would no longer eat anything that is yellow. Apparently, someone told him that the only foods that are good for you are green. I know many parents would be thrilled that their child wanted to eat green food, but when it comes to breakfast and getting sufficient sustenance in for a long day at school, it's hard. We had tantrums and tears, and even Harper became belligerent, so by the time I shoved them into the schoolyard, I felt frazzled. I picked up a few bits and pieces at the local convenience store and hurried home to give Lupin a ten-minute walk.

And now, here I am walking up to Linette's front door. I wonder how long it will take until I stop thinking of this house as the Walkers'. I ring the doorbell, and this time it takes a little longer for her to appear, but when she opens the door, it's with a big smile on her face.

'Lovely to see you,' Linette says, kissing me on both cheeks as if we're long-lost friends. It smells as if I'm being enveloped in a cloud of scent. It has a touch of jasmine and something slightly synthetic that I can't identify. I can hear voices coming from inside the house, and I'm surprised. 'Come on in,' she says, leading me through the empty hallway.

She's wearing a fitted leather skirt and a cream V-neck sweater with several thin gold chains around her neck. I feel positively dowdy in comparison in my jeans and an old jumper. She pushes open the door to the living room, and I'm immediately on the back foot when I realise both Josie and Mrs Quinn are here.

'So,' Linette says, clapping her hands together, 'I thought it would be lovely if we ladies of The Close could have a little get-together.'

My smile feels very fake, and by the way she shuffles in her chair, I can sense that Josie is uncomfortable too. I'm most surprised to see Mrs Quinn. I can count on one hand the number of times I've seen her this year.

'Hello, Josie, Mrs Quinn,' I say.

'Take a pew.' Linette motions towards a brown leather armchair. All her furniture is brown leather, those extra-large types that look too big even in a reasonably sized living room such as this. I sink into it, and from its sticky feel, I realise it's probably plastic and not leather after all. 'Would you like tea or coffee, Isobel?'

'Coffee, please. Milk and no sugar.'

Linette peers into Josie's and Mrs Quinn's mugs. 'Would you like a top-up, Mrs Quinn?'

'Yes, please, dear. You're such a lovely young woman.'

Linette scrunches her face slightly and looks over at me. 'The young bit I'm not so sure about.' She laughs. 'I've offered to help Mrs Quinn from time to time when Mr Quinn has to pop out to do the shopping.'

'And I've accepted the offer,' the older woman says. 'Linette came over yesterday, and my Doug has agreed that she can help us.'

'He has?' I say with surprise. I'm relieved that Josie looks equally startled. Linette has been living in The Close for barely a week and has not only set foot in the Quinns' house —which to the best of my knowledge none of the rest of us have—but is being trusted to care for Mrs Quinn, who is suffering from the early stages of dementia.

'She's quite the dear is Linette,' Mrs Quinn says. 'She popped over the day after she moved in, bringing along a delicious sponge cake. It was scrumptious. She was a care worker in her time, weren't you, love? And you know how Doug fusses over me and doesn't like to leave me in the house alone. Quite ridiculous, really.' She takes a loud slurp from her mug of tea and carefully places it back onto the glass and chrome coffee table. I wonder whether Linette took the cake I made her to the Quinns' house.

'Anyway, where was I?' the older woman asks.

I glance at Linette, but she's leaning towards Mrs Quinn, patting her hand. 'You were telling us how I'm going to pop in when your husband is out.'

'Was I? Oh well, never mind.'

Neither of the Quinns has explicitly told us that Mrs Quinn has dementia, but she's been sighted less and less over the past few years, and Mr Quinn has hinted at his wife's illness. It must be hard for them with no children or other family living nearby to lend support.

'So what do you all do in your downtime?' Linette asks.

'You mean hobbies?' Josie says.

'Yes.'

'Farmers' wives with three children don't get any time for hobbies,' Josie says. 'Isobel has time on her hands. You used to paint, didn't you? How do you keep yourself busy these days?'

I try not to bristle because Josie knows exactly what I do. She knows that I was a high-flying architect, and I've wondered whether she feels threatened by me because now she seems to gloat that I'm a stay-at-home mother with a home beauty salon. She may have never used my services, but plenty of her friends do. 'I have a beauty business, which is going quite well.' But then I decide to change tack and be the bigger person here. 'Josie is a brilliant knitter and sewer,' I say. 'She makes all her children's clothes, don't you?'

She harrumphs. 'No time for that anymore.'

'So you're all creative,' Linette says. 'When I was at Mrs Quinn's, I discovered that she used to crochet magnificent blankets. She has one in pretty shades of mauves over the back of her sofa. I know you don't have much time on your hands, Josie, but we should try to have regular Close craft evenings. It would be fun.'

'What are your hobbies, Linette?' I ask. The coffee is instant and tepid. I don't want to be a coffee snob, but I could do with a stronger hit of caffeine this morning.

She laughs. 'I haven't got a creative bone in my body. I think my job in our craft evenings would be to provide the drinks, and then I can sit back and be in awe of all of you skilled ladies.'

There's silence for a long moment, and whilst I'm grappling for something to say, I glance around. Other than the heavy sofa and two matching armchairs along with the glass coffee table, this room is completely empty of the things that make it a home. No pictures on the walls, no nick-nacks on the mantelpiece, no cushions, absolutely nothing to give an insight into the woman living here. I wonder whether Linette intends to soften the place up or whether she's just not into home decor.

'Do you work?' I ask Linette.

'Not at the moment. I got a good settlement from my divorce, but I might think about getting back into something in the care sector in due course. I really love this house. I'm thinking about finding out whether the owners might sell it to me. What do you reckon?'

Linette looks at each of us in turn. Mrs Quinn seems to be in a world of her own, gazing out the window at the rabbits nibbling the plants in the border at the side of the overgrown garden. Josie shrugs her shoulders, so Linette's gaze falls on me.

'I'm not sure,' I mumble.

Linette leans back in her chair and stretches her legs out in front of her, kicking off her kitten-heeled shoes. She has bare legs, and even though it's warm enough in here, it's a strange look for this chilly time of year.

'What are they like, the people who own this house?'

For the first time, Josie and I catch each other's eyes. It's obvious that Linette has no idea what happened to the Walkers, and I certainly don't want to be the one to talk about their tragedy.

'Come on, spill the beans!' Linette laughs. 'Why are you all so cagey? They can't have been that bad.'

'It's not that,' Josie says, biting the side of her lip. 'They were a perfectly nice family, but their son died. It was a very difficult time for them, and that's why they moved away.'

'Oh, goodness,' Linette says, sitting up straight, her hazel eyes wide open, fake lashes quivering. 'I had no idea. The estate agent didn't tell me anything about the owners. That's awful. What are the family called?'

I will Josie not to say anything because if Linette searches for the Walkers, she'll find all the newspaper reports describing the tragic hit-and-run death of Wilson Walker. How will Linette feel about living in a home where something so sad happened, a home where the family felt compelled to move from because they had to drive past the spot their son was killed just to get in and out of their home? But Josie doesn't hold back.

'They were called the Walkers, and their son was Wilson. It was horrible.'

'Wow,' Linette says.

I notice that Mrs Quinn is still gazing out the window with a blank expression. I wonder if she even knows what we're talking about.

'I can't imagine how awful that must have been. How old was the lad?'

'Nineteen,' I murmur.

'Well, at least the Walkers had all of you lovely neighbours to rally around. I'm sure they must have really appreciated that.'

There's another long, awkward silence because Josie, Mrs Quinn, and I know that none of us really offered the sort of support that we should have done. I still feel terrible about it, and just Linette's mention of the Walkers elicits a churning feeling in my stomach. There was an inquest and an investigation, and the funeral didn't happen for a good three to four weeks after Wilson's death. Keith Walker put a little scribbled note through our door, as I assume he did to all of the neighbours, telling us that the funeral would be at three p.m. on the following Thursday. We didn't go. Not because I didn't want to, because I did. But it was the afternoon of Harry's psychological assessment for autism, a date that had been in the diary for months and months. Because those appointments are so hard to get, I knew that I couldn't change it, so I asked Mike to attend and to offer up my apologies.

Later that afternoon, after Harry's assessment, I was pulling into The Close when I saw Josie. I wound down the car window.

'How was the funeral?' I asked.

'What funeral?' she said.

'Wilson's.'

'Oh, that. We didn't go. We had a delivery this afternoon, so it wasn't convenient.'

That evening, Harry was tired and grumpy, and when Mike got home—late, as usual—he launched straight into quizzing me as to what the psychologist had said and what tests they did on Harry to establish what condition he might have and when we might get the results. It wasn't until much later that I realised Mike wasn't wearing the black tie that he normally dons for funerals.

'Was the funeral awful?' I asked. 'It must have been terribly sad.'

He frowned at me. 'Oh, you mean Wilson's. I didn't go.'

'What?' I exclaimed.

'I had a client meeting this afternoon, and I couldn't *not* attend. Besides, it's not as if we knew the Walkers well. I'm sure the church was packed full of his friends and family, and we wouldn't have been missed.'

But I felt terrible about it. I suggested to Mike that I write a note apologising for not attending, but he said that would only be drawing attention to the fact we weren't there. It wasn't until the Walkers had moved away that I discovered not a single resident of The Close had attended. It's not surprising that the family moved away just a few days later.

So no, we weren't lovely neighbours, and we certainly didn't rally around.

'How did he die?' Linette asks, bringing me back to the present.

'Let's not talk about horrible things like that,' Mrs Quinn says, flapping her hands in front of her.

'It's very distressing when people die young,' Linette says, gazing out the window. 'But sometimes, things happen for a reason.'

'What?' I can't help myself from questioning such a dreadful statement. 'There can't ever be a reason for the tragic death of a young person,' I say. I glance at Josie, who is avoiding catching my eye, but I can tell by the way she curls her lip and flinches that she's appalled by this conversation.

'Do you all believe in karma?' Linette asks.

We stare at her.

'Because perhaps the Walkers did something really bad in a past life and that was payback.'

A shiver runs down my spine. That was the weirdest thing to say. How can the terrible death of a teenage boy ever be considered karma?

4

_____

Harry is autistic. Not severely so, but sufficient to cause problems at school. We're one of the lucky families, getting a diagnosis when he is still so young and being able to give him any additional support that he might need in the future. I don't like labels, but I know that it will help him and us navigate the educational system now that we know what is making him special. My main worry for Harry isn't his educational abilities because he's intelligent and particularly excellent with numbers. It's the social aspects of school life, particularly friendships and teamwork. He has one best friend, a little boy called Bashir, whose refugee parents don't speak any English. I fear that once Bashir fully integrates into life here, he will move on from his strange friend, and Harry will be left all alone once again.

This afternoon, I sense immediately that something is wrong. Harry shuns me when I try to greet him at the school gates. He pushes me away and refuses to talk. I'm sufficiently experienced in this to realise there's no point in insisting that he tell me what the problem is, as that will only make things worse, so I chatter away, telling him about my day, listening to Harper twitter on about nothing much. Once we're home and Harper is distracted by the television, I attempt to talk to Harry.

'You can tell me, sweetheart,' I say, suppressing my over-whelming urge to scoop him up and give him a big hug. 'What happened at school today?'

I get a grunt in response, and he won't meet my eyes.

'Come on, darling. It's going to be a great week. It's Halloween on Friday, and we can go trick-or-treating.'

Harry bursts into tears, and this time he lets me touch him, stroking his head and holding his shuddering little body. It's as if his heart is broken, he is crying with such ferocity.

'Benji hasn't invited me,' he snuffles.

And then I realise. Benji Abbott is Josie's son, and they're in the same class at the local primary school. Every year, Josie organises a trick-or-treating party for a bunch of her children's friends. Clearly, Harry has been excluded. How could Josie be so heartless, especially when Harry was perfectly well-behaved at last year's party? But I know I can't show my son my sense of dismay, so I scoop him up and tell him that we're going to have a much better party, with creepy costumes and all of his favourite sweets, and eventually, he calms down. Me, less so.

I can't help but wonder whether Harry's exclusion is more to do with Josie's feelings towards me than Benji's feelings towards Harry.

THE NEXT MORNING, after dropping the children at school and firmly avoiding Josie, because I need to let my fury simmer down before approaching her, I'm pulling into our private road. The road isn't long, about one hundred and fifty metres, and the five houses are spread far apart, but even so, it causes problems. Several large potholes have developed in the tarmac, and we will have to come to some consensus as to how to split the costs of resurfacing. Before Wilson died, we had some informal discussions about the best way forwards, round-robin emails, as no one took the initiative to have a face-to-face meeting. As there are only five properties using the road, you might have thought that agreement could be easily reached, but no. Thomas Adler wanted to do a complete resurface, the Quinns didn't want anything to do with it and said they had no funds to support the project, Keith Walker said he had a friend who would fix it up for mates' rates, and the Abbotts said they rarely used the road so didn't want to contribute anything more than ten percent. And then there were Mike and me, who said we'd go along with the consensus. Nothing has been mentioned about the road since Wilson died, and I think it will be a long time before any of us has the appetite to broach the subject again. It's as I'm avoiding the first of the large potholes that I see Mrs Quinn sauntering along our private road. She's just passed our entrance and is meandering towards Thomas Adler's house. Her gaze is fixed to the oppressive metal grey sky, and despite the freezing cold, she's outside without a coat on. There's something not right. I park the car and hurry after her.

'Good morning, Mrs Quinn,' I shout.

She turns around and smiles at me. 'Hello, love. Who are you?'

My heart contracts slightly. 'It's me, Isobel Floyd. I'm your neighbour, and I live in this house.'

'Oh, yes. Isobel.' But she still doesn't look at me, so I follow her gaze up towards the leaden sky.

It's the damned drone, yet again.

This is the second time I've seen it hovering over The

Close. Last week, Lupin was in the garden, barking maniacally. I was giving a customer a pedicure and eventually had to excuse myself and go and check on the dog. A drone was hovering just above the trees, circling our garden. When I stood on the patio and waved my arms around, the drone sped off and out of sight. Today, it's higher up and not nearly as noisy, but it infuriates me. If nothing else, it's a gross invasion of our privacy, nosing around The Close, looking at our houses and gardens. I wonder whether it's even legal to be spying on people's properties like that.

'Is it a UFO?' Mrs Quinn asks.

'No, it's a drone. It's a camera in the sky, controlled by someone nearby.'

'Oh, good. I don't fancy being whisked away by Martians.'

'Aren't you cold, Mrs Quinn?' I ask. Her blouse is buttoned up wrongly, and her long grey cardigan has food stains on it.

'Yes, dear. I am a bit.'

'Why don't I walk you home?'

'Well, that's very kind of you.'

The noise of the drone fades, and the device disappears over the treetops. I link my arm into Mrs Quinn's, and we turn around to walk towards her house.

I know very little about the Quinns other than they've lived in their home for over forty years, and Mr Quinn has been retired during all the time we've been here. Josie once mentioned that he had a transport business, so perhaps he sold it. At a guess, I assume he's in his early seventies, and Mrs Quinn must be a similar age. We walk slowly along the lane for the fifty or so metres to the entrance to their driveway. The Quinns' house is red brick, and from the style, I assume it was built in the 1930s. It has a large bay-fronted window at the front, and all the window frames are white. The front door is set in an arched lobby, also constructed from red bricks, and the chimney rises far above the roof, out of proportion with the modest size of the house. The garden is big and clearly the Quinns' pride and joy because it is always immaculate. Even at this time of the year when the trees have shed most of their leaves and the rest of us just give in to the losing battle of leaves piling up on our lawns, blocking the ditches and getting stuck to our heels, the Quinns' property is devoid of leaves. Mr Quinn doesn't have anything as fancy as a leaf blower. Instead, he is outside every day in the autumn, come rain or shine, raking away the leaves and filling up his massive compost heap, occasionally burning them when the pile gets too big. But he's a considerate man and makes sure that he only has a bonfire when there's an easterly wind so the smoke blows away from the other houses on The Close.

Mrs Quinn and I arrive at her front door, and she rifles in the pockets of her cardigan.

'I don't seem to have a key,' she says.

'Is your husband at home?' I ask before realising that his car isn't in the driveway, and Mrs Quinn most likely wouldn't be wandering outside alone and confused if he were.

'No, dear. Now what did Doug say? Oh, yes, I think he's gone shopping. He had to pick up a prescription for me.'

'And you don't have a key to the house?'

'Maybe around the back, but I'm not altogether sure.'

I follow Mrs Quinn around the side of their house to the back door, which is wide open.

'Oh, that's good. It's open. I wonder why.'

No doubt she left the house without shutting the door behind her when she stepped outside to view the drone. I feel a rush of sadness as I realise her dementia is getting worse.

'I think it might be a good idea if I stay with you until your husband returns,' I suggest.

'Really?' She stares at me with a blank expression.

I realise my staying here at the Quinns' house might seem like a bit of an imposition, but I'm worried about the older woman. After the way we neglected the Walkers, I'm going to make absolutely sure that I look out for our current neighbours. We're both standing there in front of the open door, and Mrs Quinn shivers.

'Shall we go in, then?' I suggest.

'Oh, you'd like a cup of tea,' Mrs Quinn says and walks inside.

I don't really, but I say, 'If you're offering, that would be lovely.'

The kitchen is immaculate, but it looks as if it were installed in the 1950s. The cupboards and work surfaces are covered in brown linoleum, and the oven is white and blue with the brand name Moffat. Although it's spotless, the last time I saw a similar oven was in my grandmother's house.

Mrs Quinn gestures for me to sit at the circular wooden table while she makes us a pot of tea in a green teapot with a cracked lid. She takes two matching mugs from the cupboard and sits down next to me, pushing a mug towards me.

'She's a very nice lady, that one who has moved into the dead boy's house,' she says.

'Linette. Yes, I agree. It was lovely that you, me, Josie and Linette could get together.'

'Get together?' Mrs Quinn knits her eyebrows together.

'A few days ago, for coffee,' I say, realising that Mrs Quinn's short-term memory must be impaired. I'm just about to change the subject when a car door slams, and Mr Quinn strides into the kitchen.

'Yvonne!' he says and then stops totally still when he sees me. His arms hang limply at his sides, and he lets the Tesco carrier bag he's holding slip to the floor. 'What are you doing here?'

'I found Mrs Quinn wandering down The Close without a coat on, so I wanted to sit with her until you got home.'

'For heaven's sake, Yvonne. I told you to stay inside. It's not safe for you to be wandering off.' He picks up the shopping bag and turns his back to me, his shoulders hunched up under his ears. 'You didn't need to be here, Mrs Floyd,' he says.

'Please call me Isobel. I was just a little bit worried.'

He harrumphs. 'Yes, well. Thank you. But it's best if you go now.'

I'm taken aback by his brusqueness. I know he's not keen on having people in his house, but I was only doing them a favour. But then I check myself. Of course he's going to be short with me. He'll be upset and worried about his wife, concerned that her dementia is getting worse. It must be so difficult for him, being all alone to care for her.

'I'd be very happy to sit with your wife either here or at our house when you go out,' I say. 'Just to give you a bit of peace of mind.'

'Thank you, but no thank you,' he says, still with his back to me. 'We're quite able to look after ourselves.' He walks to the back door, which is just behind the table where Mrs Quinn and I are sitting. Still wearing his black anorak, he opens the door and stands back, the chill of the autumnal day causing me to shiver. I stand up despite my mug of tea being almost full.

'Goodbye,' I say, but Mr Quinn has chivvied me out before his wife can respond.

I stride back to our house, feeling somewhat aggrieved. Mr Quinn has accepted Linette's offer of help despite her being a newcomer to The Close, yet he has firmly rejected me. I'm beginning to wonder whether Mike and I have inadvertently done something to upset all of our neighbours. I wonder whether this antipathy relates to the email discussions over repairing the road, but we were the only ones not to have a strong view, and I felt we were being the most amenable. But other than that, we've had no involvement with any of them. It's extremely frustrating that I can't fathom what we might have done.

5

Back at home, I have a general sense of unease. None of us neighbours have ever been close, but it's one thing keeping a distance and quite another to be spurned. I understand Mr Quinn's reaction, but I can't so easily dismiss Josie's rejection of Harry. Despite my dislike of confrontation, I'm going to have to talk to her about it, and this isn't a conversation to be had at the school gates. As a child, I used to do anything I could to avoid arguments, hiding under a duvet on more than one occasion, running away from any foster home that was too rowdy. Mum took me in when I was nine, a damaged, painfully shy little girl too small for her age. She's never given me the full explanation as to why it was me whom she chose to adopt and not one of the other fifteen kids she'd fostered over the years. Perhaps there's a chemistry that can't ever be defined. She taught me to stand up for myself, but that dislike of direct confrontation has never completely dissipated. The only occasions I lose the inhibition is when I drink too much. According to Mike, I'm a belligerent drunk. He used to think it was funny, but it's been years since I've had a glass too many.

After I finish clearing up the breakfast things and making the beds, I wrap up warmly and walk the short distance to the Abbotts' house. Josie's new but old car is parked outside, so I know she's there.

Taking a deep breath, I rap the door knocker. It's a long minute before I hear footsteps, and for one silly moment, I wonder if Josie will spot me and decide not to open up.

'Oh, it's you,' she says. Josie has an apron around her midriff and flour on her hands.

'Sorry to bother you, but I was wondering if I could have a quick word about Harry being excluded from the trick-or-treating party this year.'

'Yes, well, I thought that with his condition, it would be too much for him,' she says, rubbing a bit of flour into her hair. 'He's very sensitive to noise, and he got upset last year, didn't he?'

I don't recall him being anything other than excited—a little overexcited, perhaps.

'He's very hurt that he wasn't invited,' I say.

'Oh, come on. Life isn't fair, Isobel. And the younger the children are when they realise that, the better. You know that better than most.' She sighs. 'Look, I'll invite him if you want me to, but I can't handle tears and tantrums.'

I don't want to feel beholden to Josie, so I grit my teeth. 'It's quite all right. We'll do our own thing.' I turn on my heel and stride away. When I reach the top of their driveway, I turn my head back towards the house, and Josie is still standing there with her arms crossed. When she catches me looking at her, she slams the door closed.

That did not go well.

MIKE ARRIVES home at a reasonable hour for the first time since I can remember and takes over the bedtime routine from me. When he comes back downstairs, I hand him a glass of wine.

'I tried to have a word with Josie about her excluding Harry from their trick-or-treating party. It was a failure. I just can't understand why she's being so off with us. Can you think of anything we might have done to upset her?'

Mike shrugs. 'Neighbours. There are always some difficulties, aren't there? Just let it go.'

'Easier said than done. I see her all the time. But it's the impact it's having on Harry that upsets me. He was gutted not to be invited.'

'These things happen,' he says with a shrug.

I grind my teeth. He is so damned unsupportive these days.

'Anyway, I've decided to have a little Halloween party ourselves. Harry can invite his friend Bashir. Can you come home early on Friday?'

Mike is fiddling with his mobile phone and doesn't answer.

'Did you hear me?' I ask, a tinge of exasperation in my voice.

'What?'

'Can you come home early on Friday?'

'No, sorry, absolutely not. I've got back-to-back meetings.'

'You haven't even checked your diary,' I say.

He scowls. 'Some of us keep our diaries in our heads, Isobel.' But that's not true. When I asked about booking that long weekend away, he told me to check with Janine.

'You're just saying you're busy because you don't want to come.'

'Come on, Isobel.' He stands up and strides towards me, putting his arms around my waist from behind as I'm standing at the stove, stirring the bolognaise. He gives me a kiss on the top of my head. 'I'd much rather be with my children than with an obnoxious client. Just let it go.' He releases me and walks to the fridge, taking out the bottle of wine to pour himself a top up.

But I can't let it go. I mull over Mike's reaction all evening, and when I eventually get to bed, he is already asleep, his back towards me.

As it turns out, Bashir's parents aren't comfortable with him coming over for Halloween. I suppose it's understandable. When you've escaped from a war-torn country, you don't want your child to be scared unnecessarily in the place that is meant to be their safe haven. I ask Harry if he'd like to invite anyone else over, but he just shakes his head and turns away. I could invite some of Harper's little friends, but if Harry isn't going to have anyone, then it will be better if it's just the three of us.

'We'll have lots of fun,' I promise him.

I make a real effort, carving several pumpkins and putting candles inside them and placing them around the front door. I bought some Halloween costumes from the supermarket, because I really can't be bothered to make them when they'll be worn for a couple of hours max, and have decorated cupcakes with hideous green and orange icing that hopefully will appeal to both the kids. On the way home from school, Harry doesn't say a word, and I just hope that my afternoon of preparations will perk him up.

'Mummy, I'm a witch!' Harper jumps up and down with excitement as she sees her costume on the kitchen table.

'That new neighbour lady is a real witch,' Harry says.

'Which new neighbour?' I ask.

'The one who's living in Ollie Walker's house. Benji told me. He said she can cast spells.'

Harper looks at her big brother with wide eyes.

'And how does Benji know that?' I try to keep my voice light-hearted, contrary to what I'm feeling.

'Because she came for tea and told him some of the spells she can cast.'

'I think she was just playing around. Witches aren't real.'

'Yes, they are,' Harry says, frowning at me.

I change the subject.

SHORTLY AFTER SIX P.M., I go upstairs to the bathroom and hear lots of chattering voices outside. Discreetly, I stand in our darkened spare bedroom and edge towards the window, pushing aside the pale blue curtains. Josie is walking along the lane with six or seven children in a variety of ghost, witch, and wizard outfits, and she's laughing raucously at something the other woman is saying, a woman who is dressed as a witch in a big black cape and tall pointy hat. It's only when she turns her head slightly towards our house that I realise it's Linette. I feel a ridiculous stab of envy that Josie has chosen Linette, a virtual stranger and a woman without children, to accompany her.

When our doorbell goes, I hurry downstairs. As much as I would rather not open the door, I know that we have to be seen to be magnanimous.

'Harry, Harper! I shout. 'There are some children here for trick-or-treating. Do you want to hold the bucket of sweets out for them?'

Harper comes running out of the living room, the skirt of her costume already ripped.

'Harry,' I say, 'come along, darling. Otherwise, we'll get tricked.'

I can't wait any longer to open the door, so I pull it open and plaster a big smile on my face. I help Harper proffer the large bowl of sweets.

'Hello, Isobel!' Linette says with a big smile. 'And who are you?' she asks, bending down to Harper's height.

'I'm Harper.'

'And where's your brother?' Linette asks.

I expect Josie to look embarrassed, but she doesn't seem the slightest bit bothered.

'He's a bit tied up at the moment,' I say, and I think I see a smirk cross Josie's face.

When the children have taken their sweets and left, I hurry back into the living room. Harry is sitting on the floor, watching *Toy Story*, a film he's seen more than one hundred times. I sit down next to him, and he lets me put my arms around him and pull him into a hug, but a moment later, he unfurls himself and edges away. My boy is hurting, but there's nothing I can do to make it better.

ABOUT AN HOUR LATER, there is the slamming of car doors, the revving of engines, and shouting voices. I run to the front of the house and look out the window once again. There are several cars on the lane just in front of our house, the loud, heavy beat of music pumping out from at least one of the vehicles. A group of young people have gathered, with more youngsters getting out of cars. What the hell is going on? I'm not sure what to do now because I can't go out to investigate, leaving the children alone in the house. The shouting gets louder. It looks like the lane is completely blocked, and my throat constricts as I realise that Mike won't be able to get home. You hear of these awful stories of teenagers stabbing people who intervene to break up brawls. Surely, that's an inner-city problem, not something that would ever happen out here in the countryside? And then the doorbell rings.

I tell the children to stay in their rooms and hurry down-stairs to look through the peephole. There are two boys and a girl standing at the door, and although it's hard to tell in the reduced light, I reckon they're in their late teens.

'How can I help?' I ask as I open the door, keeping the security chain attached.

'We're here for the party,' the girl says. She's painted her face so it looks as if she has a fang hanging over her lower lip and blood dripping down her chin.

'I think you must have the wrong address.'

'No. It's The Close. It's all over Facebook, open invitation to the Halloween party.'

'There's no one your age living here,' I say.

'What about Annamae and Tom Abbott? They live here, don't they?' the taller of the boys asks.

It's true that Jack Abbott does have two children from his first marriage, but I can count on one hand the number of times I've seen them here. They live with their mother and stay over at the Abbotts' from time to time. They certainly wouldn't be at their house now. I almost want to chuckle at the thought of Josie having scores of teenagers descend on her.

'I'm sorry that I can't help you,' I say. 'Try the Abbotts' house next door.' I shut the door.

About five minutes later, there's a thud, followed by several more, and as the security lights flood the front of the house, I realise that the youths are chucking eggs at our downstairs windows. I'm both furious and a bit scared. I'm about to open the window in the guest room, which looks out onto the front of the house, when the phone rings.

'Mrs Floyd?' the male voice says.

'Yes, it's Isobel speaking.'

'This is Thomas Adler, your neighbour. What the hell's going on?'

'I don't know. There are carloads of teenagers on the lane, saying that they're here for a party, which they think is happening at the Abbotts'. I've just had eggs chucked at our windows because I told them to clear off.'

'Right, I'm calling Jack Abbott and the police. Leave it with me.'

He hangs up before I can say thank you. It isn't until a bit later when the children are asleep and the noise outside has abated that I wonder how Thomas Adler knows our ex-directory landline.

6

The next couple of weeks are uneventful. I have plenty of clients to keep me busy, and the children are counting down the days, eager for the beginning of December when they can start their advent calendars. Mike's workload continues to be incessant, and I'm looking forward to our long weekend away, a time for the two of us to reconnect. It's much needed. Last week, Linette pushed an invitation through our door, asking us to attend a drinks party this coming Friday evening. And on Saturday, we're going to Devon, just Mike and me, for our stay in the luxurious-looking spa hotel. I'm dropping off the children at Mum's.

Mum and Dad have a birth child, my younger sister Celia. I've heard of horror stories where the birth children don't accept the adopted kids or vice versa. Celia was five when I was first fostered by Mum and Dad and seven when the formal adoption was completed. She was in awe of me, her wiser, older sister, and I was happy to have a younger sibling and be part of a real and permanent family. We've always been close, particularly so when Dad died suddenly of a pulmonary embolism a decade ago. We rallied around Mum, and anyone looking in from the outside would never have guessed that we weren't blood relations. It amuses both of us how many times people have said we look similar. We both have dark hair and dark eyes, but that's where the similarities end. I'm four inches taller than my petite sister, and at five feet eight inches, I tower over both her and Mum.

Earlier, Celia rang to confirm plans for Christmas. It's her turn to host this year, and it will be a jolly affair at her home in Suffolk.

'When will you be finishing off at the office for the Christmas break?' I ask Mike as I'm preparing supper, our normal Thursday evening casserole (although I do mix up the ingredients from week to week).

'I don't know. Why?'

'Celia wants to know which day we'll be joining them.'

'I think you'll have to count me out this year.'

I almost drop the dish I'm carrying.

'What?'

'There's so much going on, I don't think I'll have time to go away for more than Christmas and Boxing Day. Best if you go alone or we stay at home and have a quiet Christmas just the four of us.'

'You have got to be joking,' I exclaim. 'This is family time for your children, time that they can spend with their cousins.'

'I get that,' he says, his voice tinged with impatience. 'But normally, we go for several days, and this year, I can't.'

'And what else are you going to avoid? The children's nativity play, the drinks party on Friday night at Linette's?'

He ignores the sarcasm in my voice. 'I really don't feel like going to Linette's.'

'Well, we have to. Neighbours need to stick together, and you never know when you might need them. You know I feel terrible about how unsupportive we were of the Walkers. Linette is trying to bring us all together, and I think that's a good thing. We don't need to be best friends, but we should be there for each other in times of difficulty.'

Mike harrumphs, and we barely talk over supper.

MUM COMES over on Friday afternoon and does the school pickup for me. I go for a much-needed appointment at the hairdresser's, and by the time Mike returns home, I've had a relaxing bath and am getting ready for our evening out. I put on a knee-length black velvet dress and high heels. I know it might be a bit smart for a neighbourly get-together, but I feel the need to put on some armour.

'You look nice,' Mike says, raising an eyebrow. It's the first time he's commented on how I look for a very long time, and it gives me hope that our long weekend away might be healing.

'I've packed a few things in the suitcase for you,' I say, 'so we can leave in good time tomorrow.'

Half an hour later, we are striding along the lane, Mike holding a bottle of red wine and me wrapped up in a thick woollen coat. Linette has strung lights across the front of the house. It's on the verge of looking gaudy, but I keep my thoughts to myself.

'Hello!' she exclaims as she swings the door open. 'You must be Mike!' She leans forwards and kisses him on the cheek, leaving a bright red lipstick mark. Mike looks startled. 'Come in, come in!'

She's wearing a very short, very figure-hugging leopard-print wrap dress that exposes so much cleavage the edge of her lacey black bra is visible. Once again, she's bare-legged, and her feet are wedged in vertiginous stiletto heels.

'You didn't tell me you had such a handsome husband,

Isobel,' Linette says, fluttering very long fake eyelashes at Mike. I'm not sure if I should feel flattered or worried, although I doubt that Linette is Mike's type. She leads us into the living room, which is unrecognisable from when I was last here. She has hung up three large glitter balls from the ceiling and has strung long fairy lights around the windows. A large artificial Christmas tree stands in the corner of the room despite it not even being December yet. She has pushed the heavy furniture to the walls so that the centre of the room resembles a dance floor. Her camping table stands near the door to the hallway, and it is laden with glasses and various bottles of wines, spirits, and soft drinks. She also has several platters of sausage rolls and bowls of crisps.

'How many people are you expecting?' I ask.

'Oh, it's just the neighbours from The Close. I prefer intimate parties rather than big shindigs where you never get to have a proper conversation with anyone. What would you like to drink?'

After pouring me a glass of white wine and a beer for Mike, the doorbell rings.

'Mike, be a love and get the door, will you, whilst I put some music on.'

My husband does as he's told, and a moment later, he's back in the living room with Thomas Adler. I am very surprised to see him. Thomas Adler lives alone, although we often see him in his car with a blonde woman, a different one every time we pass him on the lane. He is one of those ageless men and could be anything between thirty-five and fifty-five. My longest conversation with him was the night he rang about the youths on Halloween. I can't even remember who told us, but apparently, he runs some sort of cybersecurity business from home. Keeping himself to himself, I had assumed he would be gauche and socially ill at ease. Not so.

Linette turns up the music to full volume and starts

dancing provocatively to 'Macarena' in front of Thomas. Rather than shifting away awkwardly as Mike would do, Thomas joins straight in, so much so that it's almost embarrassing to watch as the two of them writhe their bodies. Linette doesn't even hear the doorbell ring, so I walk to the door and open it.

'Hello,' I say to Mr Quinn, who looks somewhat disconcerted that it's me who is letting him in.

'The music's rather loud, isn't it?' he asks.

'Linette is in full party spirit,' I say. He follows me into the living room.

As soon as Linette sees Mr Quinn, she hops over to us and leans forwards, giving him a lingering peck on the cheek, her cleavage in full view. Despite the low light, Mr Quinn blushes.

'What can I get you to drink?' she shouts over the music.

'Just a tonic water for me,' he says.

Mike and I stand awkwardly next to the drinks table while Thomas Adler continues gyrating his hips alone in the middle of the room.

'Where's your lovely wife?' Linette asks.

'Not feeling too good today, I'm afraid, so I won't be able to stay away from her for long. I'll just have the one glass, and then I'll leave you youngsters to it.'

'That's a shame. Why don't you come and dance with me and Thomas?'

'Oh, no, dear,' Mr Quinn says, looking really quite flustered. 'I haven't danced since 1963, and I won't be starting now. You go and enjoy yourself.'

I catch Mike's eye, and he winks at me.

Josie and Jack arrive last, and I'm relieved that Linette opens the door to them herself. It's immediately obvious that they've just had an argument. Their body language is all off, and they stand apart as if they're being repelled by two competing magnetic fields.

'Sorry we're late,' Josie says. 'The babysitter was delayed.' I get the feeling she's lying. Jack shakes Mike's hand, and before long the two men are chatting but the music is too loud for me to hear what they're talking about. Josie turns away from me to talk to Mr Quinn, and then Linette is back on the dance floor, gyrating with Thomas Adler once again. I don't mind being left alone. It gives me a few moments to appraise all the neighbours.

It's not long before Mr Quinn leaves, and shortly afterwards, Josie and Linette are on the far side of the room, their heads close together. Then Linette slips her arm through Josie's, and they're skipping out of the room like two naughty schoolgirls. Neither of them glances at me or invites me to join them, so I just stand near Mike and pretend I'm listening to the men's conversation. When Josie and Linette return, they're laughing uproariously, and I feel totally excluded. I guess that's exactly how Josie wants me to feel. I edge my way into the conversation between the three men.

'Does anyone know who that drone belongs to? It's a real nuisance, setting the dog off barking.'

I know immediately that I've made a faux pas. Thomas Adler places his beer on the window ledge and crosses his arms. 'It's mine, but it's not as if it's doing any harm, is it?'

I take a large sip of wine. 'Well, other than scaring the animals. Isn't it a problem for your livestock?' I ask Jack.

'Nah. Can't say I've seen it, but then the cattle are all inside at this time of year.'

'It just seems a bit intrusive to me,' I say.

'It's not,' Thomas replies. 'It's a bit of fun.'

'A boy's toy,' Mike says with a grin. That annoys me. My husband should be on my side. 'We use them all the time for doing site surveys.'

'Exactly. I'd let you have a go,' Thomas says, 'Except it cost a bloody fortune, and you might fly it into the trees.'

'No chance, mate. I had a couple of flying lessons when I was in my twenties. A natural, I was,' Mike boasts. 'Although I have to admit that I don't fly the drone on our building site.' This isn't like my husband, and I'm confused as to why he feels the need to show off.

'Why don't you get one too, and we can have races?' Thomas says. 'And you too, Jack.'

'Rather stick to the combine harvester, me,' Jack Abbott says.

'I get that they're needed for work, taking videos of properties for sale and the like, but just flying them over people's houses, isn't it a bit intrusive?' I take another large swig of wine and realise I've lost count of how many glasses I've drunk.

'Let it go, Isobel,' Mike says. 'Sorry about my wife. She gets a bit confrontational when she's had too much to drink!'

I open and close my mouth. How dare he talk about me like that! Firstly, I rarely drink too much, and secondly, I would never consider myself argumentative, not amongst relative strangers, anyway. On the other hand, he's right. I do get a bit confrontational when I'm drunk, and this drone has wound me up the wrong way. To stop myself from saying anything more, I turn away, reckoning that it would be preferable to talk to Linette and Josie than to be belittled by my husband. I find them in the kitchen. Josie is leaning against the kitchen counter.

'Hello, Isobel,' she slurs. I wonder how much she's drunk. It's not like she's even been here that long.

Linette laughs. 'Josie has had a bit too much to drink.'

'No, I haven't!' Josie weaves her way out of the kitchen and into the hallway.

'Can I get you some more wine?' Linette asks, noticing my almost empty glass.

'I'm fine, thanks.'

'In which case, I've got some mini-quiches in the oven. Can you help me carry them through next door?'

Josie isn't the only one who's a bit wobbly on her feet. I have to concentrate really hard not to tilt the tray to avoid the quiches sliding onto the floor. I carefully place the tray on the table and then glance around the darkened living room. Josie is trying to drag Mike into the middle of the room.

'We need to dance!' she slurs, her face so close to his that he has to pull backwards. Jack is still talking to Thomas and has his back to his wife. Probably just as well he can't see, as I don't think he'd be best pleased with the way she's flirting with my husband. I think it's quite funny how Mike is trying to duck away from her.

I step forwards and put a hand on Mike's arm.

'Sorry, Josie, but I need to dance with my husband. It's our favourite song.'

It isn't.

When Josie has staggered away, Mike whispers into my ear, 'I think we should leave now.'

'No!' I say. The alcohol is relaxing me, and I do feel like having a bit of a boogie. I can't remember the last time I danced.

'Come on, Isobel. We've got an early start tomorrow.'

'You're such a killjoy!'

Linette comes over to us and starts dancing. I'm in awe as to how good her moves are considering the high heels she's wearing.

'I'm leaving,' Mike says. 'Are you coming?'

'No,' I say, dancing with my eyes closed. 'I need to let my hair down.'

Mike puts his hand on my wrist, but I shrug him off. He stomps off out of the room, and right now, I really don't care.

Josie joins Linette and me on the dance floor, and if I thought that Linette was a good dancer, this is a version of Josie I never thought I would see. She unbuttons her blouse to show some more cleavage and dances with her arms above her head, her hips gyrating suggestively. The three of us dance until I can barely stand up anymore.

'I love you all so much!' Josie slurs. 'I love you!'

And then Jack strides over to us and pulls Josie away.

'It's time to go home,' he says firmly.

'No!' Josie says, but she stumbles and collapses in a giggling heap on the floor. I rather like this drunken version of my neighbour.

But when the Abbotts leave, I glance at my watch. Thomas is standing very close to Linette, and it's gone midnight. I've no idea how long ago Mike left, but I know he won't be happy with me.

As I stumble back to our house in the dark, just using the torch light on my phone so I can see where I'm going, the world spins around me. I try to be quiet when I use the bathroom and stagger into the bedroom, but I drop my tube of toothpaste and then crash into the door.

Mike huffs and puffs when I get into bed, but when I reach for him, he pushes me away and turns his back towards me.

'Leave me alone,' he mutters.

7

LINETTE

'Come here, gorgeous,' Thomas Adler says, grasping my hand. His palm is sticky and damp from sweat. 'I'm done,' I say. 'I'm going to switch the music off.'

'Oh no you're not.' He puts an arm around my waist, and his breath is hot on my cheek. 'The only thing I'm letting you do is put on some slow music.' He moves his face closer to mine and tries to pull me towards him.

'No, Thomas.' I attempt to wriggle out of his grasp.

'You want it, don't you?' he says, pawing me with his disgusting stubby fingers. 'Let me stay the night, and I'll make love to you like no man has ever done before.'

'You're drunk,' I say.

'The only thing I'm drunk on is lust for you.' He places both palms on my buttocks and thrusts himself towards me.

'Let go, Thomas. I'm not interested. I've got a long-term boyfriend. I'm sorry,' I say as an afterthought.

He slumps backwards, and I almost stumble. 'What was all that dirty dancing, then? You've been coming on to me all evening, your tits out, your dress halfway up your arse.'

'It's how I dress,' I say coldly. I just want this creep of a man out of the house now. 'Look, it's been a fun evening and great to get to know you, but everyone else has left, and now it's your turn to leave too.'

'I don't like the thought of you staying in this house all alone,' he says, trying the gentler tack now. He licks his lips, and it makes me shudder.

'I've been here alone for the past few weeks, and I'm absolutely fine.'

He wavers slightly, and I realise that he's even more drunk than I thought. 'Come on, it's time for you to go home,' I say, beckoning him as I walk out of the room.

Eventually, he follows me to the front door, where he tries it on again, clumsily reaching for my left breast. I bat his hand away, and this time, I can't control my anger.

'Do that again, and I'll get you arrested for making an improper advance.' My voice is low and threatening.

He steps backwards. 'No need to overreact, Linette,' he says, his words slurring slightly. 'I'm going now, but if you're horny in the night, you know where to find me.'

I open the door, and the second he's on the other side, I slam it shut and bolt it top and bottom. I step back into the hall, and then I lose it.

Totally lose it.

I go into the living room and chuck one of the cheap wine glasses on the floor. It feels good, so I smash another and another, enjoying the way the glass shatters and tinkles and how the shards shimmer like icicles under the rotating light of the glitter balls. They're a bunch of total and utter bastards, every single one of these Close neighbours. Oh, how ironic that they live on 'The Close'. That's one thing they're not. Close. I hate their guts, and the effort it takes to pretend otherwise is totally overwhelming.

I remind myself that I'm doing this for Mona, my lovely

sister who was hurting so badly she felt she had no way out except to end her suffering. And Wilson. That boy had a beautiful soul, always wanting to do things for others, to make life just that little bit sweeter for his mother. Right now, I blame them all. But I will work out who was responsible for what, and I will make them pay. Oh, yes. I will make them pay with blood.

I remember how Mona sobbed when she told me that one of the neighbours must have been to blame. One of them must have seen something. How naive I was to think that Mona was wrong, that she was just desperate for an answer. Why was Wilson out there at night? How is it possible for no one to have heard or seen anything? And who would be so callous as to drive away when they knew they'd hit a young man? As if that wasn't bad enough, their behaviour in the aftermath was unforgivable. Not one of them stepped forwards to genuinely offer their sympathy, to really support my broken sister. When none of them attended Wilson's funeral, Mona became convinced that there was some conspiracy against her, that her neighbours were glad her son died and that they took pleasure in her suffering. I tried so hard to console her, to tell her that they were just thoughtless, self-centred individuals with too much money and too little heart, and surely, they didn't mean any harm. But Mona was right. I can feel it in my bones. Whoever murdered Wilson is right here in this neighbourhood. And whoever killed Wilson was responsible for taking my beloved sister too.

I stomp around the house until I find myself in Wilson's bedroom. It's empty now except for the big teddy that I gave him when he was four years old. Back then, I had dreams of owning a home, perhaps bagging myself a man and even having children. But it was only a brief window of lucid thought because then the drugs took hold again, and any possibility of being a sufficiently responsible adult, suitable to look after my young nephews, flew out the window. I don't blame Mona and Keith for keeping me away from the boys. I was a liability. What they don't know is that I kept that teddy bear in my bedsit and in the hostel, and I honestly think it saved me. That teddy reminded me that it wasn't too late to change. It wasn't too late to be a responsible aunt and perhaps even have my own kids. Except it was too late. I had less than a year of being clean, less than a year with Wilson and Mona, and now the only way I can make it up to them is to avenge their deaths.

I sit down on the floor and hug the teddy, letting my tears seep into its long, soft, honey-coloured fur. We sit there together, equally lonesome, but the teddy's beady black eyes remain dry. There is nothing in this room of Wilson's, except perhaps the markings on the wall where blue tack pulled off paint. Even the curtains are gone. Wilson was such a lovely boy. He struggled a bit at school, but he always loved animals, and according to his mum, he was forever rescuing strays, which he'd keep out in the garden because Keith wouldn't have them in the house. He was studying animal care at the agricultural college, and he loved it, being around other kids who were equally interested in wildlife and the environment. In his spare time, he'd get odd jobs doing people's gardens, walking their dogs, or cleaning out rabbit hutches. The lad was devoted to his mum. He'd do anything to help her out, and I have to admit that I sometimes thought it a bit weird. I mean, what nineteen-year-old boy would bail on a night out with his mates to help his mum put up new curtains or cook supper because she wasn't feeling up to it? I worried that perhaps it wasn't normal, but now with hindsight, I realise that he was just a lad with the most enormous heart. They say that the good die young, don't they?

I could go to sleep right here on the old carpet, my head supported by the bulging stomach of the teddy, but I force myself to get up and to let go of the self-pity. I'm not in this place for me. I'm here for a purpose, to find out why these self-obsessed neighbours never rallied around Mona. And to make them pay. Mona told me how horrible they all are. How the Quinns pulled their curtains when the ambulance turned up. How the Abbotts didn't cut down their hedge, which meant the speeding car didn't see Wilson. How the Floyds didn't go to Wilson's funeral, and how Thomas Adler owed Wilson money for all the odd jobs he'd done in Adler's garden but never paid him. I stand at the window and look out into the dark night. There are still lights on in two of the windows in the Floyds' house, but I can't see any of the other houses from here. There are too many trees in the garden, blocking the light.

I wonder what they all think about me. I never knew that I could be a good actress, but I think I am. And an investigator. I'm sure that they all just view me as that slightly quirky new neighbour, a breath of fresh air who is eager to integrate and to bring some cohesion to this little community. In reality, I'm like a Venus flytrap, one of those horrible little plants that opens up its doors and attracts people in, only to snap them shut and slowly and painfully consume its prey. But it's hard work pretending, exhausting being nice to these people whilst at the same time watching their every move, ready to pounce when the time is right. And I have no doubt that it will be, most likely sooner rather than later, because they are all hiding something. You don't even need to be a good sleuth to establish that. Soon, I will expose every one of their dirty little secrets, and I will make them pay. I want them to suffer. Truly suffer.

8

We're back home after our three nights in a country house hotel. I had hoped that it would have been the panacea for our marriage—a few days together, talking in the way we used to before the children were born, gazing into each other's eyes and really listening. But no. Mike was furious with me for not leaving Linette's party with him, and frankly, neither of us wanted to go away on a romantic weekend together. If Mum hadn't turned up on Saturday morning, all excited about being left alone with the kids for a few days and wishing us a wonderful break, I doubt we would have gone.

The journey was frosty. Mike switched on the radio, and we barely said a word until we arrived at the hotel. I suppose we reached some sort of truce because we were at least civil to each other, but there was no romantic lovemaking, no excited sharing of hopes and dreams and planning for the future. We talked about the children, particularly about Harry's autism, and Mike told me a bit about the projects he's currently designing. When I asked why he was working so hard, he became shirty and said he was paying for our lifestyle. Once again, I offered to go back to work, and once again, he said no. But then he relented and said if I really wanted to, he would support that decision. I was thrown a bit off guard by that because I would like to resurrect my career, but at what price?

And that's the perennial question, isn't it? I was so proud that I was an architect, a professional with a label and letters after my name. A somebody who everyone knew was clever and had worked hard and had achieved a lot. It was my identity. As schoolgirls, we're all taught that we need to aspire to great things, that education and the world of work will open up unlimited opportunities for us. And indeed it does ... until we have children. Then we have to choose. I wondered whether Mike might offer to be the stay-at-home parent, but it was obvious the moment I got pregnant that it would never be a possibility for us. The have-it-all option would work for some mothers, but not for me. Harry needed me, and I would lay my life down for my children, so relinquishing a job seemed like a small price to pay. But now? Now I'm missing the old me.

It isn't until I've put the children to bed and waved Mum off that I pick up the post, but I don't have time to look at it because my sister, Celia, calls. I've already told her that we're not spending Christmas with them this year due to Mike's work, and once again, she's trying to change our minds.

'But it's Christmas!' she says. 'Surely, everything's shut then.'

'I know.' I've got no answer for her.

'Why don't you come over for a weekend, perhaps in a couple of weeks' time, just you and the kids? You can tell me everything that's going on. Bring Lupin, and we'll have a long walk on the beach, and we can swap Christmas presents.'

'That sounds lovely. I'll check whether it's convenient with Mike.'

Mike saunters into the kitchen. 'You'll check what with me?' he asks.

'Celia suggested I take the kids to stay with her in a couple of weekends' time.'

'Sounds like a good idea.' He opens the fridge and removes a can of beer, then disappears into the living room. Long gone are the days when he used to want us to do everything together. It seems to me that he's only too happy for me and the children to be away for a couple of nights.

I sift through the post and see an official-looking letter addressed to Mr and Mrs Floyd. I open it. It's a letter from the council, something to do with a planning application. I have to read it twice to fully absorb what it's saying.

'Mike!' I shout, walking into the living room and rousing him from his iPad. 'You will not bloody believe this!' I walk over to where he's sitting on the sofa and drop the letter on his lap before sitting down next to him and burying my face in my hands. 'The Abbotts are applying for planning permission to build a green burial site on the field right at the bottom of our garden.'

'My god,' Mike says, looking up at me, his face pale. 'How could they do this?'

'What does it mean, exactly? What is a green burial, anyway?'

'I don't know. We need to look at the plans online, work out exactly how it might affect us.' Mike logs into the planning portal of the local council and pulls up the application. He glances through the plans and eventually hands the iPad to me.

'What are they proposing?'

'To turn the field into a burial ground and their barn into

the funeral building where they'll accept the bodies and carry out services if they can't conduct them outside.'

I swallow hard. 'But surely, they can't just bury bodies in any field they like?'

'If they get planning permission, they can.'

'What, exactly, is a green burial, anyway?'

Mike picks up the iPad again while I pace the room. 'It says that the dead will be laid to rest in biodegradable coffins, and they won't use embalming chemicals or headstones on the graves. They'll be planting more trees, and in the six acres plot, which is the field we can see from the east side of our house, they expect to ultimately bury over four thousand bodies.'

'No! Is this a piss-take?' I ask, grabbing the planning notice that Mike has dropped onto the coffee table. I sit down on the sofa next to him.

'It looks deadly serious to me.' Mike sniggers. He might think his pun is funny, but I don't see anything hilarious in this proposal.

'The implications of this are awful,' I say, trying to calm myself. 'We'll look out onto a burial site. We'll have grieving people on our boundary. The traffic will increase terribly. And what will it do to our house price? I know we don't want to sell, but surely, it'll knock tens of thousands off its value.'

Mike leans his head back and closes his eyes. His knee is jumping up and down. 'It'll reduce the value more than that. There aren't many people who are happy to live next to a burial ground.'

'I can't believe that Josie and Jack didn't say anything. I suppose that's why Josie has been behaving so weirdly towards me these past months. They've obviously been cooking this up but have a conscience about it.' I groan. 'Do you think they'll be granted planning permission?'

Mike is silent for a minute or so as he zooms in on some

plans. 'Probably. They've addressed parking, and the drainage plans look sound.'

'You mean they might actually get permission to build this?' My voice is going up in pitch, and it feels as if my chest is being grabbed on the inside.

Mike sighs. 'Yes.'

'We've got to stop them!' I say, jumping up and pacing up and down the living room. 'I don't want to live here with a burial ground for thousands of people at the bottom of our garden!' I feel totally blindsided by this.

'We won't be able to leave. We'd have negative equity on the house.'

'How can the Abbotts do this to us? They're destroying our sanctuary, and for what? Financial greed?'

'Looks like it's a good money earner. I can't imagine it's easy being a farmer, so they're probably looking for ways to bring in more money. It's not like they're doing anything to us, Isobel. It's just their way of trying to diversify, to earn additional income streams.'

'Yes, but why not build a farm shop or have shepherds' huts? There's loads of stuff they could do rather than having a burial ground.'

'And would you be happy if they built a campsite in the field or hosted festivals? I can't see you agreeing to that.'

'No, of course not.' I run my fingers through my hair. 'Why the hell aren't you more uptight about this, Mike?'

'What good would that do?'

'I don't understand. The Abbotts have totally shafted us. They didn't have the decency or the guts to come and discuss their planning proposals with us first, and we have to learn about it through the council. If this green burial actually happens, it'll destroy The Close, and I don't want ghosts floating around here at night!'

'Don't be ridiculous, Isobel. You're getting hysterical.'

'Okay, the ghost thing might be silly, but what about foxes and badgers digging up the bodies, and will the kids have to stay quiet because they'll be disturbing funerals? It's so unfair to even consider building this right next to our home. You need to go and talk to Jack and Josie, talk some bloody sense into them.'

'There's no point.'

'What do you mean, there's no point? They'll listen to you. You're a bloody architect, for God's sake. You know about this sort of stuff.'

'So are you,' he murmurs. 'Besides, I don't have any experience in this.'

'Oh, come on, Mike. Go and have a chat with Jack and see if they'd locate it somewhere else. Their farm is big enough.'

'I'm sure they'll have explored that. By the looks of the application, they've employed a planning agent and will have spent a lot of money on a feasibility study.'

'That's not the point. You need to tell them how worried we are, how much it's going to affect us.'

'And they'll just say we're nimbies. That's what neighbours who object are always called. Not in my backyard.' He tugs his left earlobe.

'So you're just going to roll over and let them do this?'

'We'll object via the proper channels.'

I throw my arms up into the air. Why is Mike being such a roll-over about this? He's normally up for a fight, happy to argue his case. This is pathetic.

'I'm asking you to speak to them,' I say. 'Josie doesn't want to talk to me, but please, will you go over there and discuss it with them? At least try.'

'No, I'm not prepared to do that.' Mike crosses his arms.

'Why not?'

'Because I don't want to fall out with the neighbours.'

'So you're just going to let them do what the hell they want and let them walk all over us!'

Mike stands up and juts his jaw forwards before picking his iPad up and walking towards the door.

'Do not walk out on me!'

'Listen, Isobel,' he says, glowering at me. 'We need to handle this through the proper channels and not start World War Three in The Close. I'm going to bed.'

'But—'

Mike walks out of the room, and I listen to his footsteps thud up the stairs.

I KNOW it might seem a bit pathetic, but I'm a mess. This house is my dream sanctuary, the manifestation of both Mike's and my hard work and where I envisaged us staying for the rest of our lives, or at least until the children are grown up. Yet I'm not sure I'm able to live next to a graveyard. I know some people don't mind, and although I wouldn't say I was especially superstitious, the concept gives me the shivers. I wonder if Josie and Jack are doing this on purpose to upset their neighbours, but then I rationalise. Of course they're not. They just want to earn a living, and to hell with anyone else. Would I do the same? I don't know, but I hope not. I hope I would have the decency to discuss it with my neighbours rather than it being a horrible shock when they receive a planning notification out of the blue.

I finish tidying up downstairs and get ready for bed. By the time I slip underneath the duvet, Mike is already asleep. But sleep doesn't come so easily to me. I toss and turn all night, my anger vacillating towards Mike, who seems so weirdly passive about it, and the Abbotts, who couldn't care less about the rest of us.

The next morning, when I'm back from the school run, I

walk over to the Quinns' house, striding quickly, eager to ensure that Josie or Jack don't see me. I ring the front doorbell.

Mr Quinn opens the door and raises an eyebrow.

'Sorry to disturb you,' I say, wondering why I often feel like a naughty child around him, 'but I was wondering what your thoughts are on the green burial site the Abbotts are proposing.'

'Oh, that. I really don't want to get involved. It doesn't affect us, so I won't be opposing it. I suppose that's why you're here, trying to rally opposition?'

'Well, not really.' And then I stand up straighter. 'Actually, yes. Our house looks right over the field, and I think it'll increase the traffic on the lane, and there'll be noise and general upheaval. Frankly, even if you can't see it, you will be negatively affected.'

'When you get to my age, you see these fads that come and go. You have to pick your battles, Mrs Floyd, and this is one battle that I won't be engaging in. If you'll excuse me, I need to see to my wife.'

Before I can say another word, he's disappeared inside, and I'm looking at a closed front door. I'm not going to give up that easily, so this time, I stride towards Thomas Adler's house. His house is a different style to that of Linette's or ours. It's made to look like a converted barn clad in dark wood with vast full-height windows at the front allowing visitors a view straight through to the inside. It reminds me of a giant-sized doll's house where everything is on display. The interior looks uber modern with a chandelier that hangs down in front of the triple-height glass window. It looks like a giant jellyfish with its tentacles extending downwards, lights shimmering despite the gloomy day.

Whatever cybersecurity business Thomas Adler does, it must pay well. A few months ago, he traded in his VW Golf for a Lamborghini. As Mike said, that was quite some leap up. Even when he's driving at a crawl, the car roars as it drives past. I think Mike is a tad envious.

He has one of those video doorbells that blinks at me when I press the buzzer. There's no hiding from visitors here. I can see Thomas running down the magnificent glass floating staircase.

'Isobel, what can I do for you?' Thomas is wearing an open-necked shirt that is undone a little too far for this gloomy morning, showing off his chest hair, matched with dark (I assume, designer) jeans and bare feet.

'Sorry to disturb you, but I was wondering what your thoughts are on the proposed green burial site.'

'Ah, that. I don't think it's going to impact me because my garden faces the other way. Honestly, I think it's a good idea. I'd choose to be buried in a wildflower meadow surrounded by trees. Got to be better than being jammed into a creepy graveyard, hasn't it?'

I suppose the expression on my face gives away my thoughts.

'I'm assuming you're not so keen?'

'No. It directly impacts us—the view, the noise, the traffic, being exposed to people's grief every day, the reduction in our house values. I'm not happy. Look, I know you don't have a problem with it, but would you be prepared to object?'

He thinks for a moment and then shrugs his shoulders. 'Sorry, Isobel, but in all fairness, I can't. I was happy to call the police the other day when all those rowdy kids turned up, but I don't want to fall out with the Abbotts. I say good luck to them.'

Why is it that none of the neighbours—Mike included—want to stand up to the Abbotts? Do they really think a green burial site is a good idea here?

'I need to hop onto a Zoom call, so if you'll excuse me,' Thomas says.

'Sure.' I turn to walk away.

I HAVE no intention of speaking to Linette because she's only renting, but unfortunately, as I'm walking past her house, she is pulling out of her drive in her battered Toyota Yaris. She winds down her window.

'How are you, Isobel? Did you have a good weekend away?'

'Um, yes. Fine, thanks.' Did Mike or I tell her we were going away? I'm positive I didn't.

'What are your thoughts on the green burial site?' she asks. I'm surprised she even knows about it.

'Honestly, I'm not happy.'

'Well, that's a shame. I think it's a wonderful idea. We'll be surrounded by the lovely souls of the departed, and they'll protect us from evil. I've always wanted to live next to a graveyard.'

I open and close my mouth because I've never heard anything quite so bizarre. Linette carries on talking.

'Josie discussed it with me quite a bit, and she might even employ me. One of my hidden skills is that I know how to embalm people, although of course they don't use embalming fluids in green burials. They just let the body decompose into the earth.'

Is this woman for real?

'I think it's a brilliant idea for everyone,' she says. 'It's so environmentally friendly, but of course, it's going to make such a difference to the Abbotts, who are struggling finan- cially. I'm probably speaking out of turn, but dear Josie is saying they might have to sell up, things are so tight, and that house has been in Jack's family for five generations. It would be a tragedy for them.'

I feel totally on the back foot now.

'Anyway, must be getting on. See you soon, Isobel.'

ON THE ONE HAND, I don't want to speak to Josie, but on the other, I want her to know how hurt I am. As it turns out, I see her outside the school gates.

'Josie, can I have a word?'

She does that demeaning eye roll, as if she's too busy to talk to me.

'We're really hurt that you didn't discuss the planning proposal with us before submitting it.'

'We all need to look out for ourselves,' Josie says, crossing her arms.

'I thought we were friends or at the very least civil neighbours.'

She narrows her eyes at me. 'If you're going to object to the proposal, then clearly, we're not friends anymore.'

9

My little business has grown nicely, manageable but sufficient to give me a small additional income. This morning, I return home after the school drop-off to see my answer machine flashing.

'Good morning, Isobel. This is Mrs Ponder. I'm afraid I'm going to have to cancel my weekly nail polish. Goodbye.'

That is strange. On the very rare occasion she has cancelled, she's asked me to call back so we can rearrange, and she's given me a reason for needing to postpone. Not worrying too much about it, I prepare my salon for my ten a.m. appointment. I wait. And I wait. I call the woman's mobile phone, but it's switched off and goes straight to voice-mail. By ten thirty a.m., I accept she's a no-show. I have one more appointment at noon. Ten minutes beforehand, the client calls me.

'Sorry, sorry, but I'm not going to make it. Apologies for not giving you more notice.' The woman sounds breathless.

'Would you like to rearrange?' I ask.

'Sorry, I'm going to have to go.'

The line is dead.

What the hell?

I have never had three customers cancel on one day.

It isn't until mid-afternoon when I'm waiting to collect the children from school that one of my friends, Keira, pulls me to one side.

'You need to know there's some gossip about you.'

'What?' I frown. What has Josie been saying now?

'There's a rumour going around that one of your customers got an infection as a result of you cutting a hang-nail, and now she's in hospital, recovering from sepsis.'

'That's not possible!' I exclaim, my hand rushing to my mouth. 'Who is it?'

'Sorry, I don't know. But the rumour mill is that you don't keep your equipment sufficiently clean. I know it's a load of rubbish, Isobel, but I thought you should know.'

'Thank you, Keira,' I say, feeling totally shocked. I have never injured a client or drawn blood cutting a hangnail, and I am meticulous about cleaning the salon and all my equip-ment. This is too horrible and clearly a malicious lie. The first person I think about is Josie. I suppose she's spreading false rumours. But what can I do about it? If I confront her, she'll just deny it, and that will make relations between us even worse.

Back at home, I let Harry out of the car, and he runs up to the back door, where the movement sensor light comes on. And then he lets out the shrillest, blood-curdling scream. I leave Harper in the car and race to the door. Harry careens into me, sobbing, gripping my legs, and burying his face into me.

'What is it?' I ask, bending down to comfort him.

He can't talk, the sobs are so violent, but he just points towards the back door, keeping his eyes squeezed closed.

'All right, darling. Why don't you go and sit in the car with

Harper, and I'll have a look what the problem is.' He's still sobbing, but he lets me put him back in the car.

'What's the matter, Mummy?' Harper asks.

'I'm not sure. Both of you stay here for a moment while I investigate.'

I take a few cautious steps towards the back door, and for a moment, I don't see what Harry was making a fuss about. And then I step backwards and nearly gag. There's a dead rat on our doorstep, its head almost severed. How the hell did that get there? My first reaction is that someone must have deposited it there, but who would do something quite so vile? It must be an animal. It certainly wouldn't have been Lupin because, firstly, I would have seen it when I left for the school run, and secondly, Lupin would be much too scared to attack a rat. A fox, perhaps? I've seen a fox lurking around the garden from time to time. That's what it must be.

And now I'm going to have to be brave because the children can see me and my reaction, and Mike won't be home for hours. Cautiously, I step over it and unlock the door. I hurry into the utility room and find a black bin liner. I hold a wadge of old newspapers and without looking too much, I grab the dead rat and put it in the bin liner, tying it up tightly with a knot. I dump it in our big green bin at the side of the side of the house, then I take a deep breath and go back out to the car.

'It's all gone now,' I say. Harry is still snivelling.

'What was it?' Harper asks.

'A cute little rat that has gone to heaven.'

'I don't like rats,' Harper says. I'm not sure she even knows what a rat is, but I make a mental note to show them the animated film *Ratatouille*.

'Benji said that a dead rat means something bad is going to happen,' Harry says.

'What?' I exclaim. 'That's ridiculous.'

'It's what the witch lady who lives over there said.'

'I don't know what nonsense you've been told, but I can promise you that's a load of rubbish. When have you spoken to the new neighbour, anyway?' I ask.

'I haven't. Benji told me.'

'And when has Benji spoken to Linette?'

'She was there at Halloween, and he said that she babysat for them last week. Benji thinks she's creepy.'

'Well, Benji is just a little boy, and he's totally wrong about the rat. Come along. Let's get inside. How about pancakes for tea?'

I FRET for the rest of the afternoon, preparing the children's tea on automatic and trying to make them forget about the dead rat. And I can't stop feeling a ridiculous tinge of envy that Josie and Linette have become such close buddies. It seems too much of a coincidence that Benji talked about dead rats and then one appeared on our doorstep. But would Josie or Linette really stoop to doing something so horrible as dump a dead rat outside our house? It seems very unlikely. Although I keep on thinking about it, fortunately, Harry is easily distracted by playing some games on my iPad, and the rat is soon forgotten. It isn't until the kids are tucked up in bed that I recall what Keira told me and the false rumours about me and my business. I wonder whether Josie might have started the rumour, but if so, why? There's one thing not wanting to be friends with me and quite another spreading vile rumours. It doesn't make sense. By the time I'm meant to be preparing supper, I simply haven't got the energy. I message Mike and tell him I'll order a takeaway when he's on his way home.

I fire up my laptop. I have a single-page website, and I wonder if I should put a notice on it denying the false allegation, but then I discount that. It would make me look guilty. It's when I'm browsing on Google that I notice I have some reviews on the salon. To my utter dismay, there are three one-stars with the most horrible, derogatory comments. I don't recognise the names of the reviewers, and they're quite obviously fake, but what the hell can I do about it?

In contrast to me, Mike seems in a cheery mood when he comes home, giving me a quick peck on the lips and asking how my day was. I tell him about the dead rat and the cancellations in my salon.

'It's all tittle-tattle,' he says. 'What Harry told you and the rumour about your business. Forget about all of it.'

But that's easier said than done. I've worked hard to build up my little business, and if it's felled by some false rumours, then I need to do something about it.

THE NEXT MORNING, the phone rings, and to my surprise, it's Linette.

'Any chance of a last-minute manicure?' she asks. 'I've got a date at the weekend.'

'Yes, of course. When would suit you?'

'Have you got any space this morning?'

I have a totally empty bookings calendar, but I don't tell her that. 'How about eleven a.m.?' I suggest.

'Perfect.'

I'm glad Linette is coming over, as it'll give me the chance to quiz her about what she might have said to little Benji. Was it a coincidence that she told Benji the meaning behind finding a dead rat? And I'm curious to know how she's got so close to Josie so quickly.

'I was surprised you could fit me in at such short notice,' Linette says, settling into the chair opposite me, a cloud of her unpleasant perfume settling in my salon.

'I've had some cancellations this week.'

'I suppose that's the problem with a business like yours. You're at the mercy of unreliable customers.'

'It's unusual,' I say as I lift up her fingers to inspect her nails. She must be a smoker because her index and middle fingers are tinged a yellow-orange.

'I heard the rumours,' Linette says.

I glance at her with surprise. 'Don't worry, I don't follow the crowds. I'm sure it's a load of rubbish, someone with a bone to pick with you. I'd ignore it if I were you.'

I get on with doing her nails, all the while wondering whether it's Josie who is feeding her and other people with fake gossip.

'Have you objected to the planning application for the green burial site yet?' Linette asks.

'No, but I have made contact with the parish council and written to our local MP. It seems that I'm the only person in The Close who is against it.' One of the other reasons I haven't put my objection in yet is that it will be on public display, and that will only serve to fuel the antipathy between Josie and me.

'You need to stand up for what you think is right,' Linette says. I bristle. I may not like direct confrontation, but I'm hardly a shrinking violet. 'If I owned your house, I'd object. It'll reduce the value of your home.'

I'm really confused because the last time we spoke, Linette implied that she was all for the green burial.

I change the subject. 'Have you seen any rats on your property?'

'Rats?' Linette asks. She jerks back slightly, and I lose my grip on her fingers. 'Why?'

'We found a dead one on our doorstep yesterday evening.'

'That's gross. No, I haven't seen any rats. I want to get a pet, so perhaps I should have a cat. Rats are a sign of bad luck,' she says, shivering slightly. 'You know the saying "rats leaving a ship"? It means that something terrible is going to happen to the occupants of the house where they're found. You need to be careful, Isobel. It might be an old wives' tale, but we need to take note of these things. Wrap up your children tightly; don't let them out of your sight.'

10

It's Saturday late afternoon. I have just given the children their tea, which was the normal struggle, and Mike is in the living room, watching some football game on the television. The doorbell rings. I hope that Mike will get up and answer it, but no such luck. It chimes again.

'Be good,' I tell the kids and hurry to the front door, glancing out of the window onto the driveway. My throat constricts as I see a marked police car. What the hell? The last time The Close was full of police officers was the night Wilson died. I try not to think about it.

I open the door to two officers in uniform.

'Hello.' My voice sounds croaky. *Please don't let it be Mum or anyone from my sister's family.*

'Mrs Floyd?'

'Yes.' It feels like my knees are going to buckle, so I lean against the doorframe. 'Is someone hurt?'

The policemen glance at each other and frown.

'No, Mrs Floyd. There's nothing to worry about,' the taller man says. 'We just need to ask you a couple of questions. Can we come in?'

I let out a breath I didn't know I was holding and beckon them inside. The relief makes me light-headed.

I push open the living room door. 'Mike,' I say, speaking loudly over the television. He turns to look at me, and when he sees the uniformed officers, the blood drains from his face. I suppose he's like me, automatically assuming the worst.

'What's happened?' He jumps up and drops the remote control, then fumbles with it for a few seconds whilst he tries to switch off the television. We all stare at each other awkwardly for a few moments.

'Sorry, sorry. Please take a seat,' I say, gesturing at the sofa. 'Can I get you something to drink?'

'No, we're fine, thanks.'

They sit down, and I follow suit, although Mike stays standing, his fingers balled up into fists.

'We've had a complaint about someone using a drone to inappropriately spy on neighbours.'

Mike snorts and then tries to cover it up with a cough. I suppose he's as relieved as I am that they're here over something so relatively petty.

'Is the complaint from here? Neighbours here in The Close?' I ask. I recall how I confronted Thomas Adler about it at Linette's party.

'In this vicinity. Have either of you seen a drone?'

'Yes. I've seen it a couple of times,' I say.

'It's Thomas Adler's,' Mike interjects. 'The dog has barked at it.'

I wonder who has made an official complaint. Perhaps it was Mr Quinn, concerned that Mrs Quinn had followed it. I wonder how far she would have gone if I hadn't found her.

'Has the drone come down low enough to look in through your windows?' one of the policemen asks.

'No,' I say. 'It's been flying quite high up, hovering just

above the trees. It's a pain but hardly worth complaining to the police about.'

'Have you spoken to Adler?' Mike asks. I notice that the colour has returned to his cheeks.

'Yes, we have. The accusation is against him. We're investigating a claim of harassment and infringement of privacy. Can you recall the last time and date you saw the drone flying?'

Mike and I look at each other and shake our heads. 'It was midweek,' I say, 'because the children were at school.'

'Not in the evenings or early mornings?'

'No, but it's dark early these days. Unless we were outside, we wouldn't have known about it,' I say.

The taller policeman stands up. 'In which case, thank you very much to both of you for your time.'

I see the policemen to the door.

'Was that really a police issue?' I ask Mike after they've left. He is back slumped in front of the television.

'We don't know what was said or done. But it all seems a bit pathetic to me.'

'I agree.'

ABOUT TWENTY MINUTES LATER, I am playing with the children when the doorbell rings again. I hear Mike get up and open the door. A few seconds later, he's shouting, 'Isobel, can you come here?'

I leave the children and walk to the hallway. Thomas Adler is standing there with his hands on his hips. He glowers at me.

'How dare you tell the police that I used my drone to spy on people through their bathroom windows!'

I recoil. 'What?'

'You rang the police and told them that I was invading your privacy and harassing you!' He jabs his finger at me.

'I did nothing of the sort,' I say.

There is spittle forming at the edges of his lips, and it looks like Thomas is going to explode.

'You can't come in here and accuse my wife of something like that,' Mike says, pulling his shoulders back. I take comfort in the fact that my husband is taller and broader than Thomas Adler.

'Don't lie to me,' Thomas says, jutting his jaw forwards. 'I know you've complained about the drone.'

'I don't like it,' I say. 'It sets the dogs off barking, and I found Mrs Quinn wandering down the lane the other week, following it. But I certainly haven't contacted the police. It was a shock when they turned up here and questioned us about it.'

'If it wasn't you, then who the hell was it?'

'The Quinns, maybe?' I suggest.

'Nope. Mr Quinn didn't know anything about a drone. The Abbotts couldn't care less so long as I don't fly it over their livestock, which I don't. So it must be you.'

'You're missing someone,' Mike says. 'What about the new neighbour, Linette? She's the newcomer on The Close. Perhaps she doesn't know how things are done in the countryside.' I edge closer to my husband.

Thomas puts his hands on his hips. 'It's not Linette.'

'How can you be so sure?' Mike asks.

'Because it isn't.' He takes a step closer to Mike. 'She's a good woman and wouldn't do anything like that.'

'So instead, you're accusing my wife? Is she not a good woman, Adler?'

'She was going around stirring up shit only a couple of days ago, wanting me to object to the Abbotts' planning application, so it sure looks like it's your wife creating the discord around here.'

'Stop it!' I say. 'I'm right here, so don't talk about me as if I'm not in the room. I haven't complained to the police about the drone, so if you're sure it wasn't anyone else, it must have been Linette.'

'It wasn't Linette,' Thomas hisses.

'I'd like you to leave now,' Mike says, taking another step towards Thomas. Mike swings his arm back, and for one horrible moment, I think he's going to aim a punch at Thomas. Fortunately, Thomas turns around and yanks the front door open, slamming it hard behind himself.

'I'm damned if that creep is going to turn up here and accuse you of doing something you haven't,' Mike says, stomping back into the living room.

'It's okay,' I say, worried that Mike seems so on edge at the moment.

'Don't know why he's so protective of that Linette,' Mike mutters.

I don't know either. I also don't know why there's so much unpleasantness amongst all of us neighbours. Why can't we all be civil to each other, supportive if not best buddies? It seems to me that all the residents in The Close are in combat mood, looking to cause discord, doing whatever they want and to hell with the consequences to everyone else. I wish I knew what lay at the root of all of this. It's not Linette's arrival, and it's not even Wilson's death, because things have been awkward for the past year. It just seems to me that animosities are close to bubbling over.

IT'S a couple of days later, and I'm walking Lupin through the woods behind The Close. It's a walk we do at least twice a day, along a public footpath that meanders through ancient woodland where we frequently see deer, foxes and squirrels. My wellington boots squelch on the thick layer of fallen leaves, and the wind gently whistles through the trees. In the spring, the ground is a mass of wild daffodils, and then the yellow gives way to mauve bluebells and white anemone, and in places, where the stream cuts through the undulating land, there is wild garlic. When we first moved here, I found the walk slightly creepy, as the mass of oak, beech and birch trees creak when they bend in the wind, and in places, the sun barely breaks through the canopy of branches. These days, the walk is my solace, giving me time to think and appreciate the ever-changing seasons. At the weekends, the footpath is busy, but during the week, seeing another dog walker is the exception rather than the rule. I like the solitude.

Today, I'm obsessing about the green burial site, trying to work out how I can garner more objections without falling out with all the neighbours. I've been spending any spare time studying the planning objection process and all the legal requirements that applicants have to adhere to. Yes, I may be called a nimby, but the thought of looking out of our house onto a stream of funerals is too horrible to contemplate. And then there's my little salon business. I had a few more cancellations for this week, but at least I still have a handful of bookings.

'Hiya!'

I literally jump. Lupin is several metres ahead of me, sniffing something and unperturbed that I have been startled.

'Hello, Linette,' I say, trying to calm my thumping heart.

'Oh, sorry if I gave you a fright,' she says. She's bouncing up and down on the spot, wearing Lycra running gear, dark purple leggings with a matching fleece top and trainers that look brand new.

'Just walking the dog,' I say needlessly.

'Well, I won't disturb you,' she says.

'Actually, I've something I wanted to ask you. Did the police drop by to ask about Thomas Adler's drone?'

She frowns. 'No.'

'Someone has accused him of using his drone to spy on bathrooms.'

Linette laughs. It's a deep, throaty chortle. 'That wouldn't surprise me.'

'Did you report him?'

'Good heavens, no. If I saw a peeping drone, I'd either pull the curtains or use an airgun to shoot it out of the sky.'

'You've got a gun?'

'It's not illegal, but it's also not something I shout about from the rooftops. It's useful to cull the pesky squirrels and to scare away over-amorous lovers.' She winks at me.

Although she's trying to be light-hearted, it sends a shiver through me nevertheless.

'Thomas Adler was adamant that it wasn't you reporting him.'

'Probably because it wasn't.'

'So you're not . . . you're not close?'

'No, Isobel, he's not my type. He came onto me, and I firmly rejected him. He's involved in some dodgy business. How else do you think he can afford a Lamborghini?'

'What sort of dodgy business?'

'Some internet business. Porn and the like, so it all adds up.'

'Adds up to what?' I ask.

'The chances are he really is using that drone to spy on people.'

I don't like Thomas Adler, but I still think it's unlikely he is spying on us all.

'He's a creep,' Linette says as she removes her phone from her bum bag. 'Look.'

I watch as she taps away and then brings up Thomas Adler's profile on a dating site. 'Look how sleazy he is.'

I agree that he does look creepy in his too-tight T-shirt and slicked-back hair, but that doesn't make him a peeping Tom.

'Anyway, after my date at the weekend, I might have snagged myself a new man.'

Lupin nudges my leg, clearly eager for me to get on with the walk.

'Your dog is such a cutie,' Linette says, holding out her hand for Lupin to sniff. He ignores her. 'I really must get around to finding myself a pet. I was thinking about something a bit more unusual, a parrot or a tortoise, perhaps. Anyway, I mustn't hold you up any longer.'

She turns on her heel and jogs away, giving me a little wave.

There is something about Linette that makes me feel uneasy, yet I can't put my finger on it. I'm unsettled, and when I tell Lupin it's time to go home, rather than looking at me with a soulful expression as he normally does, he turns around immediately and happily trots homewards. I wonder if he senses it too.

11

Mike can sleep through anything. I can't. Perhaps it's the role of a mother, to always be on alert. When I'm jolted out of sleep, my heart pounding and a sour taste in my mouth, I'm shocked to realise it's only just gone midnight. It sounds like there's a music festival going on outside. There's a heavy, loud bass going boom, boom and loud, raucous voices laughing and shouting. I hear a car door slam and then another.

'Mike,' I say, nudging him slightly. He grunts and rolls over. I decide not to wake him, as he has to be up early in the morning for work. I climb out of bed and tiptoe over to the window, pulling back our pale grey curtains. It's pitch-black outside, and as our bedroom faces onto the garden, I can see nothing. Pulling on my dressing gown, I pad silently out of our bedroom and down the hallway into the spare room, which faces the lane. To my dismay, I see there are cars parked at the top of our driveway, blocking our entrance, and Linette's house is lit up like a Christmas tree. Even from here, I can see that her front door is wide open, and people are spilling out. Music and shouts are coming from her property, and by the sounds of things, she's having a rave. Why on earth didn't she tell me? I only did her nails the day before yesterday.

I'm not sure what to do. Normal etiquette around here is prior to having a party, neighbours let everyone else in the vicinity know, apologising in advance for any disturbance, but Linette isn't from around here, and it's becoming increasingly obvious that her standards are not ours. I go back to bed. I find a pair of foam earplugs in my bedside table drawer and shove them into my ears, but it doesn't do much to stop the noise or my increasing frustration.

By the time it's morning and Harper comes into our bedroom, trailing her favourite rag doll, complaining that she's hungry, I feel like I've slept about an hour. The noise eventually died down around five a.m. when I heard car engines start up and the shouts of people saying goodbye. I can't believe that Mike and the kids slept through it all, but seemingly, they did.

I FEEL bone weary as I take Lupin on his normal morning walk through the woods, my limbs so heavy that I have to cut it short. As we're walking past the Quinns' house, I see Mr Quinn is in his driveway, sweeping vigorously. He doesn't notice me.

'Good morning,' I say.

He looks up at me and scowls.

'Is everything all right?' I ask.

He stops sweeping. He looks as tired as I feel.

'No, it's not. Bloody disgusting,' he says, holding up an empty beer bottle. 'I've found cigarette butts, empty bottles, and even some plastic cups chucked over the hedge into our garden.'

'Yes, it was quite a racket last night.'

And then Mr Quinn spots something slightly out of my view and starts running towards it, his rake held aloft.

'Get the hell out of here!' he yells as he sprints, surprisingly fast.

A young man and woman run across his front garden. They must be late twenties, the woman wearing a sparkling silver dress, a thick puffa coat over her shoulders, the man wearing skinny jeans and a fitted floral-design shirt. Mr Quinn is giving chase, waving his rake in front of him.

'You're trespassing!' he shouts. 'Filthy vermin, sleeping in my shed. I'm going to sue you for trespass, and you're going to regret ever setting foot in The Close. Get the hell off my land!'

The couple leg it out of his drive, skidding past Lupin and me and running full pelt along the lane, laughing hysterically before turning into Linette's drive.

'The bastards,' Mr Quinn says. He's red in the face and panting now, and I'm slightly worried he's going to have a heart attack.

'What happened?' I ask.

'They were sleeping in my garden shed. Disgusting.' He shakes his head. 'As if the noise wasn't enough, and then all of this litter, but to find them doing their business in my shed, it sickens me.'

'Would you like me to help you clear up?' I ask.

'No. I just want to be left alone. It's not too much to ask, is it?' He shakes his head, lifts up the rake, and strides off into his garden.

BACK AT HOME, I have a customer booked in for a mid-morning manicure. My bookings have dropped off considerably, but there's little I can do about it except tell everyone I can that someone has been spreading malicious gossip about my business. It's depressing how it takes years to build up a business, but it can be destroyed literally overnight. I'm so tired that I barely make it through the appointment, keeping my chat to the minimum. Afterwards, I call Mum.

'Any chance you could have the kids tonight? I'm exhausted and need to get a good night's sleep before driving to Celia's for the weekend.'

'Of course, love. I'll collect them from school. You look after yourself.'

I have plenty of errands to do prior to going away for the weekend, but when I finally go to bed a little before ten p.m., I sink into sleep gratefully.

'What's that?' I sit bolt upright in bed and press the light on my alarm clock. It's just gone three a.m. Mike grunts.

It's the doorbell.

'Mike, wake up!' I say. 'There's someone at the door.'

He pulls on a sweater and hurries downstairs. I stay at the top of the stairs, hugging my dressing gown around me, grateful that the kids are sleeping over at Mum's tonight and aren't being disturbed.

'Sorry to wake you, but my wife's gone missing.' It's Mr Quinn, and there's panic in his voice. 'She hasn't stopped by or anything, has she?'

'No,' Mike says, adding rather unnecessarily, 'It's three in the morning.'

'I know. I'll call the police but thought I'd better check with all the neighbours first.'

'Give me a couple of minutes, and I'll pull on some clothes. I'll come out and look for her with you.'

'Thanks, Mike. Much appreciated.'

Both Mike and I hurry back to the bedroom and get dressed.

'You don't need to come,' he says.

'It's not like I have to stay at home to look after the kids.'

'No, but you still don't need to come.'

But I do. I'm not prepared to have anything else on my conscience. I failed our neighbours once before.

It's a clear, bitterly cold night, the moon throwing a milky hue across The Close. By the time we walk out of the house, wrapped up in thick coats, hats and gloves, Mr Quinn is talking to Jack Abbott in the lane. All four of us are carrying torches.

'I was suggesting we split up,' Jack says.

'Have you checked all the neighbours?' Mike asks.

'Yes, Adler hasn't seen her. He's on a Zoom call so can't join us,' Mr Quinn says.

Mike frowns. 'At this time of night?'

'Does transatlantic business, apparently,' Jack says.

'When did you notice Mrs Quinn had gone missing?' I ask.

'About twenty minutes ago. I woke up, and she wasn't in bed. I searched the house and garden and then knocked on all of your doors. The only person I couldn't make contact with is that dreadful Linette. All the lights are off in her house, and she doesn't answer the door. Perhaps she's not even home.'

'What was your wife wearing?' I ask.

Mr Quinn shrugs. 'I don't know.'

'I think you should ring the police,' Mike says. 'It's a cold night, and she's vulnerable. We'll search everyone's gardens, but perhaps they could call out a helicopter and search for her properly.'

Mr Quinn looks really upset. I place a hand on his arm, but he shrugs me off.

'Why don't you two search all the gardens in The Close, and I'll have a wander onto the road?' Jack says.

Mike and I stick together and start off by searching our garden. From time to time I shout 'Mrs Quinn' or 'Yvonne', although it seems strange to be calling out her first name.

They have always been Mr and Mrs Quinn and have never asked us to be less formal.

'She's not here,' Mike says, stating the obvious. 'Let's move on to Linette's garden.'

I feel a sense of dread as we walk up the side of Linette's house, push open the gate and enter her garden. Our wellington boots squelch on the waterlogged lawn, and the tall trees throw long, dark shadows. I jump at the sound of a squealing rabbit most probably being killed by a fox.

'It's all right,' Mike says, squeezing my arm. But I'm terrified that we're going to stumble over Mrs Quinn's lifeless body.

And then there's the sound of a car, and I see blue flashing lights through the trees. We hurry back the way we've just come, around the side of Linette's dark house and onto the lane. The police car is parked up between the Quinns' and Linette's house. Mike walks towards the car, but something makes me turn around.

'What's going on?' Linette is standing in her doorway, wearing a white nightdress that leaves nothing to the imagination.

'Mrs Quinn has disappeared, and we're out looking for her. The police have just arrived.'

'But she's here, in my living room!'

I knot my eyebrows together. 'Didn't you hear Mr Quinn when he knocked on your door? Didn't you hear us shouting for her?'

'No. I sleep like the dead,' she says. I shiver. 'Have you been out searching for her?' She laughs as if we're some silly children, as if it's rather hilarious that we've been roused from our beds and worried about a vulnerable older lady.

I hurry to the police car and see that Mr Quinn is already talking to them.

'She's at Linette's house!' I yell.

Mr Quinn runs up the drive, his torchlight bobbing up and down. Jack, Mike and I follow him, standing a few steps behind him as Linette talks to Mr Quinn.

'Your wife rang on my doorbell earlier. She came in for a chat, and I gave her a hot chocolate. She fell asleep on the sofa, so I popped a rug over her and a pillow under her head and left her there. It was already about one a.m., so I didn't want to wake you up.' She stares at Mr Quinn with big eyes. 'I'm ever so sorry and to have wasted police time. Shall I go and wake her up?'

I can't help but wonder whether Linette did this on purpose, whether she welcomed Mrs Quinn into her home and then knowingly failed to inform her husband that she was safe. Although she's portraying herself as the Good Samaritan, it doesn't wash with me. Of course she should have rung Mr Quinn or, better still, accompanied Mrs Quinn back to the safety of her own home.

And then Mrs Quinn appears behind Linette, rubbing her eyes.

'What's going on?' she asks as she frowns.

'Come along,' her husband says, grasping her forearm. 'You should be at home tucked up in bed. You had us all worried.'

'There was nothing to worry about. I was quite safe at Linette's.'

'Let's go home,' Mike says quietly, putting an arm around my shoulders. And so we leave them all, letting Jack deal with the police.

'There was something odd about that,' I say.

'What do you mean?'

'Just that it seemed like Linette wanted to worry Mr Quinn.'

'You need to stop seeing the worst in people, Isobel. She was just being nice and probably didn't think it through.'

I don't reply. When we get home, Mike goes straight back to bed, but I'm not tired now, so I make myself a hot chocolate and sit for a few minutes in the darkened kitchen, sipping the hot drink. Something isn't right with Linette. Sometimes, she's hospitable and making every effort to be the considerate neighbour, but then she undoes all the good by creating disturbances. I can't put my finger on it, but I have a feeling that she's up to no good.

'I DON'T KNOW if I'm going to be too drowsy to drive,' I say the next morning with a yawn. Mike and I are seated at the kitchen table. I'm meant to collect the children from Mum's house and then drive them up to Suffolk to stay with my sister for a couple of nights. I'm sorely disappointed that Mike has refused to go over for Christmas, breaking our long-standing tradition. Instead, I'm going now. Celia and her family are taking a trip to Lapland, so I've no choice but to visit her now, at the beginning of the children's Christmas holidays. It's a long drive, which I don't enjoy at the best of times, let alone when I'm exhausted after two nights with limited sleep. But what choice do I have? Cancel and severely disappoint Harry and Harper, as well as my sister and her children, or drive as carefully as I can? As I'm loading up the car with Christmas presents and our luggage, a ridiculous amount for a two-night stay, I hear the loud and grating sound of an electric saw. I walk up onto the lane to see what's happening, and there's a truck parked alongside the Quinns' entrance. Halfway up one of the massive leylandiis that delineate the edge of the Quinns' and Linette's properties is a man strung up with ropes, using the saw to lop off large branches. As I'm watching, Linette appears, seemingly from nowhere, as she's prone to do.

'The Quinns have agreed to chop down the leylandii,' she says, looking rather smug.

'Really? I'm surprised.'

'Why?' Linette asks.

'Mona Walker, who used to live here, was desperate for the Quinns to take down those trees. Every year they grew taller and denser, and Mona said they were blocking the light into their bedroom and kitchen. But the Quinns refused to have them touched. You did well to persuade them.'

'What was Mona like?'

'I'm afraid I didn't get to know her well. I believe she suffered from SAD disease and really struggled from the lack of light.'

'Did anyone try to help Mona by getting the trees cut down?'

It's a strange question, and I furrow my brows as I look at Linette. She's wearing a thick duffel coat and leggings. It makes her look top heavy.

'It's just, if you knew that she suffered from the lack of light, I was wondering what you did to help her?'

I open and close my mouth because I have no answer to that.

'Where are you off to, anyway?' Linette asks.

'Sorry?'

'I saw you loading up your car with luggage and Christmas presents.'

I try to suppress a shiver. What's she been doing? Spying on me? It's none of her business where I'm going.

'Ah, yes. You're off to see your sister, aren't you?'

'How do you know?' I ask.

She taps the side of her nose. 'Drive carefully, Isobel.'

12

LINETTE

I've got the measure of these awful neighbours. And mostly, I'm furious with Isobel. If she'd shown an iota of the amount of care towards Mona that she's showing towards Mrs Quinn, perhaps things would have played out very differently. I'm sure she's only showing Mrs Quinn concern because I led the way. How I loathe women like her, all comfortable in their middle-class domestic bliss, with her two children and pathetic little business. Why doesn't she do something useful like helping out in a charity? It's not like she needs the money.

I watch as the taillights of her car disappear down the end of the lane and wonder about her husband. I haven't had much dealing with Mike, but he's certainly shifty. I am positive he's hiding something. Now that she's away, I'm going to take the opportunity to get to know him. As they say, knowledge is power.

I go back upstairs and sit cross-legged on the floor in Wilson's bedroom. I feel closest to both him and Mona in here. The essence of her has gone from the bedroom she shared with that brute of a husband. I often wondered about

Keith. Did he take a hand to my sister, or something worse, perhaps? A belt, maybe. I never had any proof that he hit her, but then Mona was too proud to let on about something like that. To be honest, when they told me that she had died through suicide, my first assumption was that Keith had done it or at least driven her to it. It wasn't until I went around to see him at the new house they were renting in Crawley that I realised I was mistaken. Keith Walker was a broken man. He could barely breathe, let alone function. Poor Ollie, just thirteen years old and having to keep it together for his remaining parent. I felt bad for doubting Keith's affection for Mona, but at the same time, I knew in my gut that he felt guilty for letting her die. Perhaps that's why he was so devastated, a big man like him unable to prevent the deaths of his oldest son and his wife.

I could have made life hell for Keith, but I decided it wasn't in my interest and certainly wasn't in the interests of Mona. I needed him on my side to help me find out the truth, so I did everything for him and Ollie—their cooking and cleaning and making sure that Ollie got to school, and I even arranged the funeral. Keith was grateful. A bit too grateful. When he made a crass advance and suggested that I might like to take on my deceased sister's conjugal duties, I let rip. He realised his mistake soon enough, and in a way, it worked to my favour. His guilt spilled over, and here I am in his old home on a nominal rent because he knows that my benefits won't allow me to pay him any more. It's what Mona would have wanted, and he sees that.

Mike doesn't get home from work until nearly eight p.m. I've been sitting at the window, waiting for the lights of his car. I wonder what he's been doing all this time. Playing away or eating out, perhaps. I'll give him an hour, and then I'll pop over there for a cosy little chat.

It's just before nine p.m. I've carefully applied mascara and lipstick and am wearing a figure-hugging dress. I'd have preferred to put on some high heels, but I'm not stupid enough to go snooping around someone's house in the dark wearing heels, so boots will have to do. Wearing a dark coat and with the light of my phone, I walk across the road towards the Floyds' house. I have no intention of going in until I've worked out exactly what Mike Floyd is doing, so I tiptoe down their drive and then stand still for a few long moments until I get my orientation as to which room is which and where he might be in the house.

But then, to my delight, I realise I'm not alone. I have stood outside this house on many an occasion since I moved into The Close, and I had my suspicions before, but now they are being confirmed. There's a dark figure creeping down the drive, a hood pulled up over his or her head, boot-clad feet lit up by the feeble light of their mobile phone. Who could it possibly be? The person stops still, glancing around, but I'm good at hide-and-seek, and there's no way that I'm going to be detected. Clearly thinking the coast is clear, they carry on walking, glancing over their shoulder to check there's no one else coming down the driveway, and then the person sneaks around the side of the Floyds' house and does a final little scurry towards the back door.

I smile with glee when I realise it's Josie who has set the floodlight off and made the dog bark. Silently, I follow her, tiptoeing until I have perfect vision of the door. She knocks once.

After a few moments, Mike opens the door. I have a clear view of his face, and he doesn't look happy. Not one little bit. Well, that's a surprise. I thought he'd be pleased to see her. I daren't get any closer to overhear their conversation, but from the hushed whispers and Mike's frantic gesticulations, it's obvious that he's trying to send her away. But dear Josie isn't having any of that. Oh, no, she's standing her ground and trying to stroke Mike's face with her right hand. So my suspicions were right. And then he takes hold of her wrist and pulls Josie inside, slamming the door shut behind her. I tiptoe up to the back door, hiding in the shadows, and then shimmy around the side of the house until I see them in the kitchen, talking animatedly, standing so closely together their noses are practically touching. I crouch down directly underneath the window in the kitchen, where I can hear every word they're saying, especially as Mike is now raising his voice.

'No, Josie, I can't.'

'I don't think I can live without you,' she says.

'Please, think of Jack and your children. They need you in the same way that Isobel, Harry and Harper need me. It was good whilst it lasted, but it is over now. We agreed. Come on, don't make things any harder than they already are.'

She whispers something that I can't hear, and there's silence for a while. I wonder if they're smooching in the kitchen, but then I hear a sob.

'All right,' she says. Her voice sounds choked. Aw, poor Josie with a broken heart. 'If you change your mind—'

'I won't, Josie. And you know it's for the best.'

And then I hear footsteps and know I need to scarper fast. I race across the driveway, setting the floodlights off again, and swoop into the dark bushes, my heart beating furiously. I'm enjoying this spying game and the adrenaline rush it brings.

'What was that?' Josie asks. She's standing in the open doorway now.

'A rabbit, probably. They set off the lights all the time.'

'I'm glad you're being so understanding about the green burial application,' Josie says loudly. For a moment I'm confused, and then realise this is probably her cover, her reason for popping over to see her lover-boy neighbour just in case anyone else, or specifically her husband, might overhear her.

When she's disappeared into the night, I stand up and stretch. What should I do? Go and have a little chat with Mikey or plan how I can weaponise the information I've just obtained? On reflection, I decide that it's better I remain in the shadows, both metaphorically and literally. I trot back to my house, and I'm not in the slightest bit bothered that I got all tarted up for no reason. I have information, and I will take great pleasure in working out how best to use it.

13

The weekend away at my sister's was the tonic that the children and I needed. They let off steam playing with their cousins while Celia and I put the world to rights. Harper was entranced by her youngest cousin, Celia's nine-month-old baby girl, and asked if we could have a baby too. I tried to keep my expression neutral when I explained that was out of the question.

I told Celia about Linette and all the other neighbours and the unfortunate goings-on, and Celia laughed. 'Let it go,' she said. 'Neighbours are neighbours. You don't have to be their friend.' But I don't want to feel awkwardness around them. I want it to go back to how it was between Josie and me a couple of years ago.

Although we were only away for two nights, by the time I return home, I feel fully refreshed. Today, we're going to visit a Santa's grotto in a garden centre on the edge of town. I expect it'll be heaving, but it's an annual tradition, and the children are beside themselves with excitement at the prospect. Mum has come over early and is entertaining the kids whilst I take Lupin for our regular walk through the woods.

I'm on my way back from walking Lupin through the woods. When I get to the end of the muddy footpath, I attach his lead before we stroll along the lane. We're about to turn into our driveway when I spot Linette standing at the bottom of her drive, waving wildly. To my bemusement, she has a pig standing next to her, not one of those cute pot-bellied pigs but a large one, the sort that you see on farms. Around its neck is a fluorescent pink collar with a lead attached.

'Come and meet Twiglet!' she shouts.

I walk towards her, but Lupin is very reluctant to get anywhere near the pig.

'I've got a new pet!' Linette exclaims. 'The breeder promised me that she'd be good on a lead, but I don't think she wants to go for a walk.' Linette tries to tug on the lead, but the pig is going nowhere.

I can't help but laugh. When Linette was talking about getting a pet, it never crossed my mind that she would get a pig.

'Are you allowed a pig under the terms of your lease?' I ask, thinking how horrified poor Mona would have been to have a pig in her garden.

'I got special dispensation, so don't be a killjoy.'

'Sorry, it's just a pig is quite an unusual pet.'

'They're as intelligent as dogs, I'll have you know. If you'd like to bring your kids over to meet her, then feel free.'

'Thank you,' I say, knowing full well that I have no intention of Harry and Harper meeting Twiglet and risking an enormous pig trampling them.

Back at home, Harry and Harper are dressed in anoraks, hats and mittens, ready to go to see Santa. They chatter excitedly in the car and tug my hands as we walk into the garden centre. As expected, the queue is long despite having booked timed slots, but the kids don't seem to mind waiting as they gape at the magical winter wonderland animatronic animals and dance to the repetitive Christmas songs piped over the Tannoy system.

When Santa asks Harry whether he's been a good boy this year, he looks at me for reassurance.

'He's been a very good boy,' I say.

Harry beams.

'And what would you like for Christmas?' Santa asks.

Harry recites the names of a couple of toys on his Christmas list, and then he lowers his voice and steps a little nearer to Santa. 'I'd like some more friends too, but I don't know if you can give those to me because they don't fit in a stocking, do they?'

I have to blink hard to stop the tears from flowing, and it feels like my heart is going to split open.

THE NEXT MORNING, I'm in the kitchen laying the breakfast table while Mike is upstairs. He lets out a string of expletives; then he comes running down the stairs, wearing just his boxer shorts and a shirt.

'Isobel! Have you looked outside at the garden?'

'No,' I say. It's only just getting light, and I let Lupin out at the side of the house, as I always do. I turn and walk towards the window. 'Oh, my God!'

The mess is horrific. Our flower beds are mounds of earth, plants and roots scattered across the lawn. The lawn itself has been dug up, and there is soil everywhere.

'When did you last look in the garden?' Mike asks. His hands are on the top of his head, and his shoulders are hunched up.

'I don't know. I was out most of yesterday with the children. By the time we got home, it was dark, and I wouldn't have noticed the damage if it had already been there.' I pause and sigh. 'I think I know what did this,' I say. 'Linette has got a pig, and I expect it got out.'

'A pig in a residential area! That's ridiculous. It shouldn't be allowed. Are you sure?'

'Totally. I saw her with it yesterday morning. With the excitement of seeing Santa, I forgot to tell you.'

'In which case, I'm going over there now to tell that woman she can pay us damages and get the garden sorted out. It must be hundreds, if not thousands of pounds of damage.'

'Don't have a fight,' I say, but Mike has disappeared upstairs.

A COUPLE of minutes after Mike has rushed upstairs, the doorbell chimes. Frowning, I walk to the door. It's Linette, looking bashful, wrapped in a giant black puffa jacket that swamps her.

'Twiglet got out of her pen last night, and I was wondering if you'd seen her.'

Before I can say a word, Mike appears at my side, dressed in his shirt and suit trousers but barefoot. 'Your bloody pig has decimated our garden. It's totally trashed, and you're liable for the damages. It's irresponsible to be keeping a pig in a domestic setting.'

'Calm down,' Linette says, which only infuriates Mike further.

'Did you listen to a word I said? You need to walk around the house and see the damage. This needs cleaning up imme-diately, so I suggest you find a gardener and make good.'

'I'm sorry about any mess, but I'm really worried about Twiglet. She could have got onto the main road. She's created a bit of muck in Jack's field, and he's not happy either.'

Mike throws his arms up into the air. 'Get this sorted, Linette; otherwise you'll be receiving a solicitor's letter.'

Linette opens her mouth as if to say something and then clearly thinks better of it, turning around and stomping off.

'That's a fine way of making friends with our neighbours,' I say, flapping the tea towel that I didn't know I had put over my arm.

'Why would we even want to be friends with someone who has an out-of-control pig? Let's hope that Jack captures the bloody animal and shares the pork chops around The Close.'

'That's horrible, Mike! How can you say such a thing?' I'm shocked by his reaction. Yes, I know he's upset, but it's hardly a catastrophe. The garden can be made good easily enough, and normally, Mike is overly compassionate towards animals.

He ruffles his hair with his fingers. 'I don't mean it, really, but pigs are meant for farms, not back gardens.'

'Why don't you go and have a word with Jack? If the Abbotts have got damage too, then perhaps you can tackle it together.'

He grunts.

'So?'

'No, I'm not going to.'

'Why not? It makes sense for you to join forces on this.'

'I'm quite capable of handling Linette alone without needing Jack for moral support.'

'It's not that—'

'Let it go. I need to hurry up; otherwise I'll be late for work. We can discuss it later.'

ONCE AGAIN, Mike's reaction confuses me. He seemed to get on with Jack just fine at Linette's drinks party, but now he's keeping his distance again. I know he has a huge amount of work on at the moment and some tight deadlines looming, but he is reacting weirdly.

Despite my business trailing off, I have had a few new appointments booked with people rushing to get their nails done before Christmas. Mum has offered to have the kids for the day, and I have agreed to collect them from her house later on. I need to give Lupin a quick walk first, so I hurry off for our normal amble through the woods. Someone is having an enormous bonfire, the heavy, acrid scent of burned leaves enveloping The Close, particularly bad in the Quinns' house and garden, where their house is cloaked in a dark grey fog. Mr Quinn appears out of the smoke, coughing and spluttering.

'That bloody woman. She's burning a mountain of leaves, and the smoke has engulfed us. It's so thoughtless of her. When I have a bonfire, I make sure that no one is going to be affected by it.'

'Yes, it is bad,' I say, squinting to see him as the smoke stings my eyes. 'Her pig got out and ruined our garden and the Abbotts' field last night. Have you seen it?'

'A bloody pig! What the hell is this place coming to? No, I haven't seen it, and if I do, I'll report it. I'm going over there now to tell her to stop burning those leaves until the wind changes. It's terrible for my wife's asthma.'

It hits me then. Is Linette doing all of this on purpose, or is it just unfortunate that she's upset all her neighbours at the same time? I don't suppose she could encourage the pig to do damage, but it's a possibility. When I'm returning from my walk, Josie is driving up the lane. I gesture at her to slow down, and as I'm standing in her way, she has no choice. She rolls her eyes as she lowers her window.

'How bad has the damage been to your field?'

'Bad enough.'

'The pig wrecked our garden. I'm not quite sure how to

approach Linette about it. What do you recommend?' I
reckon that as Josie is so chummy with Linette, she might be
able to suggest the best way to talk to her without having a
massive fallout.

'You're asking me?' she says with a harrumph.

'I thought—'

'We're not friends. She's a nosy bitch.'

That startles me. The last I knew, she and Linette were
tight buddies.

'She's been burning leaves, and the smoke has enveloped
the Quinns' house,' I say.

'I know. I can smell it.'

'She's quite a divisive character, isn't she?' I comment.

'You know, Isobel, for once, there's something you and I
can agree on.' She winds up her window and drives away.

I can't stop thinking about Linette during my appointments. There she was so eager to befriend us all, and now she
seems to be causing upset. It is extremely strange. Does she
have an agenda, I wonder, or is she just a meddling type of
person? Perhaps she's lonely, or perhaps she's never lived in
an area like this and doesn't know the ways of country living?
But she's piqued my curiosity, and I want to know more about
her. What sort of woman moves into a big house with no
furniture, a house that must command a high rent, and then
buys a pig as a pet?

When my last client has left, I fire up the laptop and type
Linette Smith into Google. Unfortunately, her name throws up
over a million search results. I narrow the search, looking for
someone of that name in Crawley and then look on images,
but I can't find our Linette anywhere on social media.
Perhaps she changed her name back to her maiden name
after her divorce. I have no way of finding out what her

married name was. And then my imagination really goes haywire. Is Linette Smith really her name? Does she have an agenda? Or am I overthinking this? I put the laptop away and get ready to go to Mum's. After Dad died, Mum downsized to a new build house on one of the smaller developments on the other side of Horsham. It's convenient for her because she can take the bus into town, and she's within easy distance of most of her friends. I normally take the ring road, which is dual carriageway and faster, but on a whim, I decide to go through the centre of town and make a stop-off.

The Walkers had an estate agent's 'house to let' sign at the bottom of the lane for a while after they moved out and I'm wondering if the estate agent might be able to throw some light on Linette. I park the car in a multistorey and stride towards Strathearn Estate Agents. I'm greeted by a middle-aged woman who looks like she's just stepped away from a week under a sun bed. I'm not quite sure where I'm going with this one, but I'll wing it.

'Have a seat,' she says, gesturing at the chair on the other side of her desk. 'How can I help you?'

'You had a house available for rent, Number Two, The Close. I was wondering if you could tell me whether it's still on the market, or if not, when the lease might be up for renewal?'

'That one rings a bell. Let me have a quick look.' She types rapidly and then frowns.

'My colleague was dealing with that, and it was taken off the market two months ago.'

'You mean it was rented out?'

'No. The owners took it off the market. They said they'd changed their minds and didn't want to rent it out after all. There was some suggestion that they'd put it up for sale, but that hasn't happened yet.'

'So Linette Smith, the person who is renting it now, didn't come through you?'

A look of displeasure crosses the woman's face. I suppose she thinks she might have been cheated out of a commission. 'What did you say the tenant was called?'

I repeat myself, and she types something into her computer, no doubt wanting to check that the introduction didn't come via their agency.

'We don't have anyone of that name on our database,' she says, more to herself than me.

'Are you interested in renting a house in that area? Because I can do a search and see what we have available.'

'No, thank you. It was that house in particular that I wanted to rent.'

'If you leave your name and address, I'll pop your details in the database, and we can contact you if Number Two, The Close comes back onto the market.'

'I'll leave it for now,' I say, standing up and grabbing my handbag. 'But thanks for your help.

She tilts her head to one side and gives me a strange look. I throw her an awkward smile and hurry out of the estate agent's before she can ask me any further questions.

The big question is, where did Linette come from? Was she introduced via another estate agent, or is she a personal friend of Keith Walker? And does it even matter?

14

The green burial site application is never far from my mind, but with all the pre-Christmas rush and the stress around Linette and the Quinns, I haven't gotten around to submitting my objection. Now I have to get it done; otherwise it'll be too late. I go onto the planning portal and see that there have been a few objections, but not nearly as many as I would have expected. There have also been some supportive comments, which is unusual. I note with some disgust that Linette has written a gushing note of support. The parish council does have some concerns, and Highways haven't commented yet. I would imagine that their support or objections would carry the greatest weight because increased traffic on our narrow lane will be of concern. I take some time composing my letter, relating all of my points back to the planning laws and the local plan. I'm grateful that my job as an architect means I have a reasonable knowledge of planning law, and above all, I'm aware that emotion carries zero weight. The only objections that count are those that clearly contravene planning laws. When I'm happy with my response, I click *Send* and then lean back in my chair.

Everything has changed so much in the past year, and although Wilson's death was a catalyst for some things, the rot started well before. I really think life was better in The Close when the neighbours had nothing to do with each other.

THE CHILDREN and I are on our way home from doing a supermarket shop in Horsham. It's always difficult shopping with Harry. The lights and the noise and the row after row of brightly coloured objects often create overwhelm. We've had numerous meltdowns over the years, but more recently, Harry seems to be coping better. The trick has been to let him push the trolley and keep him occupied with counting games. I'm driving along the main road when to my amazement, I see a large homemade banner saying *STOP THE GREEN BURIAL GROUND*. I wonder who put that up. I then turn left to drive onto our lane, but ahead of me are a number of stationary cars in a traffic jam. My heart sinks. Please, not another accident.

I stop the car. Ahead of us is a small crowd of people holding banners. From here, I can't see what they say. We sit there for three or four minutes, and then the car in front of me tries to turn around, doing what must be a ten-point turn. I edge forwards, and a young man with a beard, wearing a blue parka and ripped jeans, walks up to the driver's window. I lower it.

'What's going on?' I ask.

'A demonstration against the green burial site. Do you live here?'

'Yes, on The Close, the next turning on the left.'

'What, next to the Abbotts?'

'Yes. And you are?'

He ignores my question. 'Are you a supporter of the green burial site?'

'Absolutely not.'

He smiles, revealing a gap where a couple of his molars should be. 'In which case, we'll let you in.' He walks towards the car in front of me and gets the driver to edge towards the left verge. He then beckons me through. As I drive past the waiting cars, I'm stunned to see that there must be twenty to thirty people all holding homemade banners. Some are wearing skeleton masks and look positively terrifying.

'Harry, can you check out something on my phone?' I fumble in my bag and chuck the phone onto the back seat. I don't want the children looking at the people in the masks, but I'm too late.

'Mummy, what are those scary people doing?' Harper asks. I glance in the rear mirror. Both children are staring with wide eyes, my phone, which is normally an object of great interest, discarded on the seat between them.

'They're just some silly people playing dressing up like at Halloween.'

The man in the ripped jeans pushes the crowd of people to one side, and I see that they've chalked messages, which I can't make out, on the Abbotts' drive and have strung police tape saying *Crime Scene Do Not Cross* across their entrance. For a brief moment, I actually feel sorry for Josie and Jack.

'What's happening, Mummy?' Harry asks.

'The Abbotts want to set up a new business, and these people are objecting to it.'

'What new business?'

I wonder how I can explain it in a way that they will understand but not freak them out. 'Where people go when they die.'

'They want to put heaven in their garden?' Harper asks.

I smile. 'Something like that.'

'But that'll be nice, won't it? We'll be able to see Grandma,' Harper says.

I let out a puff of air. Mike's mother died last year, and we're still finding it difficult to explain to the children where she's gone. I can see how one little fib rolls over into a big, fat lie, a bit like a small lump of snow that becomes a snowball, and then it's so large nothing can get past it until it creates an avalanche, destroying everything in its path.

I hurry the children into the house. Lupin seems very happy to see us, although he starts barking loudly when I have the back door open. The protestors are making a racket, shouting, 'No to the green burial ground!' and, 'Let the bodies rot in a proper graveyard!' and, 'Protect our fields and wildlife!' In fact, they're so noisy, that even with the doors and our double-glazed windows closed, I can hear exactly what they're saying through our double glazing. Despite our differences, I feel sorry for Josie. If she's home, it must be scary for her and the kids to have such venom directed towards them. After ten minutes or so, I telephone her.

It rings and rings, and then eventually, she picks up the phone.

'Josie, it's Isobel. Are you all right?'

'No, I'm bloody not all right. I suppose you're gloating now, aren't you? Who did you pay to organise a demonstration like this right outside our front door?'

'What!'

'I know you did this. You're the only person who is against the green burial ground, and you know what, I'm actually quite impressed that you have the wherewithal to find people like that. You know, one of those women actually spat at me, and she was trespassing on our property.'

'This is nothing to do with me,' I say, staggered that she might think it could be.

'Whatever. The police are on their way, and they'll get to the bottom of it. You'll be charged, you know.'

'Josie, this is nothing to do with me, I promise. I was genuinely worried about you, which is why I called.'

'If you didn't organise this, then who did? That's what I want to know. And I will find out, rest assured.'

And then she hangs up on me. I'm still staring at the phone in shock when I hear the police sirens. They get louder and louder, and at the same time, the shouts reduce in volume.

When the children are settled in their playroom, I go onto my laptop and check out the objection letters to the green burial ground on the council's website. I don't know any of the names, but the addresses suggest they're all local to this area. I simply can't imagine anyone organising such a protest. Except Linette.

Could it have been Linette? I think back over all the things that have happened since she arrived on The Close. The noise and rubbish from her party. The pig and the damage it caused. The smoke from her burning leaves. The youths turning up for a Halloween party. The dead rat on our doorstep. The complaint about the snooping drone. How she blew hot and cold about the green burial application. The bad reviews about my salon business. In isolation, I might think these events were all just unfortunate niggles, misunderstandings and thoughtlessness, but I can't help but wonder whether this is part of a more concerted campaign. Yes, something terrible happened here long before Linette arrived, but more recently, it's as if all of us neighbours are being pitted against each other, being made to feel uncomfortable in our own homes. I try to ignore the feeling of unease.

I take our shopping bags out of the boot of the car, and there's now quiet outside, not that I intend to hang around to find out what's going on. Back in the kitchen, I unpack the shopping, and then I line up all the ingredients for us to make stained-glass-window shortbread biscuits, those little shaped ones that have windows of melted sweets in the middle that we can hang on the Christmas tree.

'Harry, Harper, it's cooking time!' They both rush into the kitchen. I help them put on little aprons that Mum gave them last Christmas, and then I measure and whisk the ingredients while Harry and Harper wait impatiently. I've just given them each a mound of dough to roll out when the doorbell rings.

I hurry to the door.

My heart sinks when I see Linette. At least the protestors and the police have gone.

'Isobel, I've got something difficult that I need to tell you.'

'It's not a good time. I'm cooking with the children.'

'I don't think it can wait,' she says. 'I've been mulling it over for a little while, but if I were in your shoes, I would want to know without any delay.'

I feel cold dread wind its way from my throat to my stomach.

'What is it?' I whisper.

She beckons for me to walk away from the door, away from little eavesdropping ears.

'Okay, I'm just going to say it.' She glances up at the pewter sky and takes in a big gulp of breath. 'Your Mike and Josie Abbott have been having an affair.'

The sides of the house seem to sway, and my legs weaken. I lean my back against the cold brick wall.

'No,' I murmur.

'I'm sorry to be the one to tell you, but you need to know.'

'You're talking a load of nonsense,' I say, immediately pulling myself together. 'I don't know what it is that you want from all of us, but ever since you've arrived on The Close, things have gone wrong. It's like you're trying to get a rise out of us, to anger us, set us off against each other. You think you're some puppet master, don't you? But you're not. You're just a sad, meddling woman, and I'd like you to leave me alone.'

Linette gapes at me, but I turn around, walk through the door, and shut it firmly in her face.

I stand there for a few long moments, my knees trembling.

'Mummy, are you coming?' Harper shouts.

'I just need to use the bathroom,' I say, slipping into the downstairs loo next to the back door. I sit on the closed toilet seat for a while and realise tears are streaming down my cheeks because it suddenly all makes sense. Mike has been so stressed for so long, to the point of pushing me away, whereas Josie has done her best to avoid me, yet when we've spoken, she's been confrontational and awkward. Why the hell didn't I see this before? And at Linette's party, Josie was drunk and dancing provocatively with Mike, and when that happened, Mike was out of there like a shot.

Yes, it all makes sense. But why? What can Josie give Mike that I can't? It's not as if she's a younger, prettier version of me. She's a harried farmer's wife juggling businesses and children. Or is it my fault because I've taken my eye off our marriage and focused all my attention onto the children? Should I have been making more of an effort? No, I'm the injured party here. And then I wonder. Are they really having an affair, or is Linette just trying to create more discord in The Close? What should I do? Confront Mike or Josie?

This is ridiculous. I'm believing a strange woman I barely know over my husband. The trouble is, once that little seed of doubt is planted, it's impossible to kill it off. My head is spinning, and my throat is choked. I'm going to have to try to forget about this for another couple of hours because the children need me.

I splash cold water onto my face and wipe away my tears.

When I walk into the kitchen, there is flour all over the kitchen counter and on the floor while the children are giggling and splattering clouds of flour over each other.

'What have you done!' I snap. 'I leave you for a couple of minutes and you destroy the kitchen. Just get out! Go to the playroom now.'

Harper's bottom lip trembles, and she bursts into tears while Harry runs out of the room.

I close my eyes and take a deep breath. What the hell am I doing, taking out my anger on the kids? I never lose my temper like this, at least not with the children. I know how very important it is that I remain on an even keel for Harry. But Linette has really got to me.

I throw my arms around my little girl and wipe away her tears. 'I'm sorry, darling. Mummy didn't mean to shout at you.' I take her hand. 'Come on. Let's go and find Harry so I can say sorry to him too.'

15

After apologising to the kids and persuading Harry to return to the kitchen, which takes an awful lot of grovelling on my part, I force myself out of self-pity and help the children cut random shapes into the dough. When the biscuits are in the oven and the children are seated in front of the television in the living room, I set about cleaning the kitchen. Is Linette right? I give myself a stern talking-to. What she said is nonsense. Surely, I can't believe a woman I barely know, a woman who has been divisive and thoughtless? Mike is my husband. I love him, and I've known him intimately for nearly a decade. Would Mike cheat on me? I remember discussing fidelity in the early stages of our relationship, and he said he could never stay with a partner who cheated on him. But what did I say? I think I was so in love back then that the thought of either of us cheating on each other was inconceivable. But now? No. Mike wouldn't do that to us. Nevertheless, he has been working very long hours, but an affair with Josie? She's an attractive woman, especially when she dresses up, but she's so busy all the time and makes sure we all know that. When would she even have time to have an affair with Mike? It just doesn't stack up. Yet Mike has definitely been different this past year.

And how would Linette even know? Has she been following Mike or Josie, or has Josie confided in her? I find that hard to believe.

When Mike comes home from work, I don't say anything to him. I can't, not yet. Not unless I have concrete evidence. I just have to pretend that everything is normal and do some more digging myself. But I watch him covertly. Yes, he definitely looks tired all the time. But he's still my Mike, the man I fell in love with the moment he stepped into my office for that interview over a decade ago.

I was a rising star in the architect's firm I worked for, mainly because I won a great big contract early on in my career. It was serendipitous, being in the right place at the right time. My flatmate had invited me to her brother's wedding, and to my dismay, they mingled up the guests to such an extent that the old sat next to the young. On my right was a man the same age as my father. When I told him I was a newly qualified architect, his eyes lit up. He explained that he was a developer seeking outline planning consent for a butterfly farm and leisure centre adjacent to his big, independent garden centre on the south coast. We talked throughout the whole meal, so much so that I said no more than hello to the younger man sitting on my left. I shared my idealistic visions for creating low-carbon-footprint leisure facilities that integrated the environment, and he hung off my every word. He introduced me to his wife, describing me as a young, visionary architect. I blushed but then promptly forgot all about them as I danced the night away. On Monday morning, my senior partner summoned me. He and I were going to meet Simon Cartright to pitch for a ten-million-pound leisure complex project. It wasn't until Mr Cartright greeted us in his conference room that I even realised he was the man I met at the wedding.

And so began my rapid trajectory in the architect's firm. I was made the youngest-ever partner, much to the chagrin of some of my superiors. I don't think I was an especially good architect. I just got lucky along the way and grasped all opportunities that presented themselves. The firm was growing rapidly, and it was apparent that I needed an associate. Human resources presented me with a shortlist of three. When Mike walked through the door, I couldn't take my eyes off him. I blustered through the interview, asking questions like an inexperienced idiot. Honestly, I have no idea if he was the best candidate. I just knew that I needed to see him again. He accepted the job. That first Monday morning, I spent more time getting ready for work than I'd ever done in the past, so it continued for three months. We were awkward around each other, ridiculously polite, deferring to each other's opinion. None of this was helped by the fact that he was an excellent architect, one year older than me, and I had an inferiority complex, wondering how it was possible that I could be his boss.

We both attended the leaving drinks of our office manager. It was held in a bar in Brighton, a sleazy dive of a place that stank of cigarette smoke despite no one being allowed to smoke indoors for the previous four years. Back then, most of our colleagues had partners and commitments, and Mike and I were the last to leave. He suggested we go and get something to eat. We never made it to a restaurant. Over the next few weeks, we kept up the pretence of arriving and leaving the office at different times, but it wasn't long before someone caught us in the stationary cupboard—yes, such a cliché, I know. It soon became apparent that one of us would have to leave the firm. Mike said it had to be him. He was the last in, and I was a partner. And so I gave him the most glowing reference, and off he went. The day he started his new job was the day we moved in together. Six months later, we were married. For a long time, I worried that those six months at CS&P would be a stain on Mike's CV. But I needn't have worried because a year later, he was made a partner at his current firm in Horsham, and he's won awards and contracts that have made him an architectural star. Meanwhile, what am I? The fallen star?

Perhaps Mike has lost respect for me? Perhaps that's all that is wrong in our relationship, and if so, that's fixable. I just need more time to mull things over and work out how I'm going to improve our marriage. Or perhaps this is all a big lie concocted by Linette to cause strife, and if so, I'm determined to understand why she is so intent on stirring and causing misery.

The next morning, Mike is off early for a site meeting in Southampton. The children are with Mum again, and I have a couple of free hours. I decide to go through Mike's receipts. He is meticulous with his banking, filing receipts and bank statements in a shared filing cabinet kept in our small study next door to the dining room. We keep all of the documents relating to household expenses in it. I manage our day-to-day expenses, taking money from our joint account, paying for food and the children's clothes and utility bills and house maintenance. Mike rarely checks it because he knows I'm careful with money and would never overspend. What I don't have access to is anything that he does at work—his hotel bills for nights stayed away for on-site visits, his company car expenses. And if he is having an affair and charging things to the firm, there is no way I will ever get hold of that evidence. But Mike is too law-abiding for that. I simply can't see him charging anything to the firm that isn't totally above board.

Nevertheless, I go through every item on our joint account, looking for anything out of the ordinary. There is nothing odd. I then go upstairs and rifle through his jacket pockets, because that's where spurned wives find evidence, isn't it? Again, there is nothing. Where else would he store evidence of a night away or a fancy meal for two? I look in his bedside table drawers and then return to the study and remove absolutely everything from the filing cabinet, placing each folder out on the ground in front of me and meticulously going through every document. But of course Mike wouldn't keep anything in a shared place. If he has documents he wants to hide, he could easily pop them into his briefcase and take them to work. And that's when I remember. I gave him a new briefcase for his birthday three months ago. I recall watching him transfer a pile of papers into the new briefcase, but he left some old papers in the original one.

I find the tattered brown leather case wedged between the filing cabinet and the chair. I pull it out and open it up, taking out some random papers. And that's where I find it. A garage receipt. It's from a garage in Croydon, one I've never heard of, and weirdly, it's not for either Mike's or my car. It's a registration number that I don't recognise. The receipt is handwritten, although the name of the garage, *Fawcett Bros Repairs*, is stamped at the top. It just states *repairs to bonnet and bumper* and lists the registration number. And then I notice the date, and I gasp. Grabbing the receipt, I run to the kitchen and find my phone to check my diary.

My god. The repairs took place the very day after Wilson's accident.

I sink into the kitchen chair. Surely not. Surely, Mike didn't do something quite so horrific as to kill that boy and never admit to it? I glance again at the registration number. It is vaguely familiar, but why? I pour myself a glass of water from the tap, and then it hits me. Was it Josie's old silver Audi? Is that the registration number? I rack my brains to try to remember, but how many of us can recall the plates of our neighbours' cars? But if it was Josie's car, then it confirms exactly what Linette was saying. Mike and Josie were having an affair. And worse than that, Josie's car might have been the vehicle that killed Wilson.

The full horror of this makes my stomach cramp and causes me to double over. How am I going to know for sure? Josie has changed her car, and how on earth can I find out what her old registration number was? I pace up and down the kitchen and decide there's only one thing I can do—visit the garage in Croydon and just hope that they have a record of the type of vehicle associated with that number plate. I tidy away all the files and put the papers back into Mike's brief-case. I should really make myself a sandwich, but I don't feel like eating, so I take a banana and flask of water, lock the house, and walk out to my car.

'Isobel!'

My heart sinks when I see Linette hurrying towards me. She's such a troublemaker, and I don't want anything to do with her.

'Have you seen Twiglet?'

'Nope.'

I press the remote control to open my car doors. Linette still hasn't made good on the damage the pig created in our garden, even though she has promised to refund us any expenses. Our gardener has been on holiday but is due to come next week to attempt to tidy up the mess. Mike has done the lion's share of it, though.

'Thomas Adler has been playing with his drone again, and I think it spooked Twiglet. She's gone AWOL.'

'Look, Linette. You need to either keep control of that pig or get rid of it. If it destroys our garden again, Mike will take out a restraining order and report you for criminal damage. We've all had enough.'

'No need to get all lawyerly with me, Isobel. I'm just

trying to fit in with you lot and be a good neighbour. But sometimes we get things wrong. Have you spoken to Mike about Josie yet?'

'It's none of your bloody business.'

I'm furious now, so I get in the car and slam the door, reversing out of our drive a bit too quickly. When I glance in my rear mirror, I can see Linette staring at me. To hell with her.

It takes me nearly an hour to get to the garage in Croydon, by which time I'm beginning to doubt whether it was even a good idea. There is probably some perfectly rational explanation as to why Mike has that receipt. Perhaps it's from a car at work, one of Mike's associates, maybe. When I eventually find Fawcett Bros Repairs, it's in an industrial estate, a run-down premises with a heap of old, knackered-looking cars at the front. Why on earth would anyone bring a car here? I park up, thinking that my black Golf looks rather smart for a change, and walk into the premises. There's a door with a glass panel, which I push open, but no one is behind the small counter. An unpleasant smell of burned rubber and sweat makes my nostrils twitch. I press an old-fashioned brass bell on the counter, and just when I'm about to press it again, a man in his sixties dressed in mid-blue overalls appears, his hands and face covered in grease.

'Yes?' he says.

'Sorry to bother you. I have a receipt from some repairs you did on a car about seven months ago.' I take out the receipt and place it on the counter. 'I was wondering if you had a record of the make and model of the car.'

'What are you, a cop?'

'No.' I laugh awkwardly. 'It's for my office. It was an employee's car, but I don't have a record as to the make and model.'

He narrows his eyes at me, and it's perfectly obvious that

he thinks I'm up to no good. He crosses his arms in front of his chest.

'We don't keep records like that. This is enough for the tax man and should be good enough for you. See, it was paid in cash. I've got work to do.'

He turns on his heel and disappears into the back.

I curse under my breath. I didn't handle that well. In my general panic this morning, I hadn't even noticed that the payment had been made in cash. That makes it even more suspicious.

Back in the car, I'm angry with myself. Of course the man at the garage wasn't going to hand over any details to me. I was naive to come all this way and waste half a day in the process. As I head back towards home, I try to recall details of Josie's silver Audi, but for the life of me, I can't remember the number plate. I think of all the events we've been to together when she brought her car. Could there be a photograph somewhere of her car, showing the number plate? School outings, fundraisers. Yes. Josie organised a car boot sale two years ago to raise funds for a new playground at the kids' primary school. We went to that, and I always take photographs of the children. Could I have any pictures of her car? I've been quite diligent about backing up photos from my phone to my laptop at home. I'll have to look later.

But my mind keeps on wandering back to Mike. I can't bear the thought of confronting him, knowing that if he says yes, our world will be destroyed, but I'm not sure I have any option other than to ask Mike straight out whether he has had an affair with Josie, and worse than that, whether he had anything to do with Wilson's death. I'm not even sure I'm going to be able to get the words out of my mouth. Yet I need to know.

The journey home passes quickly as I mull things over. I turn left into The Close and slam my foot on the brake.

Ahead of me are blue flashing lights. Three police cars. An ambulance.

Not again.

'No!' I say out loud before calming myself as I remember that neither Mike, Harry nor Harper are at home. It's not us. Nothing has happened to us. I ease the car forwards at a snail's pace, and a uniformed policeman walks towards me, his hand outstretched.

I wind my window down, and he leans in.

'What's happened?' I ask.

'Do you live here?'

'Yes, in number three.'

'I'm sorry to tell you that there's been a serious incident.'

'What! What's happened?' My stomach clenches.

'I'm afraid I'm not at liberty to divulge any details. If you could drive very slowly, I'll escort you to your house.'

My heart is hammering as I drive behind the policeman, who is striding towards our house. He steps to one side at the top of our driveway, indicating for me to stop. The police cars and ambulance are blocking the road further ahead.

'Can I take your name, please?'

'It's Isobel Floyd.'

'Is there anyone else at your home right now?'

'No. My children are staying with my mother, and my husband is at work.'

'In which case, please stay in your house, and a colleague will come and talk to you shortly.'

'Is someone hurt?' My fingers are gripping the steering wheel so tightly, my knuckles are white.

'Please just stay in your house for now, Mrs Floyd. And keep the doors and windows locked.'

16

I spend the next few minutes pacing the kitchen and intermittently stroking Lupin. What has happened? Obviously, someone on The Close has been hurt. Otherwise, all those police and an ambulance wouldn't be here. I'm about to call Mike when the front doorbell rings.

It's two police officers, a woman and a man, both dressed in uniform.

'What's happened?' I ask again.

'Can we come in?'

'Yes, yes, of course.' They follow me into the living room, but unlike last time, none of us sit down.

The mixed-race policeman, in his early forties at a guess, has chiselled features and kind eyes. He gets straight to the point. 'I'm sorry to have to tell you that the resident of house number two, a Linette Smith, we believe, has been found dead.'

I'M NOT sure what happens next. I don't think I faint or pass out, but a few minutes later, I find myself in our kitchen with the policewoman, drinking a cup of sugary tea. I have no recollection of the handsome policeman leaving the house. All I notice is that the kitchen is a mess. I never finished tidying away the breakfast things, and there's a stack of dirty dishes in the sink and a mountain of ironing that needs to be done in the plastic basket on the countertop, not that I suppose this policewoman cares. Nevertheless, I wish I had tidied up a little in those few minutes straight after I came home.

She's a wiry woman, with streaks of grey in her short, straight hair and a wide gap between her two front teeth.

'How are you feeling now, Mrs Floyd?' she asks, peering at me anxiously.

'I'm all right. It's just such a shock.'

'Yes, it's truly terrible when something like this happens. My name is DC Cathy Dopler. Can I ask you a few questions, please?'

'Yes, yes. That's fine.'

'Where were you today?'

'Um, I was here this morning. Mum collected the kids, and I took Lupin, our dog, out for a walk. Then I did some paperwork at home, and I drove to a garage in Croydon. I wasn't there long and came straight back here.' I gasp as I remember. 'I saw Linette just as I was leaving. She said the pig had disappeared again.'

'And what time was that?'

'I don't know, exactly. About midday, probably.'

'How did Linette seem?'

'Normal. Worried about the pig.' I don't tell the policewoman that we'd had a few words and I had stormed off when she quizzed me about the supposed affair between Mike and Josie.

'It's a possibility that you might have been the last person to see Linette alive.'

I swallow hard. This is truly horrible. That house must be cursed. Two deaths in the past year, all related to Number Two, The Close.

'What happened to her?' I ask as I stretch my fingers around the warm mug to heat up my freezing cold hands. Then I wonder if I really want to know.

'She was fatally wounded in the head.'

'So it's a murder?' I murmur. I'm trembling now.

'We're treating it as a suspicious death at this point.'

'What was she hit with?'

She pauses for a moment, and I realise that I've assumed that Linette was hit. Perhaps she wasn't. Guns aren't common in the UK, but perhaps she was shot or stabbed.

'How did she get fatally wounded in the head?' I ask. My hands are trembling.

'We don't know as of yet what the exact cause of death was. This will be an ongoing investigation, and we will need to formally interview everyone who lives here and those who knew Ms Smith.'

'Yes, of course. Who found her?'

'Mr Abbott.'

'Oh, poor Jack. That must have been awful.'

'Mr Abbott mentioned that Linette Smith's pig has caused a lot of damage to property in The Close. Can you tell me more about it, please?'

'Yes. The pig pretty much wrecked our back garden, and it did lots of damage in the Abbotts' field. You don't think . . .' I let my voice trail away. There is no way that Jack would have beaten Linette up over damage to a field. That's ridiculous.

'There will be a lot of police presence here over the next few days as we search the crime scene, and inevitably, even though we'll try to keep the media away, there's likely to be journalists camping out along the lane.'

'My kids are with my mum. I'll make sure they stay there for a few days.'

'And your partner?'

'My husband will be home later. He's at work. He went to Southampton early this morning.'

'Can you give me both your and your husband's contact details, please?'

I suppose this is routine, but I still feel a shiver of unease as I write down our mobile phone numbers.

'We will need to interview you formally. It's totally routine, just to find out as much as we can about what happened to Ms Smith. Have you any plans to go away?'

'No.'

'I would appreciate if you would refrain from discussing the case with anyone else whilst the investigation is ongoing.'

I nod. Poor Linette. She's a case now. I may not have liked the woman, but it doesn't mean I don't feel desperately sorry for her.

When DC Dopler leaves, I feel horribly alone and for the first time scared. I'm not sure if I'm scared for myself or just spooked because such a horrible thing has happened in The Close yet again. I wonder if the police know about Wilson's hit and run, but I assume they must do. There can't be that many tragic deaths in this semi-rural smart neighbourhood. It's a time like this when I wish I hadn't fallen out with Josie. We could do with sitting together over a glass of wine and consoling each other. When my tea is cold, I call Mum.

'Can you keep the kids for a night or two, Mum?'

'What's happened?'

'The new neighbour has been murdered, and The Close is teeming with police.'

'Murdered! Oh, my goodness, how terrible. Are you safe, darling?'

'Yes, I'm fine. Mike will be back soon; it's just I don't want the children to know. In fact, the policewoman said I shouldn't discuss it with anyone, so you'll need to keep this to yourself.'

'Are you sure you don't want to come to stay here too?'

'I think it might look a bit weird. I'll stay put and will keep you posted. Can I speak to the kids?'

After a quick chat with the children where I make up a silly lie that I've got some unexpected work to do and that Grandma wants to keep them for a couple of nights, I pick up the phone to Mike. He answers on the second ring, which surprises me, as he doesn't often respond when I call during the working day.

'Are you in the office?'

'In the car.'

'Something terrible has happened. Linette has been murdered.'

'What?' he exclaims. And then he is totally silent, and I wonder if he's still on the line.

'Mike?'

'Yes, I can't believe it. I'll be home in five minutes. Lock the doors.'

I smile wryly. I really don't think I'm in any danger with all of this police presence on our doorstep, but I do lock the doors and ensure all the windows are closed too. I walk upstairs and look out the spare bedroom window. There are at least four police cars and a black van. I suppose they're going to put Linette's body in it, and I shiver. At least I can't see one of those white tents they put up to secure a crime scene. I wonder if Jack found her inside or outside.

When Mike pulls up into the driveway, I run downstairs to open the door to him, and he pulls me into his arms and hugs me so tightly I can barely breathe. I wonder if this is what it takes to repair our marriage, another horror right on our doorstep.

'Are you all right?' he asks, breathing into my hair.

'Yes. It's just so horrible. The police think I might have been the last person to see her alive.' I feel a kernel of panic then, because I told that policewoman I had been to a garage in Croydon, which of course is the truth, but if they mention it to Mike, how on earth will I explain that?

'Come on, let's have a drink.' Mike pulls me by the hand into the kitchen. He goes into the larder and takes out a bottle of red wine. I sit down whilst he uncorks the bottle and pours us each a very full glass.

'Mum is keeping the kids,' I say.

'Thank goodness for your mum.'

I smile wryly. Mum wasn't sure about Mike when we first got together. A keen feminist, she couldn't understand why I was the one to give up my job to look after Harry. But their relationship has improved over the years, and sometimes, I think she has a better rapport with Mike than with me. She fusses over me, forgetting that I'm no longer that little lost girl with a troubled background that she adopted all those years ago. I have to bite my tongue to remember that she only wants the best for me, and remember that her concerns are an expression of love. Mike is blunt with Mum and tells her to stop worrying, that he's here now, and indeed, he was until this past year. Sometimes, I think that Mum worries that my lack of a decent maternal role model in my early years might impact how I treat my kids. It's Mike who consistently puts her mind at rest and tells her I'm a great mum. And that's a relief because I'd be lying to say it hadn't crossed my mind. They say that the maternal bond is instinctive, but until my babies were put into my arms, I wasn't sure I believed it.

Mike hands me a glass of wine and then squeezes my shoulder. 'Are you sure you're all right?'

'It's just the shock of it, for something so dreadful to happen right on our doorstep yet again.'

'I know,' Mike says, sitting down next to me. 'But she was a bit weird, that Linette, wasn't she?'

'Unconventional perhaps, not like the rest of us here, but why would anyone want to kill her? I can't believe that there have been two deaths right here. It's too horrible. Perhaps that house really is haunted.'

'I don't think new builds can be haunted!' Mike sighs. 'They say lightning doesn't strike twice, but sometimes it does. I guess two horrible but unrelated things can happen in the same place.'

We both take large sips of wine. 'Are you hungry?' I ask.

'Not really. You look really shaken up, love. Why don't I make us an omelette?'

Mike is a weekend and dinner party cook, happy to whip up some fancy dishes when we have people over but reluctant to do the slog of the day-to-day cooking, which is particularly hard due to Harry's peculiar demands. I can't remember the last time he made supper, but tonight, I'm more than happy to hand over the reins.

We're just tucking into a mushroom omelette with a second glass of wine when the doorbell rings. I look at him with alarm. We've stayed sitting in the kitchen for the last couple of hours and haven't looked out at the front of the house to see what police activity is still going on. Here, we can pretend that everything is normal on The Close.

'I'll go,' Mike says.

'Don't open the door unless it's the police.'

'It's fine, love.' He pats my hand and walks out of the kitchen.

A couple of minutes later, he returns accompanied by DC Cathy Dopler and a colleague of hers, who introduces himself as DC Peter Cardon.

'Sorry to disturb your supper, but could we ask you a few questions?' Cathy Dopler asks.

'Yes, of course,' I say, standing up. I don't feel like eating the omelette, anyway. 'Can I get you a drink?'

'A cup of tea would be lovely,' she replies. 'He'll have milk with two sugars, and I'll have just milk, please.' I wonder whether they work as a couple all the time and what it must be like dealing with such horrors on a daily basis. Then again, murders in this supposedly tranquil corner of Sussex are hardly commonplace.

'As I mentioned when we met earlier, we are talking to all the neighbours here to find out if anyone saw anything and to establish timelines. I'll take a few notes, if that's all right with you.' Both Mike and I nod. 'What was Linette's relationship like with all the neighbours?'

'She was really friendly,' I say.

'So you spent a lot of time with her?' DC Cardon asks.

'Well, no. Not really. She invited me over for a women's get-together shortly after she moved in and then invited all the neighbours for a drinks party.'

'And what happened at that drinks party?'

I glance at Mike, but he's avoiding looking at me. 'We had a nice time. We drank a bit and danced. It was a fun evening.'

'Was there anyone Linette got along with particularly well?'

'Um, she seemed to be doing a lot of dancing with Thomas Adler, and he was still there when the rest of us left.'

'What do you think was the nature of their relationship?' DC Cardon asks while DC Dopler shifts forwards in her chair.

'She might have had a fling with Thomas, although she strongly denied it. He certainly seemed keen on her.'

'Really?' Mike says, frowning at me. 'Are you implying—'

I suddenly realise what I've said. It's always the boyfriend or the husband who are the prime suspects. 'I mean, I'm not sure, obviously. They just seemed to get on well, although

Linette denied it, and really, I'm talking out of turn here because I don't know.'

DC Cardon frowns, and that makes me feel even worse.

'And what was your relationship like with Linette?' DC Dopler asks Mike.

'It was perfectly civil. As my wife said, she invited us all over for a pleasant evening. She hasn't been living here for very long, so obviously we don't—didn't—know her well. And this is the kind of place where people keep themselves to themselves.'

'Do you know if Linette had any visitors?'

'Yes, she had a party and had loads of people over.'

'When was that?'

I rack my brain but can't remember exactly when. 'I think about two weeks ago.'

A loud beep comes through DC Dopler's radio. She stands up. 'We need to go, but we'll be back to talk to you again tomorrow. As I mentioned previously, as this is a live investigation, please do not discuss this with anyone else.'

DC Cardon stands up too. 'Thanks for the tea.'

Mike sees them to the door.

'Why didn't you tell them about our run-in with Linette over the pig?' I ask. 'Isn't that withholding information?'

'Don't overreact, Isobel. They didn't ask, so I'm not going to volunteer unnecessary details.'

I pick up our plates with the half-eaten omelettes and scrape the congealed leftovers into my compost bin, putting the plates and cutlery into the dishwasher. 'But our relationship with Linette wasn't very friendly. We should have told them more about the pig.'

'It's fine. Stop stressing. I'm sure the police have more important things to investigate than the mess the pig caused to our garden.'

I bite my tongue because I think Mike is wrong. We

should have told them because now it makes us look like we're withholding information. And the more I think about that, the more I think about the receipt for the car repair. Is my husband withholding information from me as well as the police? Could what Linette said be true?

Mike goes to bed before me. I tell him I'm not tired, which is a lie. I am bone-weary exhausted, but my brain won't stop whirring. I take the garage receipt out of my handbag and stare at it, hoping that it might reveal some magic information, and then I shove it back inside again. Linette is dead. There is a brutal murderer out there, and right now, the police have their eyes on us, the neighbours in The Close.

As I'm pacing up and down the living room in the semi-darkness, I have a terrible thought. Linette knew about Mike and Josie's affair, if indeed they were in a relationship. She told me about it. Could she have told Mike? Could Mike have gone into a rage and killed her? I groan. Of course he wouldn't. Mike is a gentle man, carefully collecting spiders and daddy-long-legs and putting them outside, soppy over Lupin, distraught on the one occasion he accidentally hit and killed a rabbit when driving his car. But what about Josie? If Linette told me, perhaps she told Josie too and threatened to tell Jack? What was it that Josie called Linette? *A nosy bitch.* I was shocked by that. Could Josie have bashed Linette's head in? It's more likely a prospect than Mike doing it. She's happy to wring a chicken's neck and pluck the pheasants that Jack shoots in the autumn. And I suppose it could have been Jack too. If Linette told him that Josie and Mike were having an affair, perhaps he lashed out at her in an uncontrollable rage, killing the messenger. It seems unlikely, and I've got no reason to suppose that Jack is the violent type. Nevertheless, I assume he'll be a key suspect, being the person who 'found' Linette and reported her death to the police.

I get ready for bed and tiptoe into our bedroom. Mike is

snoring softly. I try to sleep, but just as I'm about to drop off, I see Linette's bloodied head in my mind's eye and jerk awake. Of course, I must sleep eventually because I'm jolted by voices. Mike's side of the bed is empty, and I'm startled to see that it's just gone eight a.m.

'Isobel,' Mike shouts up the stairs, 'the police are here again. Can you come down?'

I dress quickly in yesterday's clothes, run a brush through my hair, and hurry downstairs. DCs Corden and Dopler are standing in the hallway, and I wonder if they've had any sleep.

'Just a few more questions,' DC Dopler says as they follow us into the kitchen, and we all resume our places at the table. 'Can you tell us exactly what damage Linette's pig caused to your property?'

I glance at Mike, who doesn't meet my eyes. 'There was some damage to our garden,' Mike says. I notice the hint of reluctance in his voice and just hope that the police don't sense it too.

'Considerable damage, we understand,' DC Corden says, his eyebrows rising. 'And what was your reaction to that?'

'The pig dug up our flower beds and some of the lawn and the Abbotts' field. And yes, I did demand that Linette sort the damage and pay us accordingly,' Mike admits.

There's a beat of heavy silence.

'But I didn't have anything to do with her death,' Mike says. 'It was just a petty argument between neighbours.'

'An argument that you failed to mention when we spoke to you yesterday.'

17

I switch on the kettle and make everyone a cup of tea, then take my place at the table opposite the police.

'According to the Quinns, Linette Smith was a very helpful neighbour, unlike everyone else on The Close,' DC Cardon says.

'That's not fair. I offered to help Mr Quinn look after his wife when he was out, but he declined the offer. Did he mention how annoyed he was about the smoke that enveloped his house when Linette burned wet leaves?' I decide not to mention his reaction to Linette's party and the guests who made out in his shed.

'Yes, he did tell us that,' DC Dopler says. 'It seems that Linette ruffled a few feathers during the short time that she was living here. Is there anything else that you would like to tell us?'

Mike and I glance at each other and shake our heads.

'It would be helpful if you could both stay at home today. Unfortunately, the media have already caught wind of events, and the first journalists have turned up. We've put a police cordon at the bottom of the road where The Close joins the lane, so hopefully, you won't be disturbed. If you have any questions or need to leave your house today, please let one of us know.'

'How long are you going to be here?' I ask. 'It's just that our children are staying with my mother.' I'm missing them horribly and have an overwhelming need to hug them and make sure they're safe.

'We're not sure at the moment, but certainly, our forensic team will need at least another twenty-four hours. There will likely be continued police presence thereafter.'

'I'll ring the office and work from home today,' Mike says.

'THIS IS HORRIBLE,' I say as I close the door. 'It's a bit like when Wilson died.'

Mike nods. 'But even worse. I'm going to work in the study.' He turns and walks away from me.

I had expected a bit more of a dialogue with Mike, and it makes me wonder. Is he clamming up because he knows more than he's letting on? No, this is ridiculous. I can't be doubting my own husband.

I just hope he doesn't notice if I've inadvertently rearranged the order of any of the files in the filing cabinet. I make myself some toast and another cup of tea and then return upstairs. After a quick shower, I ring Mum and chat with the children. They seem relaxed and happy, as they always are with Mum, who spoils them rotten. And then like a voyeur, I look out the spare bedroom window, where we have the best view towards Linette's house. There are fewer police here now, but then a silver saloon car drives slowly along the lane and turns into her driveway. A man gets out of the car, and it isn't until he turns around and faces our house that I get a jolt of recognition. It's Keith Walker. Even though he's a big man, he looks thinner than the last time I saw him.

It's hard to tell from this distance, but it's as if his face is more lined, his shoulders and back sloping. I feel for him, having to visit his home where there's been a murder after leaving it because of the death of his son. I hope he manages to sell the house.

As I walk downstairs, I can hear Mike on the phone. Lupin looks at me expectantly, but he's going to be sorely disappointed today. His daily walk will be replaced by some ball throwing in the garden. I can't stop thinking about the garage invoice, and it makes me feel guilty because I should be thinking about Linette and her horrible demise. I sit at the kitchen table and fire up my laptop, searching through my photos from the past two years. When was that car boot sale? After ten minutes or so, I find the picture I was looking for. The photo is of our car, the boot open, showing all the junk that I was hoping to sell—boxes of old toys, a toddler's bike, a tent and some camping equipment that we've never used. And there is Josie's old silver Audi, right next to our car. Fortunately, her boot is closed, and I can just about make out the first three digits of her number plate. DG1.

I think I was praying that the number plate wouldn't match, that I was putting two and two together and making five. But I wasn't. It's the number plate on the garage invoice, and it confirms that my husband had something to do with getting Josie's car repaired. Why? And the day after Wilson was killed . . .

I slam the lid down on my computer, knowing that I'm going to have to confront Mike. Dread pools in my stomach, and my hands feel weak.

And then the doorbell rings.

I wait for a moment in the hope that Mike might answer it, but as I tiptoe into the hall, I can hear him talking on the phone. Taking a deep breath, I open the door.

'Mrs Floyd?'

'Yes.'

'What can you tell me about Linette Smith?'

'What? Who are you?'

'I write for the—'

Too late, I realise he's a journalist. I thought the police had kept the journalists away from our houses.

'Sorry,' I say, shutting the front door. But he puts his foot in the door, an ugly black shoe with a soft rubber heel.

'Please talk to me,' he says. 'It'll be worth your while.'

'I've got nothing to say other than it's devastating. Please remove your foot and leave us alone.'

'Did you know that Linette Smith was Mona Walker's sister and that tragedy has hit the Walker family for the third time?'

'What?' I say, feeling weak. I take a step backwards into the hall, and he pushes the door open further.

'Do you think the house is cursed?'

'Go away!' I say, fury now overtaking the shock. 'Get off our property now; otherwise I'll shout for the police.'

He removes his foot from the threshold and holds his hands up in a gesture of peace. I slam the door in his face.

I am trembling from head to foot. It all adds up now. Linette was a relative, and that explains why the house was removed from the rental market. But why didn't Linette tell us she was Mona's sister? And why was Linette killed? Did Keith Walker do it?

I hear Mike saying goodbye to someone, so I walk into the study.

'Not now, Isobel,' he says without looking up at me.

'It was a journalist.'

'Please, love. I'm on a really tight deadline. Can we discuss it later?'

I hesitate. I want to talk to him now, but I recognise that look, the way his shoulders are bunched up and his forehead furrowed, with those reading glasses slipping down his nose. All I want is to ask Mike about the affair, to know for sure if what Linette said is true, but I can't ask him. Not now. The last thing I can afford to happen is for Mike to be storming off in his car with some journalists in hot pursuit. I'm going to have to hold my tongue and wait for a more appropriate time.

I'M FINDING it very hard to be normal around Mike. He doesn't seek any physical contact. Hugs and spontaneous shows of affection have slowly evaporated over the years. A couple of days ago, that saddened me and increased that feeling of loneliness, but right now, I'm glad. Just the faintest brushing of skin when he passes me a fork across the table sends my mind and body into a tailspin. This is the man I love, but does he love me back? How honest is he? What has he done? Yet again, I have another restless night, missing my babies. I wake up cold and clammy with a racing heart after a horrific dream where I see Mike and Josie in a passionate embrace. Linette is standing there, ghostlike, watching them. They see her, and they both rush towards her, knives outstretched, and then there is a river of blood, and I awake screaming. Yet I can't have been screaming because Mike is fast asleep next to me, his chest rising and falling gently.

The next morning, it's all over the news. A local woman was brutally murdered on the outskirts of a village near Horsham, an affluent rural community where murders like this never happen. The article in the local paper is the most in-depth. It confirms that Linette's real name is Lyn, and she was Mona Walker's sister. And then I have another shock.

Mona Walker is dead, and she died of suicide.

The article speculates that the poor woman couldn't survive after the terrible death of her eldest son. Three deaths within half a year in the same family. The headlines yell, *Is The Close Cursed?*

I want to scream. Of course it isn't. This is just the terrible tragedy of one family, but nevertheless, it worms its way into my mind. The Abbotts' green burial site is mentioned too, something that I'd forgotten about in the midst of all this horror. I go back upstairs and look out the window towards Linette's house. The police are still there. Keith Walker is on his mobile phone, pacing up and down his drive. I wonder whether he stayed there last night, but surely not? It's still a crime scene. It just seems odd that he's back here again.

'Isobel!' Mike shouts up the stairs. I jump, as if I'm a voyeur peeking out illicitly. I hurry to the top of the stairs. 'We've had an email from Jack Abbott. He's suggesting that all the neighbours of The Close get together this evening to discuss everything.'

'To discuss what?'

'The impact Linette's murder is having on all of us, I suppose. How we can pull together to combat the negative publicity. How to get rid of the bloody journalists who are camped at the bottom of the road. How to protect our children from this mess. And how to make sure this doesn't impact our property prices.'

I bite my lip. It seems callous in the extreme to be thinking about our property prices. Nevertheless, it might be a good idea to see everyone in the same room, to see whether there are any guilty faces, to assess how Mike and Josie are together.

'What time this evening?' I ask.

'He's suggesting six thirty p.m. when it's dark and to meet in their barn so that we're not seen by the police or the media.'

'Why should the police be bothered about us getting together?'

'I don't know. Perhaps they'll think we're in cahoots some-how. It might look odd.'

'Cahoots over a murder?'

'I don't know, Isobel. It just seems like a good idea.'

I shrug my shoulders.

JUST BEFORE SIX THIRTY P.M., Mike and I slip out our back door. There is only one police car remaining, parked in Linette's drive, and fortunately, I can't see any press. We walk quickly, our feet lit up by Mike's mobile phone, heads down. It's cold, and with every step, our breaths make little puffs of mist as we stride the couple of hundred metres to the Abbotts' house. The wall lights are on outside their house, and there's a sliver of light visible under the door of their large black wrought-iron barn, the same barn I assume they plan to use to conduct the burial services. I shiver at the thought.

Mike knocks on the door and opens it. We're the last to arrive. Jack is the nearest to the door and nods his head in greeting. Josie is wrapped up in her Barbour jacket, a thick tartan scarf around her neck and a black beanie on her head. She's talking to Thomas Adler and Mr Quinn, both of whom are clad in thick anoraks. I've never been inside the barn before. It's cavernous with piles of hay bales stacked many metres high at the far end. There's lots of farm machinery too, a large tractor, a quad bike, and other pieces of equip-ment that I don't recognise. A whiff of manure combined with the scent of hay is surprisingly comforting, but it's as cold in here as it is outside, and I wish I were also wearing a pair of gloves and a hat.

Near the door is a selection of six mismatched wooden chairs that have been placed in a semicircle. It reminds me of a secretive cult meeting, or the gathering of an underground resistance movement, and I have to stifle a snigger. Inappropriate indeed.

'Take a seat, everyone,' Jack says. 'Sorry about the cold.'

I sit between Mike and Mr Quinn. 'How's your wife?' I ask him quietly.

'She's taken this hard and stayed in bed ever since it happened.'

'I'm sorry.' My gaze flits between Mike and Josie, looking for any signs that might indicate something beyond neighbourly acquaintances. So far, neither has even glanced at the other.

'Thanks for coming,' Jack says, leaning forwards in his chair, his elbows on his knees. He hasn't shaved for a few days, and the look suits him.

'I just thought we should have a conflab, bearing in mind everything that's happened. I saw Keith Walker's been here.'

'Not surprising since he owns the house,' Thomas says. 'Poor sod.'

'Let's face it, he's not the easiest of characters, and we've all had our run-ins with him over the years, but you've got to sympathise with him,' Jack says. 'First his son is killed, then his wife dies, and now the sister-in-law.'

What does Jack mean saying, 'We've all had our run-ins with him'? I can't recall any incidences where Mike and I had issues with him. In fact, other than the brief conversations about the resurfacing of the road, I don't think we've ever shared more than a few words with him.

'Do you think we're suspects?' Josie asks. She's sitting on her hands, and her right knee is bouncing up and down.

'Of course we are,' Jack says. 'They're going to look at the people closest to her, her neighbours, a boyfriend or lover—'

'Talking of which,' Thomas interrupts, his eyes narrowing. 'The police have questioned me, asking if I had an affair with Linette. They gave me a right grilling, and I want to know who suggested that. To put the record straight, nothing ever happened between us. I wouldn't have minded if it did, but it didn't, so I'm pissed off in the extreme that I've been singled out.' Thomas stares at all of us in turn, and I have to look away. Should I admit that it was I who told the police that he and Linette might have been having a relationship? There's a beat of silence, and Mike doesn't say anything, so I don't either.

'I've been thinking about it,' Thomas says, rubbing his hands. 'There's a common denominator here, isn't there?'

'What do you mean?' Jack asks.

'Keith Walker. Son, wife, and sister-in-law. I mean, it was mighty odd that Wilson was running away from his house at one a.m. Why was the lad doing that? Was he running away from his dad? Maybe his death wasn't random.'

'You're right,' Jack says. 'That was odd. But do you think Wilson's and Linette's deaths were related? Are the police reopening Wilson's case?'

It's then that Mike and Josie exchange a look. The problem is I can't decipher it. It was a millisecond of shared understanding, or was it? Am I just reading something into it?

'I don't know what the police are doing, but it would make sense to relook at Wilson's death,' Thomas says.

'Why would someone hit and kill Wilson and then murder Linette?' Mr Quinn asks. 'Are you suggesting that Wilson's killing was intentional?'

Thomas raises his shoulders and sighs. 'Who the hell knows? Look, guys, without this sounding ruthless, I'm seriously worried about the value of our houses. I've got a hefty mortgage on mine, and if I can't sell it, I'm up shit creek.'

'Are you planning on selling?' I ask.

'Not today, but who knows what's around the corner?'

I zone out because there's not a lot we can do about that,

and surely, our safety is of primary concern. Right now, there's a murderer out there who at best killed Linette, and if Thomas's theory is correct, perhaps deliberately killed Wilson too. And there is a possibility, slim, perhaps, but still a possibility, that the murderer is Keith Walker or one of us sitting right here. I shiver.

'Do you want my jacket?' Mike whispers.

I shake my head. 'It's fine. Thanks.' I shove my hands under my thighs and keep my eyes on Josie, but she's chewing the side of a nail and looking at her feet.

There is still that garage receipt, and I can't get it out of my head. Did Josie hit Wilson, and Mike helped her out by paying to get her car repaired without Jack knowing? Or were all three of them in on it together? At least that would mean that my husband wasn't having an affair. But if he loaned them money to pay for the car repairs, that means all three of them are complicit in an unlawful death. And was Linette blackmailing them because she knew what had happened? I still shudder to believe that one of those three could have bashed Linette to death. Surely, it could only have been Jack? Yet the police haven't detained him. I shake my head to dispel the confusing thoughts. When I get home, I need to look through our bank statements again to make sure there haven't been any more recent unexplained outgoings. Previously, I only checked the transactions shortly before and after Wilson's death.

'Isobel, what do you think?' Thomas asks. I've totally zoned out and didn't hear what they were saying.

'Sorry, I missed that,' I say.

'What do you think about putting an electric gate at the entrance to The Close?'

I glance at Mike, who shrugs his shoulders.

'I don't love the idea,' I say.

'It would help ensure that none of the green burial traffic go via The Close by mistake,' Jack says.

I clench my teeth. That dammed green burial again.

'It depends on how much it costs,' Mr Quinn says.

I glance at the Abbotts. I thought that money was an issue for them, but they seem for the idea. I guess they think they'll be minting it from their burial business.

'Why don't we sit tight for a while and see what the outcome is with Linette's death,' I suggest. 'Once they've arrested someone and it's obvious that this area is safe, then it might not be an issue.'

'I agree with Isobel,' Mr Quinn says. I'm quietly pleased that he and I seem to be of like minds for the first time.

A strange noise comes from behind Josie, and it's when she reaches behind her that I realise she has a baby monitor with her. One of her children is crying. Jack stands up.

'I'll go,' he says. 'We can always meet again. Let's all stay in touch, okay?'

The rest of us nod, and I'm just pleased that this little uncomfortable meeting is over.

'Where are your kids?' Josie asks. I wonder if she hopes that I've been a bad mother and left them home alone.

'With my mother, where they'll stay until the police leave.'

Everyone stands up, and I walk slowly towards the door, blowing into my icy-cold hands. When I glance around, I see that Mike and Josie are talking, their heads close together, their voices so low that their words are indistinguishable. Thomas Adler holds the door open for me.

'Are you coming?' I raise my voice as I turn to look at Mike. He steps away from Josie rapidly and strides towards me. Something has gone on between those two, but whether it's an affair, I don't know. What I do know is that I'm determined to find out.

18

On the short walk home, Mike puts his arm around my shoulders, and for the first time ever, I feel a physical revulsion towards my husband. Or perhaps it isn't revulsion but jealousy. Whatever it is, this can't go on. I tense up.

'What's up?' he asks.

'We need to talk.'

Mike doesn't say anything, but he removes his arm, and we remain silent whilst he puts his key in the lock and opens the door.

'What is it?' he asks as he bends down to greet Lupin.

'Sit down,' I say, taking off my coat and placing it over the back of a chair. I take my normal chair at the kitchen table. My heart is thudding, and my throat feels dry. I need to know, but at the same time, I don't want to. Mike hangs his scarf up on the coat hook by the back door and then walks into the kitchen, sitting at his normal place. I flex my fingers in my lap, wondering how to start this conversation.

Mike is peering at me with a perplexed expression.

'All right, I'll say it. I know that you're not happy, that you haven't been for a while. The past year, we've barely seen you. I know you've been working hard, but I think that you've been using that as an excuse to be away from me. We used to have no secrets from each other. We used to make love regularly. It's like you're slipping away, and I need you to tell me why.'

I stare at Mike, but he avoids my gaze. He opens his mouth and then closes it again as if he's changed his mind. I wait and wait, the silence becoming more painful every second it continues.

'Come on, Mike. Talk to me. If you can't tell me what's really going on, then who can you tell?'

And then he shocks me. He shoves back his chair and stands up, turning his back to me. 'I don't want to be having this conversation right now.'

'Well, I do! I want to know what's going on with you. Have you got a problem with me, or is it something else? You need to tell me, Mike!' I'm silently begging him to admit to what he's done, to be contrite, to tell me that it was all a terrible mistake and that he loves me. Or if I've got it all wrong, to be dismayed and put all my worries to rest. Mike does neither.

He speaks through gritted teeth. 'Just leave it!'

'Look at me!' I demand. I stand up and try to reach for his arm, but he pushes me away and strides out of the kitchen. I expect him to turn left to go into the hallway, but he doesn't. He grabs his coat, the one he only just hung up, fumbles in his pocket, and produces his car keys. Without saying a word to me, he walks out the back door, slamming it behind him. I wait a beat and then run after him, but I'm too late. He is in his car, the engine already started, and I watch with dismay as he reverses out of our drive and speeds away.

I can't believe it. I thought we might have an argument, that he might tell me that he doesn't love me anymore, but it never crossed my mind that he would say nothing and just storm off. I sink down onto the floor, and Lupin trots over to investigate my unusual position. I bury my face into his coat and let the tears run. What has Mike done? Is it so very terrible that he can't tell me? It feels as if my heart has been ripped out of my chest, as if the ship I thought I was sailing on has just capsized and I'm lost at sea.

At some point, the phone rings. I haul myself up off the floor, wipe my wet face, and go to answer it, hoping that it might be Mike ready to explain what the hell is going on.

'Mummy!' Harper exclaims.

'Hello, sweetheart. You're up late. Are you having a lovely time with Granny?'

'Have you got a cold, Mummy?'

'Just a little one,' I lie.

'When are we coming home?'

'Soon, sausage. I miss you.'

'I miss you too, Mummy. Night, night.'

There are fumbling noises, and then Harry comes on the line. 'Can I speak to Dad?'

That's typical Harry, talking with no filter. Normally, I can handle it because I know this doesn't mean that he doesn't wish to talk to me, just that he'd prefer to talk to his father right now. But today I have to swallow a sob.

'Dad's not here right now. He had to pop out. Are you having a lovely time?'

'Yes.' And then the line goes dead.

Mum calls back a couple of moments later. 'How are things?'

'It's tough, Mum.'

'Your voice sounds funny. Are you all right?'

'Yes, okay. Think I might be getting a cold,' I lie again.

'Well, I don't want you to worry about the kids. They're doing just fine. Both of them are ready for bed. You look after yourself and Mike, and I'll bring them back whenever the coast is clear.'

'Thanks, Mum. I've got to go now.' I don't, but I know that if I don't hang up immediately, I'll burst into tears and tell Mum exactly what is going on. I can't let that happen.

AFTER ANOTHER GOOD SOB, I pour myself a large glass of white wine. I know what I need to do, but it's not what I want. But that's what happens when the love of your life breaks your heart. It forces you down a path not of your own choosing. Mike doesn't call me. I consider calling him or at least sending him a text message, but then I think I will come across as needy and apologetic. It's not me who has done anything wrong. All I wanted to do was have an honest conversation about our relationship. He totally overreacted. I go onto the Find My Friend app on my phone, but either Mike's phone is off or he has disconnected the app. And then I wonder if we ever set it up properly. I'm not sure I've ever followed him before, because why should I? I've never had reason to suspect my husband until now.

When I've polished off another glass of wine, I run myself a hot bath. By the time I've finished, it's gone eleven p.m., and Mike still hasn't returned. I try to quell my feelings of panic and go to bed. I read for a long time and eventually nod off into a light sleep. I'm jolted awake by the sound of a door closing. Leaving the light off, I sit up in bed and illuminate my alarm clock. It's 1.43 a.m. I wait, listening to Mike's footsteps, expecting him to gently open our door to use the facilities in our en-suite bathroom. But he doesn't. I can hear the taps running because the tank makes a gentle gurgling noise in the attic whenever someone runs a tap in any of the bathrooms. I wait, expecting him to come into the bedroom. After twenty minutes, the whole house has settled back into silence. Where is he?

I switch on my bedside lamp and tiptoe out of our bedroom and along the upstairs corridor. The only door that is shut is the one leading into the spare bedroom. The linen cupboard door is slightly ajar, and some of my neatly stored sheets are rumpled. Mike must have made up the bed in the spare room. Did he do that not to wake me or because he didn't want to sleep in our marital bed? Shivering from the chilly night in our cold house, I hurry back to bed.

The next morning, I'm awoken by Lupin barking. A surge of adrenaline courses through my veins as I wonder what's happened. But when I glance at my clock, I'm shocked that it's 7.43 a.m. The poor dog must be hungry. I hurry downstairs, but Lupin isn't barking because he hasn't had breakfast. He just wants to be let outside. The dog is wearing his collar, and it's obvious that Mike has been up and gone without waking me. He's left his breakfast things in the sink, and an empty tin of Lupin's dog food stands on the kitchen counter. I look around the kitchen, but there's no note. Then I check outside. As expected, Mike's car has gone, and by the looks of things, so have the police. I wonder whether they've finished their investigations and things are back to normal.

As I get ready, I feel weighed down by disappointment. I decide to give Mike one more chance and call his mobile. I wait as it rings, but he lets it go to voicemail. I leave a short message.

'I hope you're okay, Mike. Please call me.'

After getting dressed and forcing myself to eat a piece of toast, I call his work. His direct line also goes to voicemail, and although that's not unusual, it's rare he doesn't answer when he's at his desk. I call again and ask to speak to Janine, his secretary and office manager. She answers on the second ring.

'Hello, this is Isobel Floyd.'

'Isobel, how are you?' she asks as if she's genuinely happy to speak to me.

'I'm fine. And you?'

'All good. How can I help you?'

'Can I have a quick word with Mike?'

'Sure, I'll just put you through.'

The Four Seasons by Vivaldi is piped down the phone. I wait and I wait, and then Janine comes back on the line.

'I'm sorry, Isobel, but Mike has just gone into a meeting. Can he call you back later?'

'Sure,' I say, but I know she's lying. Mike doesn't want to speak to me.

I CONSIDER WALKING over to Linette's house to see if there are any police still there but decide that what I have to say is more appropriate to be shared at the police station. The whole way to Horsham, I have my doubts. I know that if I say something, I am doing the right thing, but if I don't speak out, then I am potentially protecting criminals and failing to do the one thing I've always sworn I would be—honest. But what if I'm turning my husband in to the police? Could I live with myself? I park my car in The Pavilions car park and sit there for a couple of minutes. I could just turn around and go home and forget that horrible nagging doubt in my mind, but I don't. I get out of the car and go to the pay-and-display machine to purchase a ticket. I then walk down Hurst Road towards the police station. All the while, a voice is screaming in my head, *What the hell are you doing?*

This is a small and quiet police station in a low-rise red-brick building with a handful of police cars parked outside. I force myself to walk forwards and to push open the door.

The duty sergeant looks up as I walk in. 'How can I help you?'

'I would like to talk to someone about a hit and run. I think I might have some evidence.' My heart is hammering, and I feel queasy.

'Which hit and run?'

'Wilson Walker. It happened about seven months ago.'

The man's eyebrows rise. 'And your name is?'

'Isobel Floyd. I'm a neighbour of the Walkers and live opposite the house where Linette, I mean Lyn Smith, lived. The recent murder.'

If his eyebrows went up a moment ago, now he looks even more taken aback. 'Just one moment, please.'

I pace around the small lobby, and eventually, another policeman appears, also in uniform.

'Mrs Floyd, my name is DS McConley. If you'd like to follow me, we can have a chat in private.'

I follow him down a short corridor, and he holds open the door to a small interview room that is just big enough for a table and two chairs. The room has that institutionalised smell of disinfectant and sourness. He pulls out one of the chairs for me and sits down opposite me. He places a biro and a small notebook on the table and then looks at me expectantly.

I freeze.

It's not too late to get up and walk out, but then he smiles, and there's something about his sandy-coloured hair and kind eyes that remind me of how Mike used to be.

'I found an invoice for a car repair dated the day after Wilson Walker died.'

'All right,' he says slowly. 'And whose car was damaged?'

'Josie Abbott's car, our next-door neighbour, and I think it was paid for in cash by my husband. And the garage was miles away in Croydon. I found the invoice in his old briefcase.'

'And why would your husband be paying for Josie Abbott's repairs? Did he cause the damage?'

'No, I don't think so. His car was fine.'

'So could he have been driving her car?'

'No. I'm not sure. That's the thing, it doesn't make any sense.' I rummage in my handbag and produce the receipt, smoothing the crumpled piece of paper out on the table in front of me before sliding it across to DS McConley.

He looks at it slowly before leaning back in his chair.

'Why don't you tell me what you think happened, Mrs Floyd?'

'I'm scared that either Josie or Mike, or possibly Josie and Mike together, hit Wilson Walker in Josie's Audi. Mike then organised to get the car repaired at this garage in Croydon, which is nowhere near where we live, and they might have been covering this all up.'

'And why would your husband and Josie Abbott be in a car together at one in the morning, which was the time when Wilson Walker was hit?'

'You know about his case?'

'Of course, Mrs Floyd. Fortunately, we don't get too many tragic hit and runs in this area.'

'I was told a week or so ago that they might have been having an affair. It's possible they were together.'

'And where were you when this happened?'

'In Suffolk with my sister. She had just had a baby. Mike was at home alone with our children.'

19

As I'm driving home after my visit to the police station, I think back to that dreadful time when Wilson died.

My sister, Celia, had given birth to a baby girl two months earlier. Her lovely husband had rung me up in a panic. Celia couldn't stop crying, stayed in bed all day long, and was generally a mess. With the help of Mum and my friend Keira, I organised a rota for Harper and Harry, filled the freezer with some pre-cooked meals, and dashed off to Suffolk. I was only gone for two nights, but with the amount of organisation required and the terrible drama that happened whilst I was away, it felt like I'd been gone for a month.

Wilson died the second night I was away, and I found out when Mike rang me the next morning. The police had blocked off the lane, so he couldn't get the children to school, and he couldn't get to work. He told me not to hurry home, but I did the opposite. I wanted to be with my babies. By the time I returned, there was absolutely nothing to show that a tragedy had occurred. No marks on the road, no flowers left at the site, no police signs. As far as I knew, it might never have happened.

BACK AT HOME, I heat up some soup and realise to my dismay that I have a client this afternoon. Although many customers have cancelled on me, I've had some new bookings in the last couple of days. I think it's a mixture of needing to get manicures and pedicures done for the holiday period combined with the curiosity and voyeurism of visiting a place where a murder took place. How ironic that Linette's death may have done me a favour.

I feel terrible about what I told the police, but in my heart of hearts, I know it was the right thing. The thought of telling Mike is horrific. Nevertheless, I ring him, but once again, there is no answer. I send him a message asking him to come home early. Surely, he will respond to that.

Somehow, I get through a long appointment of doing both a manicure and a pedicure for a woman who is going to Dubai for Christmas. By the time she has left, it's gone four thirty p.m. I'm furious that Mike hasn't returned my call, both from the message I left with Janine this morning and my text message this afternoon. I telephone Janine again.

'Hello, Janine. Mike hasn't returned my call. Please, can I talk to him?'

There's a very long pause during which I wonder whether we've been cut off. Eventually, she says, 'Can you hold on a minute, Isobel?'

Once again, I listen to Vivaldi for what seems like forever.

'Isobel, this is Peter talking.'

'Hello, Peter. Is everything all right?' Why has Janine put me through to the firm's senior partner?

'Um, no, not really. Mike left with two policemen about half an hour ago. Do you know what's going on?'

I think I'm going to faint. I hang onto the countertop and take a big gulp of air.

'I don't know,' I say. 'I'm sorry.' And then I hang up.

My God, what have I done? Have I just handed in my innocent husband to the police? Is this the end of our marriage, the end of our lives together? If so, it's all my fault. I should have waited to talk to Mike, to listen to his side of the story first. What the hell was I thinking? I am trembling from head to toe as I pace the house. He will hate me, and so he should. What spouse offers up their husband or wife to the police, dumping them right in it? I don't deserve him. How I wish I could wind back time just a few hours.

I'm sitting on the bottom step of the stairs when there's a loud hammering on the back door. I don't want to talk to anyone right now. The hammering continues, and then I hear a shout. 'Isobel! Come out, now.'

I hurry downstairs and open the door to Jack. His cheeks are tomato red, and his jaw is set forwards. I have never seen him look so disturbed.

'What's happened?' I ask.

'That's what I need to ask you. Josie's been taken in by the police for questioning, and apparently, Mike has too.' He pushes past me into the kitchen. I feel sick. 'Josie can't possibly have had anything to do with Linette's murder. It's just not possible!'

He is pacing in exactly the same way I was.

'Sit down, Jack,' I say. He does as I tell him, sitting there with his knee bouncing up and down, a faint aroma of manure coming from his dirty clothes.

'It's not to do with Linette,' I say. 'It's about Wilson Walker.'

'Wilson?' he exclaims.

'I'm so sorry. I think that Josie and Mike were having an

affair, and they hit Wilson in Josie's car. I found a receipt for repairs to Josie's Audi in Mike's briefcase.'

'What?' He shakes his head. 'No, that doesn't make any sense. I know things have been tough between Josie and me, but an affair? No, she wouldn't do that.'

'Her car went into a garage in Croydon the day after Wilson was hit. Do you know why?'

He frowns. 'No. I don't remember her not having her car. You must be mistaken.'

'I don't think so,' I say quietly.

'Did you tell the police this? Did you dump them in it?'

I can't meet his eyes.

He stands up and knocks his chair over. 'What the hell have you done, Isobel?' I think he's going to come for me then, and I back away, but he doesn't. He walks straight past me and out the back door, leaving it wide open so that the cold, damp air seeps through into the house.

I WANT to talk to someone, anyone, but who? Who can I tell about this terrible thing I have done? I wait for Mike to come home, but he doesn't. I don't even know who to call at the police station. How does one find out whether one's husband is being held in custody? This is so far out of my comfort zone it's almost laughable.

For the second night in a row, I go to sleep in an empty bed, restless and scared. I try to reason. The police wouldn't be questioning Mike and Josie unless they had reason to do so, but all of this is because of me. Because Mike and I argued.

The next morning, I'm awake early, and I'm grateful that I am, as just before eight a.m., Mike walks through the door. He looks terrible, his face grey with stubble, his work clothes creased and dishevelled. I look at him, terrified as to what he's going to say, terrified that this is the end of our marriage.

He slumps into the chair that Jack sat on only a few hours ago.

'I assume the police found out about the garage bill because you gave it to them?'

I nod and whisper, 'I'm sorry.'

'You're sorry?' he asks, staring at me with watery eyes. 'It's me who should be begging you for forgiveness. I am so sorry, Isobel.'

This is not what I expected. I stand very still. 'What have you done?' I whisper.

'Josie and I have admitted to the hit and run.'

'No!' I exclaim. I don't want to believe this. This is Mike we're talking about. My reliable, dependable, steady Mike.

'We had an affair, and I'm so sorry.' He groans and runs his fingers through his hair. 'We had been sitting in the car in the lane. I'd been trying to break things off. Josie wanted . . . well, I knew we had to stop. The last thing I wanted to do was hurt you, and she'd given me an ultimatum. Her or you. I chose you, Isobel. So we were there in the car, and she got all upset. I mean, really upset and angry too. She started driving off without the headlights on. She hit Wilson, but it would have been impossible to miss him. Neither of us saw him until it was too late. He just ran out right in front of the car. It was horrible. So horrible.'

I can't take in what he's saying. My husband is admitting that he and his lover killed a boy and failed to report it to the police, failed to even call an ambulance. Who is this man I thought I knew? And what was he even doing out that evening?

'Where were the children? I was away that night.' My voice sounds distant and weird.

'They were safe, asleep in bed.'

'You left Harper and Harry alone in the house!' This shocks me more than anything. My husband, the man who I thought was sensible and caring, left our children alone. I find that even more distressing than the affair, than the hit and run. He made our babies vulnerable. I'm not sure I will ever be able to forgive that.

He reaches for my hand, but I pull it away, shaking my head. 'I'm sorry, Isobel. For everything.'

'How long?'

'How long, what?'

'How long were you having an affair with Josie?'

'Not long.'

'I want to know, exactly.'

He sighs. 'About two months, maybe a bit longer. I didn't mean to, honestly, Isobel. It's just you were so occupied with the children, and well, we weren't talking much, and Josie, she was just there.'

'Did you sleep with her?'

He nods.

'How often?'

He hangs his head. 'A few times.'

'Where?'

'Not here. Never here,' he says forcefully.

'As if that makes it any better,' I say. I thump my hand hard on the table. 'You lied, you cheated, you killed, you put our children at risk.'

'I'm so sorry, Isobel,' he whispers. 'Will you ever forgive me?'

'Linette knew.'

'Linette knew what?' He stares at me, those beautiful green eyes wide open.

'That you and Josie were having an affair. Did she threaten either of you? Blackmail, perhaps?'

'What! What are you saying?' Mike looks confused, flabbergasted even. My husband may have lied and cheated, and perhaps I don't know him any longer, but this reaction, I'm almost sure it's genuine. I am nearly positive that Linette didn't say anything to him.

'Are you saying what I think you're saying, that Josie or I killed Linette because we wanted to shut her up?' He shakes his head violently. 'No. I swear that Linette never said anything to me. I swear that I could never kill anyone.'

'But you did, didn't you? You killed an innocent young man on the cusp of adulthood. You've been lying to me for the past nine months. Why should I believe a word you say?'

He looks utterly crestfallen. I think my husband is broken, but right now, I don't care. I'm fuelled by anger.

'Wilson's death was an accident, Isobel. He was fine when we left him, absolutely fine. Josie was driving slowly, and we didn't hit him hard, I promise you we didn't. There was very little damage to the car. He got up from the ground and talked to us. He said he was fine.'

'But he wasn't fine, was he? He died.'

'He might have had internal injuries, perhaps. I don't know.' Mike's voice trails off.

'Perhaps if Josie had had her lights on—' I say.

'There was nothing we could have done to avoid hitting him.'

Mike is trying to get me to look at him, but I can't. How can I bring myself to look into the eyes of the man I thought I loved when he's telling me this? 'So what's going to happen now?' I ask after a long silence.

'It's likely that Josie will be charged with dangerous driving because she was driving with her lights off, but even so, there was absolutely nothing she could have done to avoid hitting Wilson. The reality is both of us are potentially facing jail time for failing to report an accident. According to the police, they are reopening the investigation into Wilson's

death, and we have to await the decision of the Crown Prosecution Service as to what we'll be charged with. I'm so sorry,
Isobel. I'm sorry I have let you and the children down. I have
been a terrible father and a terrible husband.'

Mike is staring at me with big, imploring eyes, but I can't
look at him. I just want all of this to disappear, for me to wade
out of this horror, for him to tell me it's all been a distasteful
joke.

Except it hasn't.

'Do you think you could forgive me?' he asks, wringing
his hands.

I stand up and pace the kitchen. 'I don't know. This is
such a shock, Mike. I thought you were a good person, but
this . . . this isn't the man I married.'

'I know. I will do anything, absolutely anything to rebuild
our marriage, to bind our family back together again.'

'To be honest, Mike, even if you don't go to jail, I'm not
sure we have a future together.'

'I know you think this now, but I pray you might change
your mind.'

'I need time. Lots of it. I don't want to look at you or talk
to you. Do you understand?'

He nods his head slowly. 'I'll carry on sleeping in the
spare room and keep out of your way for a few days. I could
move out to a hotel if you want me to, but I think that might
look suspicious as far as the police are concerned.'

I put my face in my hands and try to think, but it's as if my
brain is stuffed with cotton wool.

'You can stay here for now, but I don't want to see you,' I
say. I walk out of the kitchen, upstairs to our bedroom and
lock myself in the bathroom. I sit on the toilet and burst into
tears.

20

You know when something utterly devastating happens to you that there will always be a before and after. It might be a cancer diagnosis or a death or the day your spouse says they're leaving. I know for sure that last night was my proverbial line in the sand. How can life ever be the same when you discover your husband isn't the morally upstanding man you believed he was? How can I stay married to a man who not only cheated on me but, way worse, neglected our children and then failed to report an accident? Could they have saved poor Wilson? Did they get out of Josie's car to help him? It's so repugnant, it makes me nauseous.

I can hear Mike downstairs. There's the rattling of Lupin's bowl and the clinking of crockery. I will wait until he has left for work before going downstairs, but then it hits me. Has he even got a job? Surely, Peter will suspend him until the outcome of the case against him. How can they employ an architect with a criminal record? And there goes our financial security and, quite probably, this house. I should never have quit work because it's obvious that I'll have to return, and how easy will that be after six years away?

About ten minutes later, there's a knock on my bedroom door.

'I've left you a tray with breakfast on the floor in the hall,' Mike says. I can't remember the last time he brought me breakfast in bed. Perhaps two or three years ago on my birthday?

I don't answer, and eventually, I hear his footsteps descend the stairs.

Mum rings, and I tell her to bring the children home this afternoon. I can't find the words to tell her what has happened, to destroy her illusion that her daughter is married to a fine, upstanding man.

Mike has made an effort. He has boiled me an egg and made me toast with marmalade plus freshly juiced orange juice, but it all tastes like cardboard, and I barely touch it. I carry the tray downstairs and look outside. As expected, his car is still in the drive. I tiptoe along the hall to the study, where the door is closed, and wait for a moment, but I can't hear anything. As I'm walking away, the floorboard creaks.

'Isobel,' Mike says, hurrying out of the study, 'can we talk?'

'No. I've got nothing to say to you right now.'

'But the kids?'

'They're coming home later, and I expect you to act totally normal around them.'

'Of course I will. I'll do anything to mend all of this.'

I can't help but let out a sarcastic grunt. 'A bit late for that,' I say, walking back to the kitchen. 'Come on, Lupin, let's go for a walk.' I don't turn around to look at Mike.

It's bitterly cold outside, so I pull on a black woollen hat, wrap a thick black scarf around my neck, and stride up our drive. I hope I blend into the dark woodland. I keep my head down, eager to avoid anyone, but I still get accosted by Mr Quinn.

'Good morning, Isobel.'

'Hello,' I say, barely slowing down.

'I was really shocked to hear that Mike and Josie were taken in for questioning by the police.'

'How did you find out?' I asked, horrified that he knows.

'The police constable at the Walkers' place isn't exactly discreet,' he says. 'Think he's a bit lonely keeping guard all by himself. Mind you, now that Keith Walker is moving back in, I expect they'll let him go. The forensics have left. But I couldn't believe it when he said about Mike and Josie being hauled in for questioning. It must be a truly awful time for you.'

'Not the best,' I mutter, wondering how I can walk away without causing offence.

'It must be a mistake, mustn't it? I can't imagine either of those two doing anyone harm. I saw Josie driving off with the children this morning, so obviously they've been released.'

'Yes, I need—'

I jump as a car appears behind me, an electric car, silent and startling. I step to one side to let the silver Tesla pass, but it doesn't. The window winds down, and Thomas Adler sticks his neck out. Has he got yet another new car?

'How's everyone doing?'

I silently beg Mr Quinn not to say anything, but it's in vain.

'Poor Isobel, as if she hasn't got enough to deal with. Her Mike and Josie Abbott got taken away and questioned by the police.'

'They what?' Thomas exclaims. He looks smug, and I have an overwhelming urge to swipe him in the face.

'They've been released without charge,' I say through

gritted teeth, although I'm not sure whether that's strictly true.

'I told that police constable standing guard outside the Walkers' house that neither Josie nor Mike could have anything to do with Linette's demise,' Mr Quinn says.

'I don't suppose the police would bring them in for interview unless they had good reason to,' Thomas says. He's grinning broadly now, and I can sense his relief that he's off the hook for Linette's murder. I have no intention of correcting him and explaining that they were brought in to discuss Wilson's death, not Linette's murder, and I'm glad when he speeds off down the lane.

'It's a right mess, isn't it?' Mr Quinn says. 'My heart bleeds for the Walkers. A true tragedy. And Linette, she may have been a pain, what with that blasted pig and the stench from her bonfires and the noise from her parties, but to die like that is just horrible. I'm just glad that your Mike and Josie Abbott have been let go and aren't implicated.'

I wish the man would belt up. He seems particularly loquacious today, and I suppose he's loving all the gossip. You can't ask for anything more exciting than a murder at a neighbouring house, can you? I must get away from all of this dreadful speculation.

'It has nothing to do with Linette,' I say quietly. 'Please excuse me, but I need to get on with the walk. The kids are coming home later.'

'Yes, yes, of course. You take care, Isobel.' And for the first time since I've met Mr Quinn, I see some tenderness in his eyes, or perhaps it's pity. Either way, I soften towards him.

'Thank you, and please send my best regards to Mrs Quinn.'

.   .   .

THE FOOTPATH IS sodden with decomposing leaves and mud, and although Lupin makes easy work of it, this isn't the head-clearing walk that I need. I almost slip twice, my wellington boots unable to grip properly, and I reckon it's a bit of a metaphor for my life right now. Everything seems horribly out of control and scary. I simply can't fathom how Mike could have kept quiet about his part in Wilson's death. It's just too horrible. I'm cold despite wearing a thick woollen jumper that Mum knitted me for my birthday, and decide to turn homewards sooner than normal. I want to get ready for the children coming home, baking them a cake with green icing to appease Harry and spaghetti made with green pesto pasta. Lupin doesn't seem to mind too much and follows at my heels. I'm walking along the lane, just about to turn into our driveway, when to my horror, I hear shouts.

There are two people fighting right in front of our house. I run forwards, trying to see who it is, and then scream, 'Stop!'

Mike and Jack are fighting on the drive next to the olive tree in its terracotta pot that stands to the side of the front door. Jack draws his right fist back and slams it into Mike's jaw. Mike crumples onto the gravel drive.

'Stop!' I scream. As I rush towards them, letting go of Lupin's lead, I see there's another man on the lane. It's Keith Walker standing there with his arms crossed in front of his broad chest, a smile on his face.

'Help stop them!' I screech at him, but he doesn't move, not even flicking his eyes towards me. I race towards Jack, who is drawing his leg back to aim a kick at Mike. 'Stop!' I shout again, tugging at Jack's shirt.

And then something snaps inside him, and Jack steps backwards, his arms hanging loosely at his sides.

'I'm sorry, Isobel,' he says, rubbing his palms over his eyes. 'I'm just, it's just . . .'

'I know,' I whisper. After all, Jack and I are in the same situation. I really don't blame him for beating up Mike. I bend down towards my husband, but other than a bloodied nose, which to my inexpert eyes doesn't look broken, I think Mike is fine. A bruised ego, perhaps, but then he deserves that. I glance up and see Jack walking away, his shoulders slumped, his feet dragging as if they each weigh a tonne. And then I glance around to look for Keith Walker, but he's vanished.

Mike is being licked by Lupin now, so I call the dog to my side and watch as my husband struggles to get up from the gravel driveway.

'What happened?' I ask.

'Jack turned up at the door and asked me to come outside, and then he threw a punch.' He wipes his bloody nose on the back of his hand. 'I deserved it.'

I can't disagree with that.

'Where's Josie?' I ask.

He shrugs. 'I don't know. I haven't seen her.'

'But you knew she'd been questioned too, and I assume you had a little conflab first.'

'Yes, but you've got to believe me that it's been over for months. I love you, Isobel, and the reason neither of us said anything about Wilson was because we wanted to protect our families.'

'So why did you have an affair in the first place?'

Mike opens and closes his mouth. Blood is still seeping from his nose.

'Don't bother,' I say, tugging on Lupin's lead and striding into the house.

I SPEND the next few hours getting ready for Harry and Harper's return home. I simply can't wait to have my babies in my arms, to hold them tight and breathe in their beautiful scents. I tidy up their rooms, change their sheets, bake a revolting-looking green cake, and wait patiently for Mum to turn up. I do everything I can to avoid Mike, leaving the kitchen when he comes in to make himself a sandwich, skirting around him when we meet in the hallway. He tries to talk to me, but I don't want to hear what he has to say.

And then, at long last, Mum's Tiguan is in the drive, and I run out to help her unstrap the kids from their car seats.

'Mummy!' Harper screeches, diving into my legs. As is his way, Harry is more reserved, but when I bend down and tilt my head to one side, opening up my arms, he also runs into them.

'You're squeezing me,' he says, trying to wriggle free.

'That's because I missed you so much.' I let him go.

'I missed you too,' Harper says, reaching for my hand. Harry doesn't say anything, but I know he feels the same way.

I make Mum a cup of tea, and when the children are eating their supper, she comes to stand next to me on the other side of the kitchen.

'How are you doing, love?'

'It's been some of the worst days of my life.'

'Not surprising. It's such a terrible thing to happen right on your doorstep.'

'Mike had an affair.'

'What? With the dead woman?' Mum looks horrified.

'No. With Josie Abbott next door.'

'Oh, sweetheart. What are you going to do?'

I debate telling her about Wilson and what Mike has admitted to me and the police, but I'm not ready to say it aloud yet. It makes me question everything, and I know it'll hurt Mum almost as much as it's wounded me.

'I don't know,' I say eventually because that is the truth.

'You know I'm here for you, and if you want to move out and stay with me, you're welcome.'

I smile. Mum's house is much too small for the three of us. Besides, if anyone is going to move out of this home, it'll be Mike. But for now, until we know what the CPS will prosecute Mike and Josie with, I want to stay here to maintain just an iota of normality.

After Mum has left and the children are playing in their playroom, I hear Mike's footsteps. I turn to leave the room, to let him have his turn to say hello to the kids, but he puts a hand on my arm. 'Please stay,' he murmurs. 'Let's do the bed and bath routine together, like we do at weekends.'

I consider walking away, but that will only hurt the children, so I nod. And somehow, we end up laughing and joking around with the children as if nothing whatsoever has happened. I know it's all pretend, but for just a few minutes, I'm able to forget what Mike has done. We both read them bedtime stories, tuck them up snugly in under their duvets, and kiss them goodnight. And then we are alone again, standing in the hall upstairs with the children's bedroom doors closed.

'Would you like me to make supper?' Mike asks.

'No,' I say because I don't want to like Mike. He needs to suffer as much as he's making me hurt. But as I'm reheating the leftovers from the children's tea, and he has retreated to the study, I wonder whether perhaps we could co-parent, live in the same house so that for all intents and purposes, the children would think everything is the same as ever, but Mike and I could lead our own lives. I could have a lover, perhaps start online dating, go back to work, and be the independent woman I was before Mike and I got together. But no, that wouldn't work, because how would I cope with the knowledge that Mike was doing the same, sleeping with Josie or whoever, leading a life beyond the children that didn't involve me? In my heart of hearts, I know that I am too jealous a person to contemplate that. Such a relationship would eat me up.

I am sitting at the kitchen table, eating the tasteless spaghetti, when the front doorbell rings. I can hear Mike walk to the door, and then there are several male voices, and my stomach gnaws, threatening to bring up the food I've only just swallowed. Lupin barks, so I get up and hurry out of the kitchen and into the hall.

There are two men standing there, but the front door is open, and beyond them, I can see three uniformed policemen and a woman in plain clothes.

'What's going on?' I ask, swallowing hard.

'We have a warrant to search your house and garden.'

Mike stands to one side, his nose swollen, and he looks utterly defeated. Where is the strong, confident man I married?

The men push past us.

'Wait!' I say. 'My children are asleep upstairs!' I try to block the staircase. 'Please don't disturb them.' The policeman in charge, the one who waved the warrant in front of Mike, steps forwards.

'Okay, guys. Do downstairs and outside first. Monica, you can oversee the sorting out of the children.'

Lupin starts barking. Really barking, loud and vicious sounding, nothing like the gentle Labrador that he is. I don't hold his collar as I normally would when we have guests, and instead, I let him bare his teeth at the men. It's to no avail. Everyone knows that a Labrador rarely bites. The policemen scatter throughout the downstairs of the house while Mike and I look at each other in horror. There are tears in his eyes.

'I'm so sorry, Isobel,' he murmurs. 'I swear on our children's lives that I've done nothing wrong.'

'Don't ever use our children to appease your conscience.' I

turn my back on him and run upstairs, followed in hot pursuit by a woman wearing a pair of grey trousers and a baggy black jumper.

I stop at the top of the stairs and glare at her. 'What are you doing?'

'Sorry, but I need to follow you. It's procedure. My name is Monica Ugent.'

I consider arguing, but what's the point? I suppose she wants to make sure that I don't hide or dispose of any evidence. A sick joke.

'Am I allowed to call my mother?' I ask with my hands on my hips.

'Yes, so long as I can overhear the conversation.'

I walk into our bedroom, sit on the side of the bed with my back to the door, and use the landline. Monica is standing in the doorway, pretending not to look at me. I can barely hold it together when I ring Mum, and if that woman weren't here, I'd definitely break down.

'The police are searching our house, Mum. Can you come and collect the children?'

'What? Why are they searching your house? What the hell!'

'They suspect Mike.'

'Our Mike? You've got to be bloody joking.'

'I can't say anything now, but I'll tell you all later.' And then I wonder. Could he have killed Linette? If he found it so easy to walk away from a dying boy, there's every possibility that he could have killed too in cold, brutal daylight. You read about these women who have no idea that their husbands are murderers, not realising that they're sleeping with a monster. Could I be one of those women, an idiot who only sees what her husband wants her to see?

'I'm on my way,' Mum says. And not for the first time, I'm so deeply grateful that she lives nearby and she is willing to scoop us up whenever we need it. When I've finished the call, I walk slowly down the stairs, followed by Monica.

'I'm going to sit here,' I say as I sink onto the bottom step of the staircase. 'I don't want any of you lot going up there.'

Monica nods. 'We don't want to upset your children,' she says as she squeezes past me and talks under her breath to an officer standing near the front door.

I've no idea where Mike is now, and frankly, I don't care. Monica walks out of the house, and the policeman turns to look at me.

'Why are you searching our house?' I ask. 'What are you looking for?'

'I'm sorry, ma'am, but I can't disclose any information. We'll need to go upstairs shortly.'

'I'm waiting for my mother to arrive, as she'll be taking the kids. Please don't disturb them.'

He's about to say something else, but I interrupt him, remembering all those crime programmes I've watched on the television.

'Have you got children?' I ask, holding his gaze.

'Yes.'

'So you'll understand how traumatising it'll be for my kids to wake up and see their house being ransacked by the police.'

He nods. 'You've got half an hour.'

'How long will you be staying here?'

He shrugs. 'As long as it takes.'

And then I hear Harry's voice. 'Mummy, what's happening?'

I rush up the stairs. 'Come along, let's get back to your bedroom.' Monica, the policewoman, magically materialises behind me.

'Why are there people here?'

'They're here for Daddy's work.' It's a ridiculous comment

but the first thing that comes into my head because I can hardly tell them the truth. 'They're going to be working on something for quite a long time, and they might be noisy, so Granny is coming to pick you and Harper up.'

'But why?'

'Because it's unexpected and it will disturb you, and Daddy needs to be quiet.' I hold Harry's hand and walk him back to his bedroom, the policewoman standing behind us. At least she's not wearing a uniform.

'Who's she?' he asks, pointing at her.

'I'm Monica,' she says. 'Pretend I'm not here.'

I would like to grunt sarcastically, but I bite my tongue for Harry's sake. My son walks towards the window and pulls back his bright blue curtain.

'No,' I say, trying to drag him away from the window.

'What are those people doing? They've got lights on outside.'

'I know, darling. It's all rather exciting, isn't it?' I feel sick as I say that. 'We need to get you dressed before Granny arrives.'

'But it's the middle of the night.'

'Not quite. Just night-time for you. Do you think I can leave you here to get dressed whilst I wake up Harper?'

He nods. I shut the door firmly behind me and just hope that he doesn't look outside or nip downstairs without me noticing. I've no idea where Mike is, and frankly, I could do with his help right now. I wonder if this will be my life now, a single mother working out how to explain that my children's father is locked up in jail.

Harper is fast asleep, so I don't even try to get her dressed and leave her in bed clutching her favourite toy rabbit. I watch her for a couple of minutes before gently closing her bedroom door. Just as I'm walking back towards Harry's room, I hear Mum downstairs.

'You will let me in!' she says in a shrill voice. 'I am the children's grandmother, and I'm here to get them, so kindly let me pass.' Despite myself, I smile wryly. Mum doesn't stand for any nonsense. She used to be the head of English at a local secondary school, and she was able to whip both the kids and their parents into their places. Every year, the school's exam results were the best in English. It wasn't just her ability to teach well but her somewhat old-fashioned attitude that instilled a work ethic and curiosity. It's probably what made her such a great foster mother too. I don't suppose she'd thrive in today's environment, so it's just as well she took early retirement. I walk into the hallway to see Monica standing at the top of the stairs.

'You can let her up,' Monica instructs the policeman.

As soon as Mum sees me, she pushes past Monica and throws her arms around me. 'Stay strong,' she whispers into my ear.

Harry's door opens, and the second he sees Mum, he rushes out into the corridor and throws his arms around her legs. Anyone might have thought that he hadn't seen her in ages when in fact it's only hours since she was last here. It feels like a lifetime ago. I'm not sure why, but Harry's behaviour is always much better around Mum. Perhaps he senses her no-nonsense attitude, or perhaps she is able to attune herself to children on the spectrum better than most of us.

'Can you get Harry into the car whilst I collect some of their things?' I ask Mum. 'Then I'll bring Harper down. Fingers crossed she'll stay asleep.'

Mum nods. 'Come on, Harry, let's go and have an adventure.'

Fortunately, Harper stays asleep, all warm and floppy in my arms, wrapped in a blanket. She awakens slightly as I get her into her car seat, but then closes her eyes again and sucks her thumb, a habit I thought she had ditched.

As I watch Mum manoeuvre her car out between the two police cars and a black saloon, I just can't stop the tears from flowing. I want to go with them, away from here. I'd meant it when I said I wanted this to be our forever home, but now I'm not sure. Now I wonder if anywhere would be better than this place. Perhaps The Close really is cursed.

I wander around downstairs, followed by Monica.

'Where is everyone?' I ask.

'They're outside,' she says.

Frowning, I move to look out the kitchen window. They've set up big portable lights that floodlight the garden, and there are several men congregated around our shed. It's near the back of the garden on the left-hand side, next to the compost heap. It's quite a big shed, with room for us to keep our lawn-mower in and for Mike to have a little workbench where he does his woodwork and general pottering around.

A moment later, two policemen walk in from outside, their expressions stern. One of them is walking in tandem with Mike. It's only when I see my husband's expression do I realise what's happened. Mike's wrists are in handcuffs, and he's attached to the policeman.

'What are you doing?' I screech. Monica, who seems to be my shadow, places a firm hand on my shoulder. 'Where are you taking him?'

'I'm sorry, Mrs Floyd, but your husband has been arrested on suspicion of the murder of Lyn Smith.'

21

'Why? Why are you arresting him?'

One of the other policemen in plain clothes stares at me and then holds up a clear plastic evidence bag. Inside is a hammer, and on the weighted head end there is congealed blood. The hallway spins around me, and my stomach convulses. I grab the spindles on the staircase.

'Do you need to sit down, Isobel?' Monica asks.

I shake my head and then lean against the wall under the staircase. I watch three of the policemen walk out our front door.

'They suspect that was the weapon used to kill Lyn Smith,' Monica says. 'I'm so sorry, Isobel.'

I notice that she's calling me by my first name now rather than Mrs Floyd. I suppose she pities me.

'It's a mistake,' I say in a hoarse voice.

'Come on, let's go and make a cup of tea,' she says. I follow her numbly into the kitchen. Some of the things on the countertops have been shifted around, but other than that, you'd never know the room had been searched.

'Mike would never do something like that. He's not a violent person.'

'You take a seat and point me in the direction of your cups.'

I watch as she makes two cups of tea, using my kettle and my cups and my teabags and taking the milk carton out of my fridge. This is all surreal. She places a china cup in front of me, but when I try to lift it to my lips, hot tea sloshes over the side and scalds my fingers.

'Are you okay?' she asks, tilting her head with concern.

Of course I'm not bloody all right. It might be masochistic, but I welcome the pain. It's a transitory distraction from the pain in my heart.

'When will they let Mike come home?'

'The hammer will be sent away to forensics, and if Lyn's blood is found on it along with Mike's fingerprints, then he will be charged with murder.'

'But of course Mike's fingerprints will be on the hammer. It's his! He keeps it in the shed.'

'Is the shed normally kept locked?'

'Sometimes. Honestly, I don't know. It's Mike's shed, and I rarely go in it.' I'm silent for a few moments as I try to digest the horror of all of this. 'And if it is Lyn's blood and they find Mike's fingerprints, then what?'

'He'll be charged and will be sent to prison pending his bail application.'

'How long will that take?'

'Things are slow at the moment. It could be months.'

'Months! Months in prison without being guilty?'

'There's a very strict protocol that the police and the justice system have to follow, Isobel. But we'll make sure you're supported as best we can during all of this.'

'This can't be right. Mike may have done some stupid things, but he's not an evil man. He's just not.'

'I realise that this is a terrible shock to you. It would be best if you could try to get some sleep. It's nearly three a.m.'

'It is?' I ask with surprise, glancing at the clock on the oven. She's right.

'Do you have any sleeping pills?' Monica asks.

'I might have one left.' It's difficult to think straight. I went through a period of insomnia a couple of years ago when I was struggling with Harry, wondering what was wrong with my little boy. My GP prescribed me some sleeping pills, and I don't recall whether I finished the strip or not.

'My colleagues and I will be working here all night, but it's important that you try to rest.'

'How on earth do you think I'm going to be able to rest with all of this going on?' I wave my hands around, but in fact, we are the only people in the house, and the last time I looked, there were just two policemen outside, looking for goodness knows what in the garden and the shed.

She tilts her head to one side. 'Unfortunately, I've been assigned to a lot of cases like this. You'll need to be strong, Isobel, for your children. There'll be a lot of media interest and speculation, and it'll be up to you to protect your family.'

'They've made a mistake,' I say.

She looks at me with sad eyes. I suppose all the wives say this. It'll be the shock and the sheer horror of realising that you've spent night after night sleeping next to a murderer. But no, Mike hasn't been convicted, he's only been charged. And it will be up to me to find him a good lawyer, to make sure that the police realise they've made a terrible mistake.

'Are you staying here?' I ask, pushing my barely drunken cup of tea to one side.

'No. But another of my colleagues will be here to keep an eye on you and to give you any support you need.'

'I'm not a bloody baby!' I say and immediately apologise. It's not Monica's fault. None of this is. It's Mike's fault.

'Have you got anywhere else you can go at this time of night?'

'I can go and stay at Mum's.' But then I realise she'll have bolted the door from the inside, as she always does at night, so I'll have to telephone her and wake her up in the middle of the night.

'I'll stay here,' I say.

'Of course. I'll make sure that you're not disturbed. It's important for you to rest, and we'll deal with tomorrow when it comes.'

I stand up and feel a deep weariness, as if my bones are too heavy, and my head is overflowing with terror and horror and utter exhaustion. 'I'll let you out,' I say.

She nods. At the door, she turns to me and hands me a business card. 'This is me. You can call me any time.'

When you imagine something truly horrific happening, you assume that you'll never be able to sleep again, or if you do, your dreams will be plagued by unspeakably dreadful night-mares. That's not necessarily true, or at least it isn't for me. I swallow a year-out-of-date sleeping pill, and the next few hours are a blissful oblivion. It's only when I wake up and realise that Mike hasn't slept next to me that I remember the horror of last night. And then I barely make it to the toilet before throwing up bile. After drinking water from the tap and brushing my teeth, I walk gingerly back into the bedroom and slowly open the curtains. There's no one in the garden, although there is police tape around the garden shed. In fact, it's almost possible to believe that last night was a horrible nightmare, except of course it wasn't.

The phone rings. 'Good morning, Isobel. This is Monica Ugent. Did you get any sleep?'

'A bit.'

'We have some news. Forensics have come back very quickly, and I'm sorry to say that the hammer does have Lyn Smith's blood on it, and the weapon matches the wounds that she suffered. It has also been confirmed that Mike's finger-prints are on the handle.'

'Of course Mike's prints are on the hammer,' I exclaim, clutching my throat with my left hand. 'I told you that last night. But who else's prints are on it?'

There's a beat of silence. 'No one's.'

'Then they must have worn gloves or wiped their prints. This is a travesty!'

'I'm sorry for the shock,' she says. There's a long beat of silence.

'What's going to happen now?' I ask in a voice that doesn't sound like my own.

'Mike will come up before the magistrates as soon as possible, probably tomorrow. He will state his plea of guilty or not guilty.'

'Of course he's going to plea not guilty!'

'And then he will be committed into the court system, and a date will be set for his plea and case management hearing in the Crown court. His solicitor might apply for bail, but it's extremely unlikely he'll get it.'

It's hard to take any of this in. 'And then?'

'He'll be held on remand in prison, Lewes Prison proba-bly, until his trial.'

'How long will all of that take?' I sink down onto the side of the bed.

'The courts are running very behind at the moment. It'll be at least six weeks until the PCMH, and it could be up to eighteen months or more before the trial, or even longer.'

I can't take this in and ask her to repeat herself. 'You mean that Mike could be held in prison for two years even though no court has found him guilty?'

'Yes, that is the system at the moment.'

'But it's so unfair!' There's not a lot Monica can say to that. 'Look, there's inevitably going to be a lot of media coverage. We'll try to keep it to the minimum, but I have to warn you that there's a lot of interest in this case, so I just want to suggest you batten down the hatches.'

'When can I see Mike?'

'Realistically, a fortnight, maybe. You won't be granted a visit until he's settled on remand in jail.'

'Okay, thank you,' I say and then think, why the hell did I just thank her? She has just told me that my life is ruined, and I'm so damned polite, I actually thanked her. And then I realise that this is all my fault. If I hadn't gone to the police with that garage receipt, none of this would have happened. I groan.

After the call, I get dressed and attempt to eat a piece of toast, but it tastes of cardboard, so I just sip a mug of sugary tea. I normally hate sugar in my tea, but this morning I need it. What am I meant to do now? Could Mike really have killed Linette? I just can't make sense of it. I don't know how long I sit there at the kitchen table, staring at the little marks and stains in the grain of the wood, recalling when some of the blemishes were made. And then the doorbell rings. Recalling that awful experience I had of being doorstepped by a journalist before and Monica's words of warning, I ignore it. It rings again. I wonder if there's a way I can disconnect it. I walk towards the utility room where we have our fuse boxes, wondering if I can flip the switch to off. But then there's a knock at the utility room window, and I jump.

It's not a journalist, it's Josie. What the hell does she want? I ignore her, but she raps on the glass, her voice audible.

'Please talk to me, Isobel. I've got stuff I need to tell you.'

I squeeze my eyes closed and think. All of this mess stems from Josie, so why the hell should I speak to her? I open my eyes and glance at her through the window. Her face is pale and her eyes red with dark rings underneath, her hair greasy and tied back with a rubber band. She looks awful, as if she hasn't slept in weeks. I motion to her to walk to the back door. 'Thank you,' she says as I unlock and open the door. She can't bring herself to meet my eyes.

'What do you want?'

'To apologise.'

That takes me by surprise. I wasn't expecting any humility from her. She follows me into the kitchen and stands there wringing her hands, her eyes cast downwards.

'I'm so sorry for everything, Isobel. I should never have slept with Mike, and it's all my fault. I came on to him, saw him as a way out when my own marriage was crumbling.'

Maybe, I think, but Mike could have said no.

'I've been a total bitch to you, and I'm a liar. I don't think I'll ever forgive myself, and I don't expect you to, but I just needed to say it. And now Mike's been arrested.'

I wonder how she knows. Perhaps it's already on the news, or perhaps she and Jack watched as Mike was hand-cuffed and hauled away.

'But we both know that Mike didn't kill Linette. He just didn't.'

'What?' I ask, startled by her comment. How does she know for sure? 'Take a seat,' I say, gesturing towards a kitchen chair. I move my cold mug of tea to one side and sit down. Josie sits opposite me in Mike's seat, but she can't sit still.

'Mike doesn't have it in him to kill someone,' Josie says. 'But I want to tell you about the night Wilson died. First of all, he was running as if the devil was after him. I mean he was sprinting so fast it was if something or someone was chasing him. What was he doing running like that at one o'clock in the morning? I got hold of the inquest report, and it detailed the extent of Wilson's injuries. Some of them were really shocking, but there is no way that my car hit Wilson that hard. Just no way we could have caused injuries like that.'

'What are you trying to say?'

'I honestly don't think I killed Wilson. I was driving really slowly, and there was barely any damage to my car, and if circumstances had been different, I probably wouldn't have bothered to get it fixed. He stood up afterwards. He talked to me, but he was in a hurry. He walked around the car, and then I drove off. I think someone else killed him.'

'What!' I exclaim, thinking that this is just Josie trying to appease her own guilt.

'I think someone else finished Wilson off, the person who was chasing him perhaps. Maybe the same person who killed Linette.'

22

J osie and I sit there for several long moments, neither of us saying a word whilst I try to digest what she's said.

'I told the police that the car didn't hit Wilson hard enough to kill him, but they didn't believe me. They think I'm just trying to fob them off. Mike will tell you the same.'

'I won't be talking to Mike any time in the near future,' I say.

Josie winces.

'Are you sure about this?' I ask. How can I be positive that Josie is telling the truth? It's not like she's going to admit that she was driving like a lunatic with the lights off and ran over a lad. This must be a cover-up.

'I'm one hundred percent positive I couldn't have killed him,' she says. 'I stopped the car. I got out of it. I talked to Wilson, and he said he was fine. I didn't kill him.' Her fingers are enlarging a hole near the cuff of her navy jumper. 'I know you must hate me. I hate myself too. I've left such a trail of destruction, and there's nothing I can do to make it better.

But I didn't kill Wilson, and I'm sure that Mike didn't kill Linette.'

'What, because you were with him when she was murdered?' I snap.

She recoils. 'No. Mike and I haven't been together since Wilson died. I just know that Mike couldn't do something like that. Wilson's death has eaten us both up, but we dug ourselves such a big hole we couldn't get out of it.'

'You mean a hole you couldn't get yourself out of, because it was you driving your car, Josie. It was you who hit Wilson and no doubt you who persuaded Mike to keep quiet about it, although why he did is beyond me. And then he cleared up your mess by paying to get your car fixed in a garage in a back alley in Croydon.'

She squirms. 'He wanted to protect you and your children. He loves you, Isobel.'

'And why didn't you stop to help Wilson?'

'Because he got himself up off the ground, wiped himself down, said he was fine. He was in a hurry to get away, so we carried on driving. It was a terrible shock to discover the next day that he was dead. It just didn't seem possible, and it still doesn't.'

'Why are you telling me all of this?'

'Because Mike is a good man, Isobel. You know that, you married him. It's my fault he's caught up in all of this, and you need to try to persuade the police that he didn't kill Linette because I'm so sure he didn't.'

'If he didn't, who did?' I ask.

Josie shrugs her shoulders.

'I'd like you to leave now,' I say, staring at her through narrowed eyes.

She stands up and shuffles towards the door. It's weird, but I feel empowered, determined that I'm going to save my family from this mess. Josie, on the other hand, looks totally defeated, as if all the strength, mental and physical, has been drained out of her. I watch as she walks up our drive, her shoulders rounded and her head slumped downwards.

I try to digest what she told me. If Wilson wasn't killed by the car, then who actually killed him? I suppose it's possible that Mike returned to the scene and bashed him over the head, but why would he do that? Wilson would have been able to identify the car, and he would have seen both Mike and Josie. If it happened as Josie explained and she got out of the car to assist Wilson, then the lights would have come on inside the car, and Wilson would have seen Mike too. It seems totally far-fetched for Mike, who doesn't like to kill a spider, to calmly walk back up our drive and, whilst our children were sleeping, bash Wilson to death. I just can't believe that. Or perhaps Josie and Mike are lying, and the young man's injuries were way worse than they assumed. Could they have cleaned the blood off Josie's car in the night? No, I simply can't accept that Josie and Mike knowingly killed a boy.

But it does change things, the knowledge that their car didn't hit Wilson hard, assuming they're telling the truth. Perhaps Josie is right and both Wilson and Linette were killed by the same person. I suppose it could be anyone, but it's most likely to be someone in The Close. What was Wilson running from? To my mind, the most likely person was his father, Keith Walker. I can imagine Keith screaming at his son for doing something wrong and then giving chase in the middle of the night. I wonder if he was a drinker. If our houses were a bit closer together, we might have known what went into our neighbour's recycling bins, but the truth is, I know very little about the Walker family. But would Keith really murder his own son? I suppose anything is possible. It depends on what Wilson knew or had done to anger his dad.

I don't know how long I sit at the table, trying to work

things out in my head, but I'm interrupted by the phone ring-
ing. I'm inclined to leave it to go to the answer machine but
then realise it might be Mum or the kids. It's not. It's DC
Cathy Dopler.

'We would like to schedule a time to interview you at
Crawley police station. Preferably today.'

'Why?' I ask.

'We have some further questions, and we believe you can
help us with our enquiries.'

'You mean prove that you've arrested the wrong man.'

She ignores my jibe. 'Would two p.m. today be
possible?'

'Do I need to be accompanied by a solicitor?'

'That won't be necessary, but of course, you have the right
to bring one should you wish.'

'And if I decline to be interviewed, then what?'

'We may arrest you for obstruction.'

'So it's not really voluntary, is it?'

DC Dopler sighs. 'Will you be attending at two p.m.?'

'I suppose so,' I say.

I NEED TO FIND A SOLICITOR, but the only ones I know are
property and conveyancing specialists who will be of no use
to me. The best I can do is work my way through a list on
Google of solicitors specialising in criminal law based in
Horsham or Crawley.

I ring two firms, both of whom have good ratings, to be
told that someone from their criminal team will ring me back
later today. That's no good. And then I consider whether I
really need one. If I find anyone able to accompany me today,
the chances are they won't be very good because good solicitors are always booked up, aren't they? In addition, I've got
nothing to hide. My resources should be spent on finding a

good lawyer to represent Mike. He's the person who really needs help.

As far as I'm concerned, I'm going to do this alone.

CRAWLEY POLICE STATION is a large red-brick building with blue metal window and door frames. It looks like a sprawling office complex, and despite everything, I can't help but wonder how I would have designed it differently. I know now that I will have to return to work, and perhaps that's a good thing. But I hesitate and stand outside for several long moments. I'm feeling increasingly nervous even though I've done nothing wrong. I wonder how Mike is feeling and whether he is here, locked away in a cell. He must be utterly terrified, assuming, that is, I haven't misjudged my husband. I take a deep breath, pull my shoulders backwards, and walk into the reception area.

'I have a meeting with DC Cathy Dopler,' I say. I'm damned if I'm going to call it an interview.

'Just a moment, please.'

DC Dopler doesn't keep me waiting long.

'Hello, Mrs Floyd. Please follow me.' She doesn't offer her hand to shake, and I'm glad to be able to keep my hands inside my pockets. In my right pocket I have a small conker that I picked up from the ground one day when walking Lupin. It's smooth and comforting as I run my fingers over it. I have to walk quickly to keep up with DC Dopler as she strides down a carpeted corridor and into a small room with a table and four chairs. It's freezing in here, and I shiver as I sit down. I wonder if this is some kind of primitive torture technique but then remind myself this is twenty-first century Britain. DC Dopler is only wearing a navy blouse, and I'm surprised she doesn't feel the cold because she hasn't got a spare ounce of flesh on her. Perhaps she's used to it. As she places a pen and notepad on the table, the door opens again, and a man enters. I can't be sure, but I think he might have been one of the policemen who searched our home. He stretches out his hand.

'DS Phil Cargo.'

I shake his hand limply. He has bright blue eyes set in an otherwise unremarkable face. His hair is receding, and he is carrying a little too much weight around his stomach.

'Right, thank you for coming in to talk to us, Mrs Floyd. You are not under arrest, and you are free to leave at any time. You have agreed to be here to give a voluntary interview, and you are entitled to legal advice.'

'Do I need a solicitor?' Panic churns in my sternum. Perhaps I should have tried harder to find a solicitor to be here with me.

'No, you don't, but you have the right to have one present should you wish.'

'But this is an informal chat, you said?'

'Yes.'

They are both staring at me, waiting for an answer, I suppose.

'It's okay. We can continue,' I say, wondering if I have made yet another terrible mistake.

'Please let us know if you need any refreshments or want to use the facilities,' DC Dopler says.

I nod.

DS Cargo starts off the interview. 'We would like to ask you some questions regarding the murder of Lyn Smith. Where were you during the hours of midday to three p.m. on the day she was murdered?'

'As I explained to you before, I went to Croydon to a garage and returned to find police in the lane.'

'Can you give us the address of this garage?'

'Yes, it's the one where Josie Abbott had her car repaired. I reported it to you and gave you the receipt.'

'And your husband, where was he?'

'In Southampton. He got back home after I did.'

'You see, that's the problem, Mrs Floyd,' Phil Cargo says. 'Your husband returned home early from his meeting in Southampton, and he wasn't at work at the time of Lyn Smith's murder.'

I can't stop my mouth from gaping. When I spoke to Mike, he was in the car and said he was nearly home. I just assumed he was on his way back from the meeting in Southampton.

'You didn't know that?' DC Dopler asks.

I shake my head.

'It seems that Mike returned early from Southampton and was at your home at the time of the murder. He has no alibi. He says he was in his garden shed at the time, planting tulip bulbs into pots, and that he heard and saw nothing. He then nipped out in his car, supposedly to get some more compost, but there are no sightings of his car on CCTV or receipts to back this up. As such, we can't prove his whereabouts.'

I try to recall my conversation with Mike. I had come home to all of the police presence, but what I don't know is what time the police turned up. Could they have arrived shortly before me? I had assumed they'd been there some time, or at least an hour, but perhaps not. And when I rang Mike, I think all he said to me was, 'I'll be home in a few minutes.' He didn't say where he was coming from, I just assumed he was on his way back from Southampton. A wrong assumption, by all accounts.

'It seems that you were the last person to see Lyn Smith alive, with the exception of your husband,' DS Cargo says.

I'm about to refute that, because how do they know that Mike saw Linette, but then I think better of it.

'Please tell us again the nature of that conversation.'

'Linette had lost her pig. She wanted to know if I'd seen it, and I said no. She was complaining that Thomas Adler had been playing with his drone again, and she was worried that it might have spooked the pig.'

I wonder if I should say anything about Linette telling me that Mike and Josie were having an affair, but then decide that wouldn't be sensible information to volunteer right now. They might think that I shot the messenger, so to speak.

'Did you speak to Thomas Adler?'

'Yes. But not on that day. I've spoken to him about his drone before. Was the pig ever found?' I ask. In amongst the horror, I've forgotten about the poor pig.

'Not to our knowledge,' Cathy Dopler says, glancing at her colleague.

'Let's recap.' Phil Cargo leans forwards and puts his elbows on the table. It makes me want to shrink further back into my chair. 'You left for Croydon at approximately midday and arrived at Fawcett Bros Repairs garage shortly after 1 p.m.'

'I think so.'

'That tallies with automatic number-plate recognition that places your car in Croydon. You were at the garage for barely five minutes before heading back home again.'

'Yes.'

'Yet in that short time period of just over two hours, Lyn Smith was brutally murdered. It seems rather convenient that you were out of the way then, doesn't it?'

'What? No. It was just a coincidence. How was I to know that Linette was going to be killed then?'

'Unless you were complicit and your husband wanted you

out of the way.' DS Cargo tilts his head to one side and raises one eyebrow.

'My husband didn't kill her, and I had nothing to do with it.' My voice is getting louder, and I can't restrain my agitation. Perhaps that's why I needed a solicitor. They might not have goaded me so much if I weren't alone. 'Is there anything else?' I ask, determined to get out of this place as soon as possible.

'Yes. Please, can you tell me about your marriage with Mike?'

I grit my teeth. 'What about it?'

'Were you arguing?'

'No, it was all fine.'

'Except it wasn't, was it? Otherwise, he wouldn't have been having an affair with Josie Abbott.'

'I didn't know about that. It was a shock,' I say, feeling a wave of shame. Is the implication that I was a bad wife?

'Were you having an affair?'

'No,' I say, feeling indignant. 'Absolutely not, and Mike's fling with Josie was only short-lived. He is very apologetic about it.'

Phil Cargo and Cathy Dopler glance at each other, and my stomach clenches again in the knowledge that they might know something I don't. Perhaps the affair wasn't really over.

'Was your husband ever violent towards you?'

'No, absolutely not. He's a gentle man. He won't even kill a spider.'

'Tell us about Mike's work,' Cathy Dopler says.

'I'm sure he can tell you that himself. He's an architect for a commercial firm. He's good at his job and works long hours.'

'But you were also an architect, weren't you?'

I nod.

'In fact, you were his boss at one time. How did that feel,

giving up work and watching your husband rise to the top of his profession whilst you were stuck at home?' Phil Cargo asks.

I open and close my mouth. I can't believe he's asking such an impertinent question. Is he implying that I might have been jealous of Mike, that I resented staying at home? Yes, of course I've had my moments, but ultimately, it was my choice. And it will be my choice if I return to the workplace.

Cathy Dopler leans towards me. 'We just need to understand the dynamics of your relationship, Isobel. It's standard questioning.'

So the good cop, bad cop routine that we see on the television is an accurate reflection of real life. 'I was fine about quitting work. Our son is on the spectrum, and I needed to be there for him. It may seem naïve to you, but I had no idea our marriage was in trouble.'

I grind my teeth together and glance up at the ceiling. It's made up of tiled blocks, and one near the centre has a large brown stain. I don't want to be here. I don't want any more of this humiliating questioning, and I remember what the policeman said at the beginning of this interview. It was voluntary. I take a deep breath and then ask with as steady a voice as I can muster, 'Can I go now, please?'

'DC Dopler?' Cargo asks, glancing sideways at his colleague.

She nods her head.

'In which case you're free to go for now. We may need you to return for further questioning.'

'I've told you everything I know,' I say.

I FEEL like I'm unravelling on the way home. There's a lot of traffic, and for a moment, I can't work out why. It isn't until I drive past a garden centre with a massive, gaudily decorated

Christmas tree that I remember we're just days away from Christmas, supposedly the happiest time of the year. I weave slightly across a lane on the dual carriageway. A transit van hoots at me, and as the driver passes, he sticks his finger up in the air. I know it's silly, but it's the final straw. I can't stop sobbing, and my vision is becoming so blurry I can barely see. For a split second, I don't care. Perhaps it would be easier if I disappear. But then I think of my children, and I know I need to look after myself. It could well be that I'm the only parent they'll have, and they will need me. I pull over into a layby to wipe my tears and blow my nose. As I'm sitting there, with traffic roaring past, I think about what the police said. Mike told them that he was planting tulip bulbs. But Mike planted tulip bulbs in October, making sure he did that before the first frost. I suppose he might have been worried that the pig had eaten them all, and he planted some more, but why would he plant them in pots? Mike always digs the bulbs straight into our borders. I've been hankering after some containers to place on the patio for ages, but Mike has resisted, saying they would look twee. Planting bulbs in containers in December doesn't make sense unless, of course, it was the first excuse that came to Mike's mind when questioned. That thought makes my stomach cramp. If Mike wasn't planting bulbs in the shed, what was he doing?

When I get home, I lock the car and walk straight around the house, through the side gate, and into the garden. The lawn is sodden, and my leather boots squelch as I walk towards the garden shed. It's still taped off with police evidence tape, and I know I'm not meant to go inside. I walk right up to the shed and peer through the window. The light is low, and it's hard to make out what's inside. I can see Mike's woodwork table, and on it is a large wooden bowl. I gasp because I know exactly what that bowl is, or at least what it's made from. Last year, we lost an oak tree in a particularly fierce autumn gale. I asked Mike if he could make anything from the wood, ideally a large fruit bowl like the ones we saw on holiday in Italy. He had laughed and said oaks may be beautiful trees, but the wood isn't suitable for carving because it splits and splinters. He had explained to me that maple is ideal, and perhaps he'd get hold of some one day and carve me a bowl. It looks as if that's what he was doing, making me a fruit bowl as a Christmas present. I suppose that's why he didn't tell me he'd come home early. He was using the rare time I was out of the house to finish my Christmas gift.

23

Nothing adds up. Why did Mike tell the police he was potting up bulbs? And where had he nipped out to that afternoon? What I want to know is where were all the other Close neighbours when Linette was killed? And why was Wilson running hell for leather out of The Close and onto the lane in the middle of the night? I am convinced that Keith Walker has got a bigger role to play in all of this than just the grieving father, husband and brother-in-law. For starters, why has he moved back to The Close? I'd have thought that he would want to be as far away as possible from this place that has brought his family so much grief.

To my surprise, I'm hungry now, so after feeding Lupin, I make myself some toast, my staple diet at the moment. I think about Mona. I remember how she had a black eye once, and she gave me some cock and bull story about walking into a bathroom cabinet. I thought it odd at the time, but Mike told me not to get involved, and as she was always a bit standoffish towards me, I didn't make any effort. Was Keith Walker beating his wife, and did he lay into his boys too? And I can't work out why Linette moved into their house. I suppose she could have genuinely needed somewhere to live, but why spin us that yarn about having recently divorced her husband and telling us how much she loved the house and wanted to buy it? The divorce bit might be true, but I still don't understand why she didn't tell any of us that she was Mona's sister. Perhaps she had uncovered whatever Keith was up to, and she confronted him, and he killed her in a fit of fury, but if so, why weren't his prints everywhere, and why did he plant the hammer in Mike's shed?

The police may be convinced that they've got their man, but I can't tally up everything I know about my gentle husband with the horrific deeds they claim he's done. I need to eliminate everyone on The Close one by one, and I want to start with Keith Walker. I know he's home because I saw him and his younger son, Ollie, unloading something from their car earlier on. I find a box of biscuits at the back of my larder cupboard, and I wrap it in some gaudy red and gold Christmas wrapping paper.

But first, I do what I had assumed I'd never do again and walk over to Josie's house. It's strange how in moments like this one notices things that normally get missed. The berries on the holly bush at the top of our drive are a vibrant, shining scarlet, the only strong colour on this cold, damp and grey day. There's a branch from an old beech tree that needs cutting back, and I'm startled as a grey squirrel jumps from one tree to another. When did I last see a squirrel? They're normally the scourge of our garden but tend to be reclusive at this time of year. I don't blame them. I inhale deeply as I walk down Josie's drive. They have two large potholes at the top, and I kick a little piece of gravel the size of a walnut. It bounces down their drive. Josie's car is parked at the front of the house, and I can hear children's shouts coming from the yard between their house and barn. I feel a momentary stab of jealousy towards Josie that stops me still. If it weren't for her, Mike wouldn't be in this mess. He wouldn't have had an affair, he wouldn't have been in her car that night, he wouldn't be incarcerated in a cell, and our family would still be looking forwards to a happy Christmas.

Josie owes me a lot, so I pick up speed and stride towards her back door. Their house is looking downtrodden with paint peeling off some of the window frames, and a broken roof tile lies shattered on the gravel near the door. I can see her children playing, hitting a ball backwards and forwards using small rackets. I wave at them, but they ignore me, so I stand in front of the door and ring the bell.

When Josie opens the door, she looks ragged, her hair still unwashed, a tea towel flung over an arm, wearing her ubiquitous jeans and holey jumper. Her eyes widen when she sees me, and I see shame in them and perhaps a little fear too. I do away with any niceties.

'I want you to come with me to talk to Keith Walker. I've got a box of biscuits to give him.'

'Why?' she asks.

'Because I think you're right and Keith is the pivot in this mess. I want to talk to him, and you owe it to me to be there too.'

'I'm in the middle of—'

'I don't care, Josie.' I'm surprised at myself. Only a few days ago, I was a little scared of Josie, wanting to stay out of her way. Now, she is the weak one, and I'm going to make sure that she does what I ask. 'I want to look him in the eyes and find out if he's set up Mike.'

She nods. 'Wait a minute, and I'll get my coat.'

She disappears into the house, leaving me on the doorstep, but reappears just a few seconds later, shrugging on her Barbour. As we walk past the yard, she tells her eldest child to be sensible, that she's going to the Walkers' house for a few minutes. We stride side by side.

'I never liked Keith Walker and felt sorry for Mona being married to that thug,' Josie says.

But like me, Josie did nothing to try to reach out to Mona, to offer her refuge if she needed it, to be a shoulder to cry on after the death of her son. It's not surprising that Josie couldn't bring herself to do that, as guilt must have weighed so heavily on her. I, on the other hand, had no excuse.

'He won't do anything to us, will he?' Josie asks. She looks as if she's shrunk slightly, and her jacket looks too big. I suppose she's been like me and unable to eat properly for the last week or so. Or perhaps more like seven months, ever since she hit Wilson.

I can't admit it to Josie, but I'm terrified, and I hesitate in front of the electronic doorbell. But I remind myself that Keith is at home with Ollie, and it's daylight, and surely, he won't do anything violent in front of his son. Although perhaps that's exactly what he did to Wilson, which is why the young man was running.

'Do you want me to?' Josie says, eyeing the plastic bell.

I don't answer but stab it with my index finger, keeping it pressed for longer than necessary. I listen to the ugly electronic song but can't place the tune.

The door swings open, and Keith is standing there dressed in a short-sleeved black T-shirt, his thick biceps on show, bare, callused feet sticking out under his light blue jeans.

He scowls at us. 'What the hell are you doing here?'

'I've got a box of biscuits for you, and I just wanted to ask you—'

He cuts me off, stabbing his finger towards us. 'Your husband, and you, Josie Abbott, killed my son, and I never want to set eyes on either of you ever again. And I certainly don't want any gifts from you.'

'But—'

'Get off my property. If either of you set foot here again, I won't be responsible for my actions!'

It's now or never. 'Where were you when Linette was killed?'

'What?' He looks shocked, his jaw slack and his forehead furrowed. 'How can you even ask me that?' he hisses through chipped teeth.

He slams the door shut, so hard that the air slices across my face, and even the paving slabs I'm standing on reverberate. Josie and I look at each other.

'That went well,' she says sarcastically.

I ignore Josie and remove the wrapped biscuit box from the plastic bag and place it on the doorstep. Josie has turned around as if to walk away, but I hear something. I stand totally still.

'What is it?' Josie asks, turning as she realises I'm not following her.

'He's crying,' I whisper.

I feel like a charlatan, a voyeur and a horrible human being. Keith is on the other side of that door, sobbing like a baby. All I have done is add to his heartache, accuse him of murdering his sister-in-law, and on what grounds? Because he looks like a boxer, because he was always standoffish towards all of us neighbours, because Mona had a black eye and then took her own life. And most of all, because I'm desperate to put the blame on anyone else rather than my own husband. Those sobs pierce me, and I have to get away from here, right now. I was wrong to come and wrong to bring Josie with me.

'Where are you going?' Josie asks as she trots to keep up with me.

'Home,' I say.

It's only when I'm back in my familiar kitchen with my arms around Lupin's soft neck do I let the emotions flow. The tears come again, as does the helplessness of my situation. Could the police be right? Could Mike have killed Linette? I shake my head and sniff loudly. No. Mike hasn't got it in him, and I'm not sure that Keith does either. That leaves the other neighbours—the Quinns, Jack, and Thomas Adler.

24

I can't stop thinking about the day Linette died. The day I found that garage invoice. When I was on my way out of The Close, I saw Linette, who was stressing because her pig had disappeared. I wonder whatever became of the pig. Did someone find it and give it a new home? And then it hits me. *Wham.* Linette said that she feared Twiglet had escaped because she got spooked by Thomas Adler's drone. Drones record video, don't they? Could Thomas Adler have recorded something relevant on his drone? Perhaps he saw what Linette did after talking to me, or it captured Mike in his shed, or even the killer going into Linette's house. If so, would he have told the police? Surely, he would have done, even if he implicated himself by using the drone illegally. There's only one way I can find out, and that's by going to see him.

After wiping my face and blinking away the tears, once again, I'm striding down The Close towards Thomas Adler's imposing barn-style house. And once again, I'm nervous. What if he killed Linette? Of everyone in The Close, he is the most likely. After all, Linette rejected his advances, and she seemed to know things about his dodgy business dealings. Am I putting myself at risk by confronting him? Should I have demanded that Josie accompany me here too? Standing with my back to his house, I take my phone out of my pocket and select the *Voice Memos* app. I press the round, red button to record and slip the phone back into my coat pocket. I just hope that the microphone will be strong enough to pick up whatever Thomas is saying.

I walk up to the front door and press the buzzer. Thomas appears quickly and swings the door open. He does away with all niceties. 'Is it true that your husband has been arrested for Linette's murder?'

'Yes, but he didn't do it. Can I come in?'

'No.' He crosses his arms.

'Do you have any drone footage from the day Linette was killed?'

'No.'

'Did you fly your drone that day?'

'Nope.'

'Come on, Thomas. I know that's not true. Linette was worried your drone might have spooked her pig.'

'I didn't fly the drone that day.'

'I'm sorry, but I don't believe you. I know that you did, and if you refuse to share the footage with me, I'm going to tell the police.'

He mutters something under his breath that I can't make out, a profanity probably.

'All right, but we're going to look at it together. And I'm only doing this because you're blackmailing me. I've had a warning from the police about the damned drone, and they'll confiscate it and fine me if I fly it over other people's houses again. I've already looked at the footage, and there's nothing on it.'

'In which case you won't mind if I have a look too.'

He scowls but stands to one side. 'You'd better come in.'

My heart is pumping now, as I'm wondering if I'm walking into the lion's den. He could easily kill me in this big house and dispose of my body without anyone being the wiser. 'I've told my mum that I'm here talking to you,' I say, hoping that might deter him from attacking me.

He throws me a weird glance. 'What, you have to check in with your mother before you do anything?' he asks. 'I thought you were late thirties, early forties, maybe.'

That's galling. He's made me older than I really am. I follow him inside, through the full-height living room with its massive ceiling-to-floor windows, and the uber trendy black leather and chrome semicircular sofas, and the largest television I have ever seen above a glass-panelled fireplace. We walk along a short corridor, and then Thomas leads me into his office.

There are four huge computer screens set up on desks arranged in an arc shape. Two of the screens roll through what looks like computer code. One screen is black, and the other has a screen saver—an aerial photo of the roof of this house and Thomas's garden, no doubt captured by the drone. This doesn't look like the office of someone peddling porn as Linette suggested, but then again, he'd hardly have his wares on display. He reaches down into a pull-out drawer underneath one of the desks and takes out a small box with a large pile of SD cards in it. He flicks through them and then removes one and slots it into the rear of the Mac with the screensaver. He wheels his office chair so it's in front of the screen.

'Do you want to sit?' he asks.

'I'll stand.' I don't want Thomas leering over my shoulder, breathing down my neck.

He takes the seat, types something rapidly into the keyboard, and then the video appears, the fifteenth

December at 12.14. The drone lifts off in Thomas's garden, rising upwards vertically and surprisingly quickly. It hovers over the top of the conifers at the bottom of Thomas's garden and then veers off to the right, towards our house. I hold my breath as the corner of our garden shed comes into view, but then it swerves away, upwards and over the field behind the house.

'Well, obviously, I'm not the murderer, am I?' Thomas laughs. 'I couldn't be flying the drone and killing off our poor neighbour at the same time.'

I don't find that comment the slightest bit funny and take a step away from Thomas. Thomas speeds up the video as the drone flies up over the fields, towards the village, swooping backwards and forwards, travelling surprisingly long distances, and then eventually, it veers around again back to The Close, and I can see that Mike's car is parked in our drive. I check the time and date stamp. 2.14 p.m. So he did get home very early. How I wish he hadn't. The drone then flies back over Thomas Adler's garden and is static for a while. Thomas fast-forwards just for a couple of seconds, and then the drone is up above the woodland where I walk Lupin. It looks so dense and dark in there, nothing visible on the ground below, and then, just when I expect the drone to descend back towards Thomas's property, it veers to the left, and I catch a glimpse of Mr Quinn in his garden. The drone then swerves again back towards Thomas's.

'Hold on a mo. What was that?' he asks.

'What?'

'I'm going to rewind and play it in slow motion.'

I'm not sure what he's referring to, as I didn't see anything out of the ordinary.

'You know, I've watched this footage three times, and it's only now I've spotted it,' Thomas murmurs more to himself than to me. He presses play again just as the drone hovers over Mr Quinn, and sets it to slow motion. 'Look!' Thomas says excitedly, pointing at the screen. 'What the hell is he doing?'

The light bounces off the spade Mr Quinn is holding. 'He's digging a hole.'

'And can you see what's next to it?'

I peer at the screen as Thomas zooms in. The image is too blurry to make anything out.

'I think it's the bloody pig! I think he was digging a hole to bury the pig in!' Thomas exclaims. He rewinds by a couple of seconds and plays it again at a very slow speed. 'Is the animal standing up or lying down? I can't tell if it's dead or alive. But look at how furiously he's digging. He must have killed the thing and then is digging a grave in his garden. Quinn is strong for an old geezer, isn't he?'

'I'm not sure. It's hard to tell exactly what he's doing.'

'It's definitely the pig. Look!' He traces his finger across the screen, but I'm still not convinced. It could be a bush. 'We've got to tell the police,' Thomas says. 'I mean, what if he killed the pig and then killed its owner? Perhaps your Mikey isn't guilty after all.'

I don't say anything for a long moment, and eventually, Thomas speaks again.

'This could change everything,' he says. 'I'll drop this footage off with the police first thing tomorrow morning.'

I'm not comfortable. Yes, Mr Quinn is certainly digging a hole, and it is conceivable that the pig is standing there next to him, but it would need a much more expert eye than mine.

'It's not *definitely* the pig,' I say. 'And just because he's digging a hole, it doesn't mean he's going to be putting the pig inside it, assuming that's an animal and not a bush or something.'

'No, but it's worth showing this to the cops, and if it is the pig, well, that makes Mr Quinn a porcine murderer at the least.'

'I do think this is a bit tenuous,' I say, stepping farther away from Thomas.

'I disagree. I've watched a lot of drone footage, and I'm ninety-nine percent sure that's the pig there. The police can be the arbiters.'

I follow Thomas to his front door, wondering what it's like rattling around all alone in this big house. It's not until I'm walking home that I wonder whether Thomas Adler could be using the drone footage as an alibi. At one point, the video was static, and he fast-forwarded it. I'm not sure for exactly how long, but he could have edited that, and what if it gave him enough time to park the drone and then nip over to Linette's house and bash her over the head before returning to fly it again? It could be feasible. But if so, what was his motive for killing Linette? She mentioned his dodgy internet business. Perhaps she had found out something very damning and was about to expose him. He must be minting it from his business because how else can he afford a Lamborghini and the new Tesla? Perhaps he needs the big house because he's storing things there? Drugs, arms or other illegal things. But that's ridiculous. It's not like we get big trucks driving up and down The Close. No, it's more likely to be his internet business dealings. Perhaps he's into cryptocurrency or some dodgy things on the dark web. Alternatively, perhaps he was violent towards Linette because she rejected his advances. I think back to that drinks party, which seems like years ago but is only a few weeks past, and how they were dancing suggestively towards each other.

And then I think about the implications for Mr Quinn. Was he really burying the pig? Even if he was, it doesn't mean he actually killed it. But if he did, well, that was callous and extreme, but I can see how he might have been pushed to violent measures by the destructive animal. The Quinns are obsessed with their garden, which is always totally pristine, worthy of horticultural prizes. If he found the pig digging up his beautiful borders, then I could imagine him bashing it over the head with a shovel. Extreme and horrible, but possibly understandable considering how it destroyed both our garden and the Abbotts' field. I wonder if Mr Quinn might be prosecuted for cruelty to animals, and if so, what would happen to Mrs Quinn? Perhaps I should warn Mr Quinn that the police will be asking him about the pig, telling him that Thomas Adler intends to show them his drone footage. Or perhaps I should just keep my head down and let the police get on with their investigation. After all, if I hadn't gone to the police with that garage receipt, Mike wouldn't be incarcerated in a cell right now. Or perhaps he would have been anyway. The police might have searched our shed regardless.

I vacillate. I don't want to be that nosy neighbour sticking her oar in where it's not needed, but on the other hand, I can't stand by and let more people get hurt. I need to know the truth. If Mike is guilty, then he can rot in jail for the rest of his life, but if he isn't, then it's up to me to see that justice is done.

25

I mull it over for hours and then decide that Mr Quinn should be warned about the drone footage. Although Thomas is adamant the drone shows the pig, I'm not sure, and just because Mr Quinn was digging a hole, it is a huge leap to think that he might have been digging a grave for the animal. I put on an extra sweater and a thick padded coat and step outside. It's starting to snow, so I pull my hood up and shove my hands into my pockets. It's nearly ten p.m., and he may be in bed by now, but it's worth a knock on their door. I shiver as I walk towards the Quinns' house. There are lights on in several windows, both upstairs and downstairs.

I knock on the back door.

'Who's there?' Mr Quinn's voice comes through the door.

'It's me, Isobel Floyd.'

I listen to the unlatching of the door and turning of keys as the door opens. Mr Quinn is wearing tartan slippers and a thick navy jumper.

'I'm sorry it's so late. There's something urgent I need to discuss with you.'

'Yes,' he says.

It's really cold now, and the snow is coming down heavily. I shiver. 'Any chance that I could come in?'

He sighs and then opens the door fully. I step inside. He closes it gently behind me.

'What's so important?'

'It's about Thomas Adler's drone footage.'

'Can you keep your voice down? Mrs Quinn is asleep.'

'Yes, of course. Sorry. Thomas has some drone footage from the day that Linette died, and it looks as if you're in your garden, and you've dug a big hole, and the pig is tied up next to it. I mean, obviously, if you did kill the pig, then we all understand why because it was a terrible nuisance.' I feel like I'm wittering, but Mr Quinn is staring at me unblinking, and it's extremely unnerving.

'You see, the thing is,' I carry on, 'Thomas plans on taking the footage to the police tomorrow, and they'll likely question you about it, so I just wanted to give you the heads-up.'

Mr Quinn blinks very slowly but otherwise remains motionless. 'I appreciate that, Isobel. It's good of you to let me know. Would you like a cup of tea? You look like you're frozen solid.'

'Um, I don't want to keep you,' I say, feeling quite uncomfortable now.

'No, no. It would be good to have a chat about all the shenanigans that have gone on in The Close and the repercussions from what happened to poor Linette. I heard on the grapevine that your Mike has been arrested. Is that true?' He doesn't give me time to answer. 'Come and have a seat in the sitting room whilst I put the kettle on.'

Their sitting room is old-fashioned with an olive-green sofa and two matching chairs. There is a brick fireplace with an electric fire standing in front of it, and in the corner of the room there is an old box-like television, the sort my grandparents used to have when I was a child. I see the mauve crocheted throw that Linette mentioned, and I feel a stab of sorrow for our dead neighbour.

'Take a pew,' Mr Quinn says, so I remove my coat and sit on the sofa but wish I hadn't because it's bitterly cold in here. The electric fire must have been on earlier because there's a lingering smell of burned dust.

'How do you take your tea?'

'Just a drop of milk, please.'

Mr Quinn walks out of the room and back into the kitchen, where I hear him rattling some china. I'm about to get up to look at some of the pictures on the wall when there's a swishing of air.

With a fright, I turn to look at the door and am shocked to see Mrs Quinn there. She's wearing a long-sleeved blue cotton nightdress that can't give any protection against the cold in this house. Her grey hair is standing on end, and her eyes are open wide, glancing wildly from side to side.

'Are you all right?' I ask, but she interrupts me by waving her right arm around and placing the index finger of her left hand across her lips.

'Shh!' she whispers. She looks agitated, manic even. 'You've got to help me!' she whispers.

'What's the matter?' I get up from the sofa and take a step towards her.

'You have to believe me!' she says in an urgent low voice, and then a clawlike hand reaches out and grasps my upper arm. 'We need to get out before Douglas gets back! Come on!'

'It's all right, Mrs Quinn,' I say gently. 'You're perfectly safe. It must have been a shock seeing me here this late in the evening.' The poor woman's dementia has evidently got worse, and I'm sorry to have upset her.

'No, we have to get out! You have to believe me! He killed her!'

I stop still, but Mrs Quinn is still tugging at me, her nails digging into my skin.

'Who killed who?' I ask, and then I go icy cold. Perhaps Mrs Quinn is telling the truth. Perhaps she is perfectly lucid, and Mr Quinn has lured me into their living room intending for me to meet the same grisly end as Linette.

'Doug killed Alice!' she whispers.

I let out a breath I didn't know I was holding. 'Who is Alice, Mrs Quinn? Is that your name for the pig?'

'What? No, you silly woman. It's my daughter. Douglas killed her and buried her in the garden, and then he killed that woman next door, Linette! You'll be next if we don't get out, right now!'

A lump gets stuck in my throat, and I stand stock-still. Could she be right? Am I really in danger? But then I hear footsteps, and Mr Quinn appears in the doorway.

'I thought I heard you, Yvonne love. What are you doing up? You're meant to be in bed.'

Mrs Quinn steps backwards, treading on my foot. 'Don't touch me!' she says to her husband. Her voice quivers, and her eyes dart from side to side. Her breathing is rapid and shallow. I think she's genuinely afraid of her husband, and it's pitiful to see.

'Come along, Yvonne. We don't want to make a fuss and scare Isobel. Let's get you back to bed.'

He reaches out for her, but she flinches and tries to cower behind me. I feel such pity for this woman who one moment is totally lucid and the next is acting like this. I have no doubt that her fear is genuine.

'It's okay, Mrs Quinn,' I say, attempting to stroke her arm, but she's trying to grab me, her fingers gripping my arm.

'We need to get away!' she says, her eyes wide with terror.

'I'm sorry, Isobel. Sorry that you need to see my wife like

this. She's getting increasingly confused these days, and it's quite hard to manage.'

'I can see that.'

'Come along, Yvonne. It's bedtime, dear.' Mr Quinn puts an arm around her shoulders, but she pushes him away with a surprising force.

'You and me,' she says, gesticulating at me. 'We need to get out of here!' she yells. And then she becomes quite hysterical, her limbs everywhere, pushing and punching Mr Quinn.

'Calm down, love!' he says, trying to restrain her. This is pitiful to watch.

'Go, woman! Save yourself!' she screeches at me, and for a split second I wonder if there's some truth in what she's saying. I scoot behind Mr Quinn so I can get to the doorway and make my escape when, suddenly, there's a crash. I spin around, and to my utter horror, Mrs Quinn is standing there, totally dishevelled in her nightdress, holding the china table lamp that until a moment ago stood on the sideboard. Mr Quinn is slumped on the floor at her feet.

'What have you done?' I exclaim.

She looks at me, her eyes blank, and then she lets the lamp slip to the floor. The white and blue porcelain base splits in two, yet the bulb and the lampshade remain intact. That single moment seems to extend and extend until I suddenly come to my senses and drop to my knees on the floor next to Mr Quinn. Has she killed him?

His eyes are closed, but he is breathing, and his chest is rising and falling. Then there's a piercing scream as Mrs Quinn realises what she's done; then she's pushing me out of the way, cradling her husband, tears flowing. 'Have I killed him?' she sobs. She's rocking backwards and forwards. 'I didn't mean to kill him, really I didn't, but he's been keeping me here as a prisoner, and I just needed to get away. And you needed to get away too. I didn't mean to kill him. Wake up, Doug! Wake up!'

'Shush,' I say, surprised how calm I'm feeling in the face of this horror. 'You haven't killed your husband. I think he's just got a concussion.'

I don't know if she hears me because she continues sobbing and rocking and cradling his head in her lap. I hurry over to the sofa and grab my coat, removing my mobile phone and jabbing in 999.

'Emergency. Which service do you require?'

'An ambulance. And the police too.'

I give the operator the address, and I think there's a pause, as if this stranger recognises it, which perhaps she does because Linette's murder has been featured on all the news. I put the phone on loudspeaker, and she talks me through how to put Mr Quinn in the recovery position, which is difficult because Mrs Quinn simply won't let go of her husband. Mrs Quinn is sobbing hysterically.

'I'm going to stay on the line with you until the ambulance arrives,' the lady on the phone says, and I reckon I have never been quite so grateful to a complete stranger. The next few minutes seem to stretch into hours, during which Mr Quinn remains concussed on the floor, his eyes closed and his body relaxed. Mrs Quinn's hysteria subsides into whimpering. And then, at long last, I hear the sounds of a siren, and I have never been so relieved to hear them get louder and louder. When I see the blue lights flashing through the net curtains, I rush towards the front door, unbolting it and pulling it open. There is a thin layer of snow on the ground, less than I had anticipated, although sufficient for the paramedics to leave clearly delineated footprints from their sturdy boots as they hurry to the door.

And then they take over, one paramedic taking control of Mrs Quinn and the other appraising the prone Mr Quinn.

The paramedic talking to Mrs Quinn turns to me. 'I've called for backup, but can you sit on the sofa with the lady so I can help my colleague?'

'Yes, of course,' I say. I take Mrs Quinn's hand and sit down next to her, throwing that mauve throw over her shoulders and wrapping her up in it. She's whimpering quietly now, her eyes closed. Just as the two paramedics are about to roll Mr Quinn onto a stretcher, there's a knock on the front door. I leave Mrs Quinn and hurry to open it. There are two policemen and a further two paramedics. I lead them all into the small living room, which feels cramped with so many people. They have got Mr Quinn onto the stretcher, and I watch as they carry him to one of the waiting ambulances. The other paramedics rush to the sofa to talk to Mrs Quinn.

'And you are?' one of the policemen asks me.

'Sorry, Isobel Floyd. A next-door neighbour.'

'Is there somewhere we can go so you can fill us in on what has happened here?'

I'm trembling now, the shock catching up with me. I lead the policeman into the Quinns' kitchen, where Mr Quinn placed two mugs of tea on a tray. They'll be cold by now.

I sit down at the kitchen table, as does the policeman, but before I can say anything, the other policeman walks in.

'One paramedic crew is taking Mr Quinn to hospital with suspected concussion and possible bleed on the brain. The other crew is staying here to assess Mrs Quinn.'

'Mrs Quinn has dementia,' I say.

'That's what we assumed. She's incoherent at the moment. They might need to give her a tranquiliser to calm her down. They'll run a full assessment.'

'Can you talk us through what happened?' the policeman asks.

'Is there any possibility of talking to DC Cathy Dopler or DS Cargo?'

'DS Cargo has been informed that there's been another incident on The Close, and he's on his way.'

'Actually, I'm here.' Cargo strides into the room, wearing a snow-dusted black jacket and blue jeans. That was quick. I wonder if the police have an asterisk next to any incident happening at our address. 'Thanks, gentlemen. I'll take over.'

He pulls out a chair and plonks himself in it. 'So, Mrs Floyd, we meet again and somewhat sooner than I had anticipated. Please explain exactly what's happened here this evening.'

'I came over to check on the Quinns. You know, with this bad weather, I just wanted to be sure they were all right.'

He raises an eyebrow, and I just pray he doesn't see through my lie. I can hardly tell him the truth that I wanted to give Mr Quinn the heads-up about Thomas's video footage before Thomas took it to the police. If Mr Quinn was doing something dodgy, it would make it seem like I was in cahoots with the Quinns, tipping them off that the police were about to be made aware of what Mr Quinn did to the pig.

'And were the Quinns okay?' DS Cargo asks.

'Yes. Mr Quinn invited me in and was making me some tea when Mrs Quinn came into the living room, dressed in her nightie, as you see her now. She seemed very distressed and confused and was saying that I needed to leave with her immediately, as we were both in danger.'

'Danger from what?'

'I think she was referring to her husband. She talked about someone called Alice, and she said Mr Quinn killed her. I wondered whether she was referring to the pig. I mean, Linette called the pig Twiglet, but perhaps Mrs Quinn got confused and called her Alice.'

'The pig?' DS Cargo frowns.

'Was Linette's pig ever found?'

'Not that I'm aware of.'

'You see, I think Mr Quinn might have killed it and buried it in his garden.'

'And what leads you to that conclusion?'

'Thomas Adler has some drone footage from the day Linette was killed. It shows Mr Quinn digging a large hole in the garden. It's a bit blurry, but it might be the pig. Thomas planned on dropping the footage off with you tomorrow.'

'He's withheld evidence,' DS Cargo mutters.

'No,' I say hurriedly. 'He didn't spot it until we watched the footage together, and I guess he didn't want to get into trouble because he's already had one warning for illegally flying his drone.'

DS Cargo harrumphs. 'And this Alice. Who is she?'

'Mrs Quinn said she was their daughter, but I didn't even know they had a daughter.'

DS Cargo frowns. 'You claim that Mrs Quinn hit Mr Quinn over the head with a lamp. Talk me through exactly what happened.'

And so I do. He stares at me intently. 'You do know that we'll be able to verify this through fingerprints.'

'Of course I do,' I say. 'I'm telling you the truth! She hit her husband in self-defence, as she genuinely thought he was trying to hurt her.'

'And you say that she was distraught after hitting him.'

'Yes. I honestly think she had no idea how hard she hit him. It was like she was having a psychotic episode.'

'All right. Please stay here until I return.'

And so I sit there, in the antiquated kitchen, shivering and wondering what sort of hellish mess I have got myself involved in. It's about ten minutes until DS Cargo returns and sits down again.

'Mrs Quinn has calmed down now, but she seems to have little recollection of what happened. Please explain to me exactly where in the garden you think you saw the pig.'

'Next to the tall leylandii trees on the border of the Quinns' garden and the Walkers' garden. The trees have been topped recently.'

DS Cargo gets up. 'Please stay here.' Once again, he walks out of the room.

DS CARGO IS GONE for a long time. I fiddle with my phone, but I don't have the appetite to go onto social media or play some mindless game. I just want to go home. Lupin is alone, and I am in desperate need of a brandy and a hot bath. Perhaps they'll get that policewoman Monica to come over to accompany me. I wouldn't mind that; I just want to get out of this creepy house. I play with the conker in my pocket and then stand up to look at the few items on the open shelves. There's a vase with a small, dusty dried-flower arrangement, but similar to in the living room, there are no photos. No wedding pictures or photos of parents long deceased. Just crockery and a pile of unopened post.

When Phil Cargo returns, I ask, 'How is Mrs Quinn?'

'She appears calmer, although still very upset.'

'Will you be taking her to the hospital or to the police station?'

'It depends on the paramedics' assessment. I might need —' But DS Cargo doesn't finish his sentence because a young man hurries into the room.

'Sir, we need to call for forensics.'

26

D S Cargo hurries out of the kitchen, and I have to wait another long fifteen minutes until he reappears. His face is stern and pale.

'Is there anyone who can stay with Mrs Quinn tonight?' Phil Cargo asks.

'I'm afraid I don't know the Quinns well enough. I don't think they have any close family.' I hesitate for a moment as I recall my promise to myself to look out for my neighbours. 'But she can stay with me, if you like, so long as that's allowed.'

'Let me have a word with the paramedics.'

'So she won't be locked up?' I ask.

He looks at me askance. 'If what you say is correct, then she acted in self-defence. I don't think it's in anyone's interest to lock up an elderly woman with dementia in a police cell, do you?'

'No, of course not. That's why I offered for her to stay with me.'

He nods and leaves the room. And so it is that about an hour later, Mrs Quinn is tucked into the bed in our spare room, the bed that was last slept in by my husband. By the time I turn the light off, she's already fast asleep, drugged up with whatever the paramedics gave her to calm her down.

I don't sleep so easily. When I hear a creak, I sit bolt upright in bed. Did I do the right thing by inviting her to stay here? After all, she hit her husband over the head, and for all I know, he may have permanent injuries. Could she do the same to me? I strain my ears to listen, but there is silence, so I sink back onto my pillow. I'm aware that some people with dementia hallucinate and might be prone to aggression. It's such a cruel disease, and I'm sad for the woman. She seemed truly broken when she realised she'd felled her husband.

THE NEXT MORNING, I'm up early, so I make a mug of tea and carry it upstairs. I knock gently on the spare bedroom door, wondering if Mrs Quinn will be confused, unsure as to where she is. There's no answer, so I open it gently. The curtains are not fully drawn, and weak morning light seeps through into the room. Mrs Quinn turns her head to look at me, her pale eyes blinking.

'Hello, dear,' she says.

'Do you know where you are?' I ask.

'Yes, dear. I know I did a terrible thing yesterday evening.' She turns her head away from me and stifles a sob. 'How is he? How is my Doug?'

'I don't know,' I say, walking into the room and placing the mug of tea on the bedside table. 'I'm sure the police or the hospital will tell us soon. What would you like for breakfast?'

'Oh, I don't want to put you to any trouble, dear,' she says, wiping her eyes with the back of her mottled hand.

'It's no problem. Shall I make some toast, or would you prefer an egg, or both, perhaps?'

'A piece of toast would be fine. Do I have any clothes?'

'Yes, we packed a little overnight bag for you before we left your house last night.' I point to the small holdall on the floor by the wardrobe.

'Oh, yes, so we did. I'll get dressed, then.'

'Do you need any help?'

'My Douglas likes to fuss over me, but really, I'm quite capable of getting myself ready. There's a bathroom through there, isn't there?' She points to the door to the en-suite.

'Yes,' I say. What a difference to last night. Mrs Quinn seems totally lucid now. 'I'll get us some breakfast. Give us a shout if you need a hand with the stairs.'

'Thank you, dear. You're definitely the nicest neighbour on The Close.'

Mrs Quinn is still upstairs, and I'm buttering some toast when the doorbell rings. Lupin barks, and I hurry to the door.

'Good morning, Mrs Floyd. Can I come in?' It's DS Phil Cargo, and I wonder if he's had any sleep. He looks dishevelled and tired, his face more lined than I recall from last night. I stand back, and he follows me into the kitchen.

'I can confirm that we found human remains in the Quinns' garden.'

'What!' I say, stepping backwards in horror. 'Who is it?'

'That we don't know as of yet. I can also confirm that we have studied Thomas Adler's drone footage, and we have found a hole that was recently dug in the location you both identified.'

'And the pig?' I ask.

'We haven't found the pig, dead or alive.'

'Mrs Quinn talked about an Alice. Could the body you found in her garden be this Alice, her daughter?' I'm utterly horrified that Mrs Quinn might have been telling the truth.

Could Mr Quinn really have been about to murder me? I assumed Mrs Quinn was hallucinating, that it was her illness talking, but perhaps she was telling the truth, and we both really were in danger.

'We will be investigating, of course. In the meantime, I would like to talk to Mrs Quinn. How is she this morning?'

'Much more lucid than last night. I think she's on her way down for some breakfast.'

On cue, Mrs Quinn hobbles into the kitchen. When she sees DS Cargo, her chin wobbles.

'How is he?' She leans against the wall.

'Why don't you come and have a seat at the table?' I say, slipping my arm into hers and leading her across the kitchen. I pull out a chair for her. DS Cargo sits down next to her.

'Your husband is still unconscious,' DS Cargo says.

'No!' she wails, rocking back in her chair.

'He has swelling on the brain, but the medics don't think it's life-threatening. He's in an induced coma now. The thing is, Mrs Quinn, we found the remains of a young woman in your garden. What can you tell me about that?'

'No, no, no!' Mrs Quinn thumps her palms onto the table, making the crockery judder. 'This is all my fault!' She pulls at her thinning hair, and tears course down her cheeks.

'What is your fault?' DS Cargo asks.

'That evening I fell asleep in Linda, Lyn, whatever the dead woman's name is, at her house. That night. I accidentally let slip to her about Alice. I didn't mean to, it's just that sometimes I forget. You know, I make mistakes. I do things I don't mean to because I'm not myself anymore. Doug tells me there's something wrong with me. But that night, I think I told her. I was so worried. I told Doug that I'd let it slip, and that's why he killed the woman. The Linda woman.'

'Linette,' I say quietly.

'Mrs Quinn, this is very important.' DS Cargo leans forwards to talk to her. 'Who is Alice?'

'My baby!' she whispers, her hand over her mouth. She's rocking backwards and forwards again.

'Are you saying that your husband murdered Lyn Smith because you told her about Alice? You knew her as Linette Smith, but her real name was Lyn.'

'Who are you?' she says, her eyes suddenly wild. 'Who are you? And where am I?' She grabs the mug of tea and tips it all over the table. Hot tea drenches the cloth and pours to the floor.

I stand up quickly and grab a roll of paper towel, dabbing the hot liquid before it drips down onto Mrs Quinn's lap.

'Mrs Quinn,' DS Cargo says, 'are you saying that your husband murdered Lyn Smith?'

'Go away, you horrible man!' She jabs her finger at the detective. 'I don't know who you are, but I don't want you here. Get out!'

'Who is Alice, Mrs Quinn?' DS Cargo asks.

'Alice, oh, Alice.' Mrs Quinn sobs, rocking backwards and forwards. 'What about Alice?' she mutters. The older lady is crying now, hot tears running down her cheeks, her distress hard to witness. I kneel down next to her and grasp her hand, but she pushes me away.

'Did your husband kill Alice, Mrs Quinn?' DS Cargo persists with his questioning, but I wish he'd leave off now. Mrs Quinn is pitching backwards and forwards faster and faster, and then she puts her hands over her ears.

'What should we do?' I ask the policeman quietly.

'I'll get social services involved, but if she calms down, are you happy for her to stay here with you? They will try to find her a temporary place to stay so long as the Quinns' home is a crime scene, or get in touch with relatives. I fear that if we

move her to a hospital or somewhere unfamiliar, that will
only worsen her symptoms.'

'It's fine,' I say. 'She can stay here for as long as she needs
to until a long-term solution can be found.' I stand up and
walk over to the kitchen counter and collect the buttered
toast, putting a plate in front of Mrs Quinn.

The older woman has calmed down now and is gazing off
into the distance.

'Would you like some orange juice?' I ask her.

She doesn't look at me but says, 'Yes, dear. That would be
very nice.'

I take a carton out of the fridge and pour her a glass.

'Would you like anything to eat or drink?' I ask DC Cargo.

'No, thanks, I need to be getting on.' He stands up, and I
follow him into the hallway.

'Now that you know Mr Quinn killed Linette and the
person buried in their garden, when will you be releasing
Mike?'

'I'm afraid that we don't know anything for sure, Mrs
Floyd. We only have the testimony of a confused elderly
woman. Until Mr Quinn wakes up and we can identify the
remains of the body found in their garden, the status quo
remains. Mrs Quinn talked about Alice as being her baby, but
the remains we found are those of a grown woman. There are
a lot of questions still to be answered, and of course, there is
the hammer, the evidence. We will need to interview you and
Mrs Quinn again, so I would appreciate if you would stay
close to home today.'

I walk back into the kitchen, feeling dejected. Mrs Quinn
is sitting stock-still, once again staring into space. But I notice
she's drunk her glass of orange juice and half eaten a slice of
toast.

'Can I get you anything else?' I ask.

'You're a dear,' she says, turning her head slowly to look at me. 'What I'd most like to do is settle into a chair and watch some television.'

'Of course,' I say. 'Why don't you come through to the living room? You'll be comfortable there.'

She follows me into the living room, and I settle her in the most comfortable armchair, placing a blanket over her knees. I switch on the television and hand her the remote control. Then I kneel on the ground and light a fire in the hearth, staying there for a few moments to warm myself up.

Mrs Quinn seems to be engrossed in some morning chat show, so I leave her and return to the kitchen to tidy up the breakfast things. It's so hard to think straight. If Mrs Quinn is right, then her husband is the murderer. He killed Linette because Mrs Quinn told her about Alice. And who is Alice? Was she really their daughter, and is it her remains buried in their garden? And then it hits me. Could Mr Quinn have also killed Wilson? If Josie is telling the truth and her car didn't fatally injure Wilson, could Mr Quinn have finished him off? Could Wilson have discovered the body in the Quinns' garden? Could Mr Quinn have realised and given chase? Is that why Wilson was running, terrified for his life? It's hard to imagine the rather gauche older man being a killer. And then I realise that I'm looking after the wife of a murderer. If the body is that of Alice, then Mrs Quinn has been complicit in her husband's killing. I think back to last night. She seemed utterly terrified of her husband. Perhaps she's been subject to his coercive control for decades. If so, it's desperately sad.

After clearing up and wandering around the house some-what aimlessly, I check in on Mrs Quinn. She has dozed off, but her eyes flicker open when she sees me, and then she smiles.

'You are a dear,' she murmurs.

'What happened to Wilson Walker?' I ask, holding my breath.

She turns away and then lets out a little sob.

'Who?'

'Wilson Walker, the young man who was your neighbour and died supposedly in a hit and run.'

'I can't tell you.'

'Please, Mrs Quinn. If you know what happened, you need to tell me. It's not fair that someone is getting the blame unnecessarily.'

She sighs deeply. 'He was in our garden with one of those lights on around his head, like the coal miners wear. It was pitch dark outside, the middle of the night, and there he was trying to cut through the roots of our leylandii.'

'Why was he doing that?'

'Because his parents were in a dispute with us. They said the trees were blocking the light into their house, apparently, but Doug loves those trees, and he refused to get them cut down. I think that stupid boy got it into his head that he would do it himself. He was studying horticulture or something or other. So there he was in the middle of the night, digging away in exactly the spot he should never have touched. Douglas saw what he was doing, opened the bedroom window, and shouted at him, told him to scarper.'

With a sense of dread, I realise what she means about digging in exactly the spot he should never have touched, but I want Mrs Quinn to spell it out herself. 'He shouldn't have dug there because—'

'Because it's Alice's grave.' Mrs Quinn lets out another sob. 'That poor boy, he ran out onto the road into the path of the oncoming car that killed him. My Douglas never meant for the boy to die.' She balls her fist into her mouth and squeezes her eyes closed.

'Who was Alice?' I ask gently, but Mrs Quinn doesn't seem to hear me.

'I still have nightmares thinking about the poor boy lying

there, covered in blood. The light on his head was still on, even though one of his eyes was missing. It was just too horrible.' And then Mrs Quinn is sobbing so loudly her shoulders are shaking, and she's rocking her body backwards and forwards, exactly as she was doing last night. Her cries get louder and louder, and she starts coughing, and I wonder if I'm totally out of my depth here and whether I should call for an ambulance. I kneel down next to her and try to hold her hands, but there's seemingly nothing I can do to console her.

'I want to go to bed.' She manages to squeeze out the words in a staccato voice.

'Yes, of course,' I say. I hold out my hand to help her stand up, but she ignores me and stands up alone and then shuffles towards the door. At the bottom of the stairs, she comes to a halt.

'Which way is it?' she asks, shaking her head as if she's trying to dislodge something stuck in her brain.

'Follow me,' I say, again holding out my hand. She waves my hand away and instead grasps the stair rail and hauls herself up while I walk slowly ahead. Back in the spare room, I quickly make the bed.

'I'll lie on top of it and have a doze,' she says as she slides her feet out of her furry slippers and swings her legs up onto the bed. When she's comfortable with her head resting on two pillows, she looks at me with an expression of surprise.

'Who are you, dear?'

'Isobel Floyd,' I say with a sense of sadness. One moment, Mrs Quinn is totally lucid, and the next, utterly confused. It also begs the question whether what she's told me is indeed fact.

And then she closes her eyes and almost immediately falls into a deep sleep. I tiptoe out of the room and carefully close the door behind me.

· · ·

I FEEL AT A LOOSE END. I want to do something to help Mike, to get him released, but what? Even if he and I no longer have a marriage, I don't want him incarcerated in a prison cell for something he didn't do, and now I need to find out why Mr Quinn put the bloodied hammer in Mike's shed, assuming, that is, that Mrs Quinn has been telling the truth. Why did Mr Quinn choose to set up Mike as his scapegoat and not one of the other neighbours? Is it because he knew Mike was in the car with Josie that night when they hit Wilson, and he thought it easiest to put the blame on someone who was already guilty? Or was it a more mundane reason, the fact that we have a shed that's easily accessible, unlocked most of the time and not visible from the road or any casual passers-by?

Mum calls, and I'm so relieved to be able to talk to her. I explain everything, and when I eventually stop to take a breath, she tells me that it's all over the news.

I walk around the house and pull all the curtains that face towards the drive. I don't want any journalists looking in, and frankly, I don't want to see what's happening outside. Mrs Quinn wakes up around lunchtime, so I make us both an omelette and heat up a bowl of ready-made soup. We spend the rest of the afternoon watching a couple of old films on the television, and then I find a jigsaw in the children's playroom. She attempts to do it, but she's exhausted and keeps on dropping off to sleep. She doesn't ask about her husband all afternoon, and I wonder if she's forgotten the horror of what's happened.

I wait for DS Cargo to return to give us an update, perhaps to ask some more questions, but the doorbell doesn't ring.

27

W hile Mrs Quinn can't stay awake, I can't sleep. I'm missing Harry and Harper so much, and all I want is to have some semblance of a normal Christmas. If it can't be here, then we can do it at Mum's. And I want Mike to be released. However angry I am towards him, he is still the father of my children, and I need to protect them.

I keep on thinking about the Quinns. Mrs Quinn still hasn't confirmed to me that Alice is definitely her daughter, and although DS Cargo returned to question her, I don't think he made much headway. I told him everything that she told me, and hopefully, that was of some help.

Mrs Quinn must have been suffering so much for keeping quiet about her husband's horrific crimes. I suppose she'll be arrested in due course as an accessory to murder. I can't imagine how such a mentally frail woman will cope in prison. As I'm lying in the cool bed, I think of the drone footage again. When exactly did Mr Quinn kill Linette? We saw him digging a hole for something, preparing to hide some other evidence, perhaps. Not that the police have disclosed anything to me, and as far as I know, neither the pig nor its remains have been found. But did he kill Linette before or after he dug that hole? Did he have time to do both?

Then I think about what Josie said, that she didn't think the car hit Wilson hard enough to kill him, that the boy was getting off the ground, that he said he wasn't badly hurt. And there was no blood on the car, despite the inquest describing lots of blood at the scene. Was Josie telling me the truth? There's something that's not right about all of this, but I just can't put my finger on it. I mull the things over and over in my head, and it's certainly not helping me fall asleep.

Eventually, I switch on the light and get out of bed. Perhaps a hot chocolate will help calm my racing mind. I pull on my dressing gown and slip my feet into my slippers and walk out into the hallway, switching on the light. As I tiptoe past the spare bedroom, I'm surprised that the door is open. I poke my head around the side, and the bedside light is on, and the bed is empty.

'Mrs Quinn?' I say quietly. There's no answer. I'm worried now as to where she might be. Did I lock the house properly before I went to bed? What if she's wandered out, all confused? I hurry downstairs to the kitchen, but the lights are off, and when I switch them on, Lupin looks up at me from his bed, one eye open, and then instantly closes it again. I check the back door, but it's locked and bolted, and the key is hanging up on the peg where I always leave it. I check in the living room, but she's not there either. The front door is also properly locked and bolted.

'Mrs Quinn!' I say, trying to quell a sense of panic. There's no answer, so I run upstairs again, looking in the children's bedrooms and bathrooms. I run back downstairs, terrified that she's fallen somewhere, perhaps unconscious. The last room I look in is the children's playroom.

Mrs Quinn is sitting in the dark, on the floor in her night-dress, tightly hugging one of Harper's big teddy bears.

'What are you doing there?' I ask, unable to keep the concern out of my voice. She looks at me with a blank expression. I hold out my hand. 'Come along, you'll catch cold down here. Let's get you back to bed.'

Mrs Quinn stands up and carefully places the teddy back onto the floor.

'Mrs Quinn, I need to ask you a question.'

She looks at me with a quizzical expression, the light from the hall throwing shadows onto her face, making her look gaunt and tired.

'Did Mr Quinn finish Wilson off? Did he kill him after he was hit by the car?'

Mrs Quinn turns her back to me. I wonder why. She admitted that her husband killed Linette and Alice, whoever she may be, so why not tell me the truth about Wilson?

'I'd like a drink,' she says before slowly turning around.

'Of course. Let's go into the kitchen. Are you cold? I can get you a blanket.'

'I'm fine,' she says.

We walk to the kitchen, and I put the lights on. Lupin lets out a sigh and ambles out of bed, obviously annoyed that his sleep is being disturbed.

'What would you like? A cup of herbal tea or a hot chocolate?'

'Tea, please,' she says. Her eyes are fixed on her hands in her lap. I'm surprised she's not shivering from cold, sitting there with just her nightdress on. I fill up the kettle with water.

'I was just wondering about Wilson,' I say. But then my words taper off, and it's as if my heart has skipped a beat. Mrs Quinn is sitting there expressionless, staring at me, but I'm remembering what she said. How did she know that there was a lot of blood when Wilson was killed and that he was missing an eye? Did Mr Quinn tell her, or did she see it for herself? Or could she have killed him herself? I have to grab the countertop as I realise what I'm thinking.

Mrs Quinn must have seen Wilson lying there. Mrs Quinn must be . . .

I turn, ostensibly to put the kettle on, but then I feel the most horrendous punch in my left shoulder, as if an ice pick has been gouged into me. I gasp, unable to catch my breath, and my knees crumple, incapable of supporting my body. I collapse onto the cool stone floor, my back leaning against the kitchen cupboards, the pain radiating outwards as if a thousand ice cubes are being held against my shoulder and then jammed deeper and deeper into my body. I'm going to throw up. I take a shivery deep breath and glance upwards.

Mrs Quinn is standing over me. Her whole body language has changed. She is standing fully erect, her head is straight on her neck, rigid, not like it usually is when it trembles ever so slightly. Is she having a manic attack? Yet she doesn't look crazy. Her eyes are still, holding my gaze, and then I see what she's holding. One of our carving knives, my blood dripping from the point.

'You're not quite as stupid as you look, are you, Isobel?'

I gasp.

'Caring, dependable little Isobel Floyd,' she says. 'Yet another nosey neighbour sticking her oar in where it's not wanted. Why, oh why couldn't you keep your trap shut? Your poor children, Harry and Harper. What silly names.' She laughs. But this isn't the laugh of the Mrs Quinn I know. It's like she's morphed into a devil woman.

'Poor little Floyd children with their daddy banged up in prison and their mummy dead on their kitchen floor.'

'Why? Why are you doing this?' I gasp. I try to get up, but the pain is too intense, and I feel like I'm going to vomit.

'Yes, I killed that stupid boy. Yes, I killed Linette because her damned pig tried to dig up Alice all over again. Can no one leave our daughter in peace?'

'Your daughter,' I murmur. I know I need to draw some strength from somewhere. If I don't, that knife will be in my heart very soon, and that will be the end. But what can I do?

And then the utility room door opens with a squeak. It'll be Lupin, wondering what's going on, probably sensing that I'm in trouble. For the first time ever, I'm so grateful that Mike never finished doing the odd jobs around the house, that he never oiled the door, because the noise makes Mrs Quinn spin around to look. As she does so, I grab hold of her ankle, yanking as hard as I can, even though the pain from my left shoulder makes me scream out loud. Lupin jumps forwards and bares his teeth, growling a low, deep snarl. Mrs Quinn lurches to avoid the dog, but I'm tugging at her ankle, and she loses her footing, stumbling to the ground. The carving knife flies out of her hand and spins across the stone floor towards me. Lupin is dancing around her, growling a deep, vicious noise, barking and jumping at her.

'Get her, Lupin!' I reach for the knife and somehow manage to haul myself to my feet. Stars fly across my vision, but I race towards the back door, adrenaline coursing through my veins, managing to unbolt and unlock the door, and then I'm outside, my slippers discarded, and the soles of my feet are cut from the freezing gravel like multiple little shards of glass.

'Help!' I scream. Adrenaline pumps harder and harder as I stagger up the drive, the pain from my shoulder radiating across my back and into my stomach. But I can't think about that, I need to get to the Quinns' house where, surely, there are some police still investigating despite it being the middle of the night.

'Help!' I yell again, but I know my voice isn't loud enough.

It's pitch dark out and bitterly cold, and there are no lights on in any of the houses. I run as fast as I can, the pain searing through my back, hot liquid pouring down my shoulder blades, into the small of my back and down my legs. My breathing is laboured, and I'm finding it increasingly difficult to gulp in the frigid night air. I hear footsteps behind me, heavy breathing.

And then nothing.

28

'Isobel, stay with us!' The voice sounds vaguely familiar, but all I want to do is to be left alone and sink into the comforting blackness. 'Come on, Isobel. The police are here, and the ambulance is on its way.'

'Josie?' I murmur, my eyelids flickering open.

'I'm so sorry, Isobel. All of this, it's all my fault.'

'It isn't,' I whisper. 'It's Mrs Quinn. You need to stop her.' And then I can't talk anymore, and I sink back into oblivion.

I AM in hospital for just two nights. The stab wound missed any major arteries and organs, and all I needed were quite a few stitches in my shoulder. As the doctor told me, I was very lucky. I blacked out from shock and pain. That's quite common, apparently. It's not easy getting myself dressed, but here I am, ready to go home, waiting for Mum to collect me.

'Did you get it for me?' I ask as she arrives in the ward.

'When do I ever fail to do what you want me to do?' Mum says with a grin. She holds up an M&S carrier bag.

'Thanks, Mum,' I say, carefully standing up and holding out my right hand.

'You're not meant to be carrying anything heavy.'

'It's a box of biscuits. I'm sure I can manage that.'

'All right, but don't do anything silly.'

I roll my eyes at her and then bend down to place a kiss on her cheek. 'I won't be long. I'll meet you downstairs in the coffee shop.'

Thanks to helpful information provided by my doctor—probably breaking data protection laws, but I think he felt sorry for me—I already know that Mr Quinn is being held on the Hortensia Ward on the fourth floor of the hospital. I walk slowly, clutching the bag in my right hand to avoid unnecessary pulling on my left side. I'm on painkillers, but the wound doesn't hurt too much. I just have to be careful not to pull on the stitches. I press the big green button to enter the ward and walk up to the nurse, who is busy on a computer at the nurses' station.

When she looks up, I ask, 'Is it possible to see Douglas Quinn? I believe he's on this ward.'

She frowns at me. 'I'm sorry, but Mr Quinn isn't having any visitors.'

I suppose I shouldn't be surprised. I take the box of biscuits out of the bag and place it on the counter. 'Would it be possible for you to give him this? Please tell him it's from Isobel Floyd. I hope he'll have a speedy recovery.'

She nods at me without smiling. I guess it's unusual to have someone dropping off a gift for a patient who is being guarded by a policeman. I turn around and walk out of the ward. I'm strolling slowly along the corridor when a voice says, 'Mrs Floyd?'

I swivel around to see DS Cargo. 'How are you?' he asks.

'I've been discharged. I wanted to see Mr Quinn.'

'Not possible, I'm afraid. He's been charged with

concealing evidence and as an accessory to murder. I expect he'll serve prison time. He should be out of hospital early in the new year.' He glances at his watch. 'Have you got time for a coffee?'

'My mum is waiting for me.' But then I pause. Mum won't mind hanging on. 'A quick one, then.'

We make our way to the coffee shop on the ground floor, where Mum is already seated at a table. I introduce her to DS Cargo.

Mum gets up and shakes DS Cargo's hand. 'You two have a seat here, and I'll wait for you back in the car, Isobel,' Mum says. 'Don't hurry.'

We stand in line in awkward silence, and then DS Cargo carries the tray with two coffees on it to a table at the back of the restaurant, out of earshot from anyone else.

'I wanted to take the opportunity to bring you up to date with the case,' he says, leaning forwards in his chair. 'Mrs Quinn is in custody. She's admitted to killing Wilson Walker. It seems that your husband and Josie Abbott's testimony was correct. He wasn't badly hurt by the car, and he did get up after they drove off, but then we assume he felt dizzy and leaned over or sat down to recover after the shock of being hit. Mrs Quinn appeared and—please excuse the vernacular —she finished him off. We don't know for sure what Mr Quinn's involvement was, but we're surmising he saw the accident from his bedroom window, and he made an anonymous phone call for an ambulance, assuming that Wilson had been seriously injured. Whilst he was busy doing that, his wife ran out of the house, took advantage of the fact that Wilson was feeling dizzy or leaning over, and murdered him by bashing him with a rock.'

'But why?' I ask.

'Because she was worried that Wilson had uncovered the remains of Alice.' He takes a sip of his hot coffee. It's still too hot for me to drink mine. 'We'll never know if Wilson actually did uncover any bones.'

'Who was Alice?'

'The Quinns' daughter.'

I can't stop myself from inhaling loudly.

'She killed her own daughter?'

DS Cargo nods. 'We managed to track down an old school friend of Alice's. It seems that the Quinns' daughter was a bit of a rebel and was forever getting into arguments with her mother. It was the summer after her A Levels, and Alice had gone off travelling. She returned home, and Mrs Quinn discovered her daughter taking drugs. We believe that she went ballistic and hit Alice over the head. Whether she meant to kill her or not isn't clear. Apparently, she told her husband that Alice had tried to attack her and that she killed her daughter in self-defence. Whether Douglas Quinn truly believed that or not, we may never know, but Mr Quinn seems to have bought the story. They buried her in their garden twenty-three years ago. Over the decades, if anyone asked where Alice was, they said she had stayed on in The Gambia and built a new life for herself. Her school friends assumed that Alice was happy with her new life in West Africa and had just moved on from the old crowd. Eventually, people stopped asking, and it became easier for the Quinns to pretend that they had never had children.'

I shake my head, trying to fathom how it might be possible to do such an abhorrent thing. 'So Mrs Quinn killed her daughter and then killed Wilson because she was worried that Wilson had uncovered Alice's remains?'

'Exactly. Naturally, we will be reopening the inquest into Wilson Walker's death.'

'But what about the hammer found in our shed and Linette's murder?'

'She admits to stealing the hammer out of your shed.

Apparently, the pig got into their garden. Mrs Quinn was livid and told her husband to deal with the pig, kill it and bury it. While he was meant to be disposing of the animal, she took the hammer and crept off to murder Linette. She was careful to wear gloves so the only fingerprints were your husband's. Fortunately, Mr Quinn didn't kill the animal but chivvied it into the woods behind their house. Later, while everyone was busy with the police and the discovery of Linette's body, she brazenly went back to your garden and deposited the hammer in the shed where she'd found it.'

'But I don't understand why. Surely, she didn't kill Linette just over the pig? And this is a woman who has quite advanced dementia. How is it even possible?'

DS Cargo sighs. 'We don't believe she has got dementia, or if so, it's extremely mild. Mrs Quinn isn't a frail old lady. That was just a pretence. I'm afraid that she acted out many of the symptoms. She missed her vocation on Broadway.'

'I can't believe it,' I say, shaking my head. 'But why? Why was she pretending?'

'It seems that Mr Quinn was genuinely worried that his wife might let slip the truth that Alice was buried in their garden, which is why he made sure that his wife stayed at home as much as possible. Mrs Quinn resented his surveillance. She wanted her freedom and was tired of the deal they'd made with each other, so she told the police that her husband had committed both of the murders so she could get him out of the picture.'

I'm finding it really difficult to understand how the fragile woman I thought I knew is in fact a wicked murderer.

'I know it's a lot to take in,' DS Cargo says.

'What I still don't understand is why she killed Linette.'

'I think the pig might have unearthed some of Alice's remains. We can't be sure, but we suspect that Linette confronted Mrs Quinn and demanded to know what was buried in their garden. We must assume that Mrs Quinn decided the only way to keep Linette quiet was to kill her.'

'So when she told me that she let slip to Linette about Alice, and her husband killed Linette to shut her up . . .?'

'That's total fabrication. Mrs Quinn is a devious, controlling individual, and her husband has been covering up her malice for years.'

We both sit there in silence for a while. DS Cargo sips his coffee, but I'm not sure I can keep anything down. I feel totally sickened about Mrs Quinn's deception and horrified to think that I had her sleeping in our house. I know I got lucky, that I managed to escape, and it was probably all thanks to Lupin. Everyone thinks Labradors are soppy dogs, but they'll do whatever they need to protect their owners.

'And Mike?' I ask eventually.

'Your husband was released this morning.'

'Oh,' I say, because what else can I say? Mike and Josie still did a terrible thing. Mike still had an affair, and I'm not sure I will ever be able to forgive him. 'Thank you for keeping me in the loop.'

'You get yourself better, and I hope you have a happy Christmas.'

'Thank you.'

I stand up and have taken just a couple of steps away from the table.

'Oh, Isobel,' DS Cargo says. 'I forgot to tell you that the pig has been found. She was foraging in the woods, and she's being rehomed on a farm, where she belongs.'

I smile.

I GET a phone call from Mike when I'm in the car with Mum, on our way home.

'I'm so relieved you're okay,' Mike says.

I remain silent.

'Is it all right with you if I come home?' he asks.

'Not really.'

'I'm so sorry, Isobel. For everything.'

'I'm sure you are, but I need time to digest things. I'd like you to move out, and we'll tell the kids you're working away. But I'd like you to be with us for Christmas. Let's make it as normal as possible for Harry and Harper. Afterwards, we can decide what we're going to do and be honest with the children.'

'Fair enough,' he says, but I can hear the tremble of emotion in his voice. 'I'll come over later and collect a suitcase of my things.'

It's six a.m. on Christmas day. I hear a car door slam and the front door open. I told Mike to get here early, in time for the frenzy of Christmas stocking opening, because it's only right that he should share the excitement.

'Has Santa been?' he asks as the children bound down the stairs.

'Yes, come and look, Dad!' Harry says, tugging Mike's hand. I follow them into Harry's bedroom, where his Christmas stocking is lying on the floor, bulging with presents.

'This is mine!' Harper says, dragging her sequinned stocking into Harry's bedroom. 'Can we start opening?'

'Of course,' I say. 'Santa Claus must have thought you've both been very good children this year.'

After lots of squealing, the presents are all unwrapped, and I leave Mike to play with the kids. I walk downstairs into the kitchen and turn the oven on, ready for the turkey. I prepared the bird last night, and it's sitting in the fridge, lifted in by Mum.

Josie delivered the turkey two days ago. It was her peace offering and her apology.

'I know you'll never forgive me,' she said, 'and I don't deserve forgiveness, but I really am sorry. Jack and I are having marriage guidance counselling. And one other thing. We're withdrawing the plans for the green burial site. Highways have objected, but the main reason we've pulled the plans is we don't think it's the right place for it.'

'Don't you need the money?'

'Of course we do, but we'll find other ways. I'm sure there are commercial activities we can do that won't upset our neighbours.'

'Thanks, Josie. And merry Christmas.'

I WONDER what will happen to Josie and to Mike. The Crown Prosecution Service will decide in the New Year whether they will be prosecuted for leaving the scene of an accident. It's a certainty that Josie will be charged with dangerous driving. I really hope they don't end up in prison. It would be shocking to have four residents of The Close in jail.

'Mike, can you help lift the turkey into the oven, please?' I shout up the stairs. It's going to be some time before I can lift anything heavy.

The children run down the stairs behind Mike.

'Do you want to give Lupin his presents?' I ask.

'Yes!' they both yell.

Lupin is getting extra goodies and extra attention this Christmas. There is no doubt that he saved my life by keeping Mrs Quinn at bay until the police arrived. DS Cargo even mentioned that Lupin could be eligible for a canine bravery award.

After breakfast, we all go into the living room. The tree is sparkly and festive, adorned with twinkling lights and multiple silver and gold decorations that I've collected over the years. Underneath it are some more presents from relatives and friends. Harry picks up an envelope.

'What's this?' he asks. It's addressed to *Master Harry Floyd*.

'I don't know,' I say. 'Open it.'

Harry rips open the envelope and removes a card. It's a party invitation with a picture of brightly coloured balloons on the front.

'Does this say I'm invited to Benji's birthday?' he asks, his eyes wide open and shoving the card towards me.

'Yes, it does. Benji is having a birthday party on the third of January, and you're invited.'

'Can I go?' he asks, bouncing up and down.

'Of course you can,' I say, tugging him towards me for a hug. After a second, he pulls away, eager to open some more presents, but I can tell how chuffed he is. Although Harry loves getting toys, I can see that he's standing up just that little bit straighter in the knowledge that he's got friends.

As for me, I have a lot of decisions to make. I don't want to carry on living here in what I anticipated to be my forever home. Too much has happened, and there are too many unpleasant memories. I will find somewhere else, somewhere smaller where I can start my life as a single mother. My New Year's resolution will be to update my CV and get a job as an architect. Mike's firm has suspended him on full pay subject to further investigations. If he gets prosecuted, and it's likely that he will, he'll lose his job. It could mean that there is a vacancy in his firm. I wonder whether I could apply for the position.

A LETTER FROM MIRANDA

Thank you very much for reading The New Neighbour.

I need to start by saying that the characters in The New Neighbour are one hundred per cent a figment of my imagination! There aren't many of us who haven't had some sort of a run-in with our neighbours, but since we've moved to Sussex, we have got lucky and have delightful neighbours. I've had my share of horror stories in the past, from the adjacent flat being used as a brothel, to an application for a massive wind turbine right next to our house in a national park (yes, I was a nimby on that occasion!), to an insomniac upstairs neighbour who paced the creaking floor right through the night. I'd love to hear your nightmare neighbour stories!

When I started thinking about this book, I spent several hilarious gin-drinking evenings with my lovely neighbours. A huge thank you to the B... Babes: Zoe, Tina, Pippa and Kajal.

Twiglet the pig is in memory of my cousin Chris's pig, Bella. She wouldn't be my first choice of a pet, but I know she brought joy! You may have noticed that Labradors feature frequently in my books. We now have two black Labs and they make sure that I take regular breaks from my writing. My thanks to Jess for giving me inspiration for the green burial site and for being such a great friend. And thank you to Becca McCauley who is always so generous with her advice.

I particularly enjoyed writing this book, not least because with the help of my fabulous editor, Jan Smith, we plotted it in record time. Sometimes thrillers are highly complicated to map out, but for some reason this one flowed easily. I hope you enjoyed reading it as much as I enjoyed writing it.

It is thanks to the amazing team at Inkubator Books that I've had another great writing year, hitting Amazon bestseller spots. Thank you to Brian Lynch and Garret Ryan, Jan Smith, Valorie, Claire, Stephen and the rest of the team. You have made my writing dreams come true.

I would also like to thank the book blogging community who so generously review my books and share their thoughts with readers. A very big thank you to Carrie Shields (@carriereadsthem_all).

Lastly but most importantly, thank *you* for reading my books. I love to chat with readers via BookBub, Goodreads or Instagram so please reach out and say hello. Reviews on Amazon and Goodreads help other people discover my novels, so if you could spend a moment writing an honest review, no matter how short it is, I would be massively grateful.

My warmest wishes,

Miranda

www.mirandarijks.com

ALSO BY MIRANDA RIJKS